I0588207

Copyright © 2025 Brian Jay Nelson

Printed in the United States of America
Paperback ISBN: 978-1-64873-540-0
Hardcover ISBN: 978-1-64873-543-1

Cover Design - Jon Barone

Publishing by Writers Publishing House
Prescott, Arizona
writerspublishinghouse.com

The Oceanids

By: Brian Jay Nelson

Thomas Nelson III
June 2011 – November 2024

In memory of our Thomas, who was with us from the start of our journey here at Large Lion. Even near the end, he still found the strength to walk up his ramp to sit near my computer, and supervise my work. We love and miss you, and look forward to seeing you once again when we take our final journey to The Summerland.

THE OCEANIDS

The mysteries that lie within the depths of our oceans, and beyond the known boundaries of outer space will always remain closed to those who choose to think inside the box. But for those who dare to imagine, the possibilities are endless.

Contents

Introduction

THEY EXIST

JUNE 18, 1966, Erie Pennsylvania

The skies were dark and clear on this first night of the New Moon, just days before the Summer Solstice. The air was pleasantly mild for this time of year, but a light jacket was still necessary on the shores of chilly Lake Erie.

Seven year old Kevin Gustafsson sat on the couch with his father Neil, in the living room of their home just a short distance away from the lake. Their attention was on the Philco black and white TV, and the military drama "Combat". Sounds of screaming men, the zing of bullets, and explosions accompanied the spectacle, as they watched with wide eyed interest.

They both jumped when there was an unexpected loud knock on the front door.

"Who in the hell can that be at this hour?" His father complained as he hurried to the door.

Kevin's mother, Nora peeked out from an adjacent room with alert curiosity as Neil looked out the window.

"It's dad! I hope everything's alright." He said as he opened the door, and looked at his father with concern. "Dad! Are you and mom, okay?"

"We're fine." Bill Gustafsson answered with an assured voice.

He was the typical grandfather type that you'd expect to see in the 1960s. He was a broad built man in his mid-sixties, with

i

a contagiously pleasant smile. He was bald, but yet very dignified as he stood there in a camel color waist jacket, and khaki pants.

Kevin jumped up from the couch, and ran to the door with excitement when he heard his voice.

"Grandpa!" He hugged him with joy.

Nora leaned on the entranceway to the room, and silently observed, as Bill greeted her with a nod.

"What are you doing out and about at this hour?" Neil asked with a tinge of annoyance.

"It was such a nice clear night that I thought I'd take a stroll down to the foot of Eaglehurst, and see if I could see the lights." He paused as he gestured toward Kevin. "I thought maybe I could get my buddy to go with me."

"Can I go?" Kevin asked with excitement.

"I don't know, dad." There might be some kids down there drinking and raising hell."

"I can handle those young ruffians." Bill intently stated.

"I have no doubt about that." Neil chuckled.

"I can check to see if Randy might want to go too." Nora suggested. "He's in his room listening to his radio."

"Oh mom!" Kevin rolled his eyes. "Randy doesn't like that sort of thing. He doesn't even believe the lights are UFO's.

"Kevin's right." Bill answered. "Randy has different interests."

Neil looked toward his wife, and sighed. "We aren't keen on the UFO thing either. I wish you wouldn't encourage Kevin's imagination, dad."

"There's nothing wrong with the boy having an imagination." He winked.

"Can I please go?" Kevin pleaded once more.

"Ok." Neil finally conceded, shooting an obvious expression of displeasure toward Nora. "Just make sure you don't keep him out too late. He has to get up and go to church with us in the morning."

"I'll have him back, and tucked in at a decent hour." Bill replied, as Kevin took hold of his grandfather's outstretched hand.

"Wait just a minute, young man." Nora warned as she retrieved a jacket that was hanging in a nearby mud room. "You're not going anywhere without this."

Kevin reacted with annoyance, as Bill grinned at Nora.

"Your mother's right. We wouldn't want you to catch a death."

A short time later, Kevin and his grandfather approached the overlook at the foot of Eaglehurst. A slight lake breeze rustled the leaves on the trees, as they paused to look out over the dark waters. They waited for a few short minutes before Kevin pointed out toward the distance.

"Look grandpa! There they are."

They both looked with awe at a cluster of bright lights at least 20 miles out over the lake. They hovered in a straight line for a time, before they descended straight down into the water at lightning speed. Once underwater, their colorful lights glowed from the depths in red, blue, and green hues.

"Wow! They went right into the water." Kevin exclaimed. "Do you really think they have an underwater base somewhere out there?"

"I have no doubt." Bill answered. "Maybe those are some sort of advanced crafts carrying supplies from another planet."

Kevin peered upward at the star filled sky. "You really think there's other life somewhere out there, grandpa?"

Bill looked upward with equal wonder. "I can say with certainty that we're not alone in this universe."

Kevin shifted his attention back to the water. "Can I go down by the water to get a closer look?"

"Your parents wouldn't be too happy if I let you go alone, and I'm not sure I could maneuver down the cliff steps at night."

"I can go by myself. I know the way by heart."

"Ok. Just be careful. That's a steep descent, and some of the steps are missing."

"I'll be careful, grandpa."

"I'll be right up here waiting for you."

Kevin hurried ahead, and started climbing down the steep cliff that led to the beach below. When he reached the bottom, he glanced out in the dark with wonder, hoping he might catch better glimpse of the lights over and under the water.

Suddenly he heard voices carrying in the night air that were conversing in a language he did not understand. They sounded like female voices, but they spoke in disjointed tones. They did laugh in a cackle that amused the young boy. He curiously pursued the chatter around a curve in the cliff, until he stopped at a clearing where large rocks protruded onto the beach, and into the water. What he witnessed in the dark was beyond his comprehension.

He could barely make out the silhouettes of what appeared to be a group of shapely young women perched upon the rocks. He moved in to get a closer look, and was surprised to see that they had fish tails, and were naked from the waist up.

"Wow!" He whispered to himself as his foot slipped on some loose rocks.

The sound echoed loudly, and alarmed the young nymphs. With lightning speed, they leapt from the rocks like seals, and splashed loudly into the water, quickly disappearing. One paused just long enough to look back toward Kevin with curiosity, before she also leaped into the water.

Though it was dark, he could tell she had blonde hair, and appeared to be in her mid teens.

With breathless excitement he hurried back up the cliff steps. At the top, he ran as fast as he could toward his grandfather, who was now resting on a park bench.

"Grandpa, Grandpa! They really exist!"

"Whoa! Hold on now!" He tried to calm the young boy. "What did you see down there?"

"Mermaids! They were sitting on the rocks, talking to each other in a strange language."

Bill looked off for a moment in thought. "Is that so?"

"It's true! One even stopped, and looked at me before she dived in the water. She had long blonde hair, and boobies."

Bill could barely hold back a chuckle, and Kevin frowned.

"You don't believe me, do you?"

Bill took a deep breath before answering, and firmly took hold of the boy's shoulders. "I believe you did see something. But you absolutely can't tell anyone else what you saw. Especially your brother." He paused. "Can I trust you on that?"

"I won't tell anybody, grandpa. I promise"

Just then, a set of car headlights headed their way. Loud music was playing on the car radio, and rowdy teens were hooting and hollering. They stopped just short of where they stood, and two young guys got out, and strutted toward them.

"Out kind of late. Aren't you, gramps?" The driver arrogantly remarked.

"Don't you gramps me, Eddie Hilbert." He replied as he stepped between the young teen and Kevin.

The young man strolled closer, and drastically changed his demeanor. "I'm sorry, Mr. Gustafsson. I didn't know it was you."

"Well, it is, and you should know that I'm not too old to grab you by the flap of your ear, and take you home to your dad." He scolded, while the other teen could barely keep a straight face.

"I didn't mean to be disrespectful." He cowered. "We were just out cruising, and having some fun. Please don't tell my dad."

Bill looked him up and down for a moment, and nodded. "Just keep the volume down, boys. There are folks trying to sleep in this neighborhood."

"Yes sir."

"And, don't forget to pick up your empty beer bottles." He soberly added. "The community put a trash can here for a reason. Use it!"

The two boys answered with an agreeing nod.

Bill then took hold of his grandson's hand. "Come on, Kevin. Let's go home."

As they walked away, Kevin looked up at his grandfather with admiration. "You really told him off, grandpa."

Bill chuckled in response. "Yeah! I guess I did."

1

AN UNLIKELY CATCH

OCTOBER 22, 2027: Freeport Beach near Northeast, Pennsylvania.

Owen Gustafsson cradled a hot cup of coffee as he stepped onto the enclosed porch of his parent's cottage. Like all the other men in his Swedish lineage, he was broad built and rugged. But despite his appearance, he was a refined gentleman with blue eyes that projected the kindness in his soul.

He gazed out at the dark, foreboding skies over Lake Erie with concern. The wind gusts had picked up over the previous hour, howling, and rattling the windows. He could see the high white caps as they crashed onto the beach below the cliffs. He knew these late fall storms could be quite severe, as the season began to transition into winter in this part of the world.

"Looks like we're in for a tough night." He commented to himself.

On the Canadian side of the lake, a small commercial fishing vessel had set out from Port Stanley earlier in the day, hoping to get one last big catch before seasons end. The small vessel tossed wildly in the high gusts and rolling waves. The crew, donning their rain gear, struggled to keep their footing on the deck as they tried to steady the small crane on the stern of the boat.

"What's taking so long? We need to get that net in, and head back to port." The captain yelled.

"The net's too full and heavy for the crane to haul it in against this storm." One of the crew members hollered back.

A huge wave crashed across the deck, nearly sweeping the men off their feet. They desperately hung onto whatever they could as the crane groaned loudly, creaking from the strain at its mooring. The entire boat heaved heavily to one side, almost disappearing below the waves.

"That net's going to pull us under. It's too rough to haul it in." The other crew member warned.

After a quick pause in thought, and a stressful sigh, the captain motioned to the crane operator. "Cut the net." He ordered. "We can't risk being capsized."

The crane immediately released the net, and the boat began to steady a bit against the storm, as it now weaved and bobbed like a cork between swells. One of the crew members patted the captain on the back.

"Well Cappy, we just lost a big catch."

"It's been a good season." He reluctantly answered. "Let's go home."

Beneath the surface, countless fish swam free from the now loose and open net. However, one large fish, barely recognizable in the turbulent waters, thrashed wildly, unable to free itself. The now weightless net was tossed violently in the rough waters, and undertow. The more the big fish tried to break free, the more it became entangled in the grip of the net.

Later that night, Owen laid awake in bed, listening to the merciless gusts of the north wind as it lashed against the side of the cottage. His mind drifted, as he imagined the violent waves of the lake, and the many ships and crews that had fell victim to its fury throughout the years.

"I hope all the vessels made it safely into port." He thought out loud.

Eventually his eyes grew heavy, and he surrendered to peaceful sleep.

The next morning, he woke to find that the howling gusts of the storm had now seized. He got up and looked out the window to see that the lake was still choppy, but had settled quite considerably.

He sat back down on the edge of the bed, and sighed. "I suppose I should walk down to the beach, and survey the damage."

A short time later, he set out in the gray misty morning, making his way down the short, but steep embankment that led to the beach below the cottage. The storm had knocked out two of the bottom stairs that his father had previously built, and he braced himself along the cliffs edge to reach the slippery rocks below.

As he reached the base of the cliff, he raised the collar of his heavy jacket to stave off the chilly north wind that blew in from the lake. The crispness of the fall morning somehow felt good to him. It had been years since he experienced Lake Erie life this late into the season. He set his sights onto the beach which was strewn with washed up debris, downed branches, and several pieces of drift wood.

The waves were still quite rough as they rushed onto the shore, and he could see that there had been quite a bit of beach erosion in the storms wake. He squinted against drizzling rain to survey his surroundings.

His eyes caught something snagged to the end of a large tree that had uprooted and crashed down from the cliffs above. He could tell it was a commercial fishing net clinging to the upper branches. But as he got closer, he also noticed a large, indistinguishable bundle tangled within the net itself. His pace hurried when he saw that it was perhaps a human body, or maybe a large sturgeon fish.

In his job as a marine scientist, Owen had grown accustomed to carrying a sharp knife on his belt to free underwater creatures who had become entrapped in nets, discarded fishing lines, and other contraptions commonly utilized by commercial, and private fisherman.

As he reached the trunk of the tree, and looked out to the top portion that extended into the water, he could see that it was something more than just a large fish bundled within the net. He saw the wet blonde hair that fully covered the face, and the twisted body covered in bottom silt, and sea weed

"Oh my God! It's a human!" He exclaimed out loud.

He immediately pulled out his knife, and waded into the cold waters. When he reached the top branches where the bundle was snagged, he began to carefully cut the netting loose. When he was able to reach through the tangled net, he brushed the wet hair aside to see the pale face of a beautiful woman. He cut away some of the heavily imbedded sea grass, and saw her shapely torso. He had thought that a large fish had been wrapped around her, but as his eyes wandered downward, he could see that the enormous green tail fin was attached to her torso.

"This can't be real." He thought.

The being opened her tired eyes just long enough to look up at Owen, completely taking him by surprise. Somehow, she had miraculously survived her ordeal. Her fragile hand weakly gripped at the confined netting.

"It's ok. I'm here to help." Owen nervously stated, as he continued carefully cutting her loose. "Please! Just stay with me."

It took a while to completely free her, and carry her to shore. As he gently set her down on the beach to evaluate the situation, he immediately checked to see if she had a heartbeat. Though still alive, she was quite beaten up, and desperately in need of care. Looking upward toward the cottage with determined eyes, he drew an anxious breath. He brushed the wet blonde hair from her face, and she slightly opened her clear blue eyes once again, to helplessly peer up at him.

"You're safe now, sweetheart." He smiled with assurance. "It's lucky that I found you."

Without further hesitation, he hoisted the almost lifeless Mermaid over his broad shoulder in a fireman's carry, and proceeded up the embankment.

By the time he reached the cottage, he was now cradling her in his strong arms. He hurried her into the bathroom, carefully placing her into the tub, before proceeding to fill it with warm water. He filled it just enough to get her body acclimated to the warmth. In her semi-conscious state, he wanted to be sure she didn't slip under, and somehow drown herself. If that was indeed possible. In all of his experience with marine life, he didn't have the slightest idea of how to deal with such a hybrid being. He took a thick bath towel, and placed it behind her head so that she could rest awhile.

A few hours later, he was in the kitchen fixing lunch when he heard a door creak open. He looked up with surprised amazement to see this beautiful, flawless woman standing there totally naked. Somehow, she had shed her tail, and now had perfectly shaped human legs. She immediately crossed her arms over her full breasts to cover herself, and cowered against the wall, trembling in fear.

"It's okay! I'm not going to hurt you."

His words did little to calm her, as her eyes anxiously searched every corner of her strange surroundings.

"Stay right there, and I'll get you something to cover yourself."

He hurried into the other room, quickly returning with a lounging robe. He draped it across her shoulders, and she slipped her arms into the sleeves. She gave him a nervous glance before fastening the belt to secure the front.

"You're very weak and unstable. Let me help you into a chair."

He very gingerly steadied her as he pulled a chair away from dining room table, and set her down. Once she was settled, he backed away to a comfortable distance behind the kitchen counter.

"Are you hungry?" He asked, placing fingers to his mouth.

She still said nothing, but continued to stare straight at him. He was baffled as to why she would not respond in some way, but he continued to try.

"Can you tell me your name?"

When she still didn't respond, he spoke to himself, venting his frustration.

"She probably doesn't understand English."
After a long moment of silence, where he was trying to think what to say next, she finally spoke.

"Katiera." He looked toward her with surprise, as she continued to stare at him. "My name is Katiera."

He walked from the kitchen, and slowly approached her. "My name is Owen."

She slightly smiled, and seemed a bit more at ease, as he took a seat opposite of her.

"Your name is just as beautiful as you are."

"Thank you." She blushed.

"You had a tail fin when I brought you here." He shook his head in bewilderment. "How is it that you now have legs?"

She only answered with a timid shrug, as she painfully tried to shift in her chair.

"I know you're hurt. I could see that the side of your torso is black and blue." He stared at her with trusting eyes. "Would you allow me to examine your injuries? I promise I won't harm you."

She subtly nodded, then loosened the belt at the front of the robe. Owen helped her to her feet, and steadied her.
"Place your hand on the table to keep your balance. I won't let you fall."

He gently placed his hands on both sides of her feminine torso, trying not to obviously stare at her perfect breast. He then began to slowly work his way down to her shapely hips, examining each rib. It was easy to detect an injury since she had very little body fat. It was also hard to conceal the fact that he was naturally aroused with her beauty.
She let out a heavy sigh, and quivered a bit as well. It was obvious that she was experiencing the same feelings.

"You have such a gentle touch." She murmured.

The comment made him slightly smile.

As he ran his finger across the rib in the bruised area, she let loose with a painful response. "Oww!"

Owen quickly lifted his hand from the painful area, and helped her back into her chair.

"Just as I surmised. One of your ribs are broken. You'll have to stay here and rest until it heals."

"But I have to go home. My people will be searching for me." She responded with great anxiety. "They have the means to instantly heal such injuries."

Owen was taken back by the revelation.

"Listen to me. I don't know where your home is, or who your people are, Katiera. But you can't swim in those rough waters, and you can barely function normally without having extreme pain. You need my help."

She could see the great concern in his eyes, and it emotionally moved her.

"If you can just get me back to the beach, I can signal them. They'll come and get me right away."

"How would you signal them?"

"With my voice." She reasoned. "I know that it's hard for you to understand. Maybe I could explain it later."

Owen pondered over the situation for a moment.

"Would they be able to hear you from the edge of the cliff?"

"Yes, I think so."

Owen paced a bit, pondering the situation.

"We'll have to wait until nightfall. I can't chance anyone witnessing it by day." He reasoned. "Until then, I have a spare bed. You need to rest."

"Could I possibly have some water?"

"Yes." He quickly went to the kitchen to retrieve it, and she eyed him with admiration.

"Do you really think I'm pretty?"

He answered as he delivered the cold glass of water. "I think you are a very beautiful wom...I mean Mermaid."

The awkward moment made her slightly laugh, though it hurt her to do so, and he couldn't help but chuckle with embarrassment as well.

Owen watched with amazement as she downed the entire 16 ounces of water in one gulp.

"Could I possibly have another?"

"Coming right up." He shook his head in disbelief.

"Owen! Wait!" She pleaded with her dreamy eyes, and motioned him closer.

He sat back down in his chair, and leaned in close. She then placed her hand gently to the side of his face, and her touch ignited a passion within his soul.

"Thank you." She smiled.

He wanted so much to kiss her passionately at that moment, but withdrew instead.

"I'll get you that water, and then I'll get you settled in the spare bedroom."

2

THE OCEANIDS

The sun had come out sometime in the late afternoon, bringing a beautiful fall day to the shores of Lake Erie. While Katiera napped, Owen went to the market to get some fresh fish, and plenty green vegetables. Through his experience with marine life at his job in Florida, he had to assume that she also enjoyed a similar diet. There were so many questions that ran through his mind. Up until this time, he had thought that Mermaids only existed in mythology. Seeing her now, as a full woman, he found it hard to imagine her anatomy as it had been when he found her that morning.

Katiera silently slipped into the room as Owen prepared supper. When he looked up and saw her, his heart raced. She now wore one of his father's flannel shirts, buttoned down just enough to reveal the top portion of her cleavage, and she was fitted fairly well into a pair of his mother's denim jeans. He smiled to himself as he also took note that she was wearing the fuzzy pink slippers he had left near the bed.

"How are you feeling?"

"Rested. But still quite sore." She answered.

"Sorry about the choice of clothes. There wasn't much to choose from."

She only smiled in response as she shuffled over to a chair to sit down. It was the type of pursed smile accentuated by perfect, plump lips. The kind that most men could only dream about. He nervously sighed as he amorously watched her, confused at how quickly this mysterious woman had begun to capture his heart.

She studied him as well as he cut and prepared the vegetables.

"Do you have anyone special in your life, Owen?"

He looked up from his work long enough to answer.

"There was someone a while back. But that's over, and in the past."

"She hurt you. Didn't she?" She asserted in a caring voice, that caused him to nervously shrug off the comment.

"Like I said. It was a long time ago." He paused, leaning on the counter. "What about you? I imagine there has to be a handsome Merman in your life."

She scoffed. "I was rather keen on a man at one time. But my best friend stole his heart."

"Ouch!" Owen responded. "Surely there were others."

"In our civilization, Mermaids outnumber Mermen 15 to 1."

"Those aren't good odds for the female."

"That's why many choose to leave, and walk on land."

"Why didn't you?"

"I visited on a few occasions. But I've yet to meet a man that I would be willing to offer myself to in a sexual manner."

Owen's eyes widened at the revelation, and he turned away, quietly mouthing the word "WOW!"

She pushed herself up from the chair, and winced in pain, before slowly pacing over to a wall full of framed pictures.

"Is this your family?"

"Yes." He answered, as she studied the faces in each picture.

"Where are they now?"

"Aside from my parents, they've all passed." He struggled a bit to continue. "My parents disappeared several years back. Just like so many other people did."

"They were taken in the rapture." She commented, before pacing closer to him with curiosity. "Yet, you were left behind." She paused as Owen finished preparing the salad. "I find that hard to believe. You seem like such a kind person."

Owen chose not to answer. But instead, looked at her with a forced smile. "I hope you like salmon, and spinach salad."

"I do." She replied with an amicable grin.

After supper, they sat side by side on the enclosed porch, and took in a spectacular sunset over the lake.

"It's so beautiful." She marveled, as her eyes remained fixated on the various hues of color that the setting sun projected onto the darkening sky and clouds.

"The sunsets are always best this time of year." Owen casually stated.

"I never have the chance to see the sunsets from my world."

"Where exactly is your world, Katiera?"

"We are Oceanids." She answered, never breaking her gaze from the lake.

"Like the Nereids and Oceanids that I read about in Greek mythology?"
Katiera nodded, and continued.

"We're originally from the planet Aquis." She paused to glance at Owen. "But my people have been here for centuries." She turned her gaze back toward the lake, and gestured. "We live out there in a place called Station 37."

Owen was flabbergasted. "I have so many questions. I only wish you could stay a little bit longer."

Katiera looked into his eyes, as she took hold of his hand, and entwined her fingers with his.

"If you'd like, perhaps I could visit again sometime."

The two were like magnets, gravitating as they eyed each other amorously. Owen could no longer control his desire as his lips slowly met hers. They softly kissed, savoring the moment that seemed to last much longer. Suddenly Katiera pulled away in almost an embarrassing fashion, hyperventilating from the rush of passion.

"It's getting dark. I should really go call out to my people now."

Owen was still dazed from the passionate moment, and awkwardly tried to regain his composure. He helped her from her chair like he was handling a fragile package, and she took notice of the gentle way he went about it. She sighed, letting loose of whatever penned up passion she was also holding.

"I'll go with you." He offered.
A smile graced her lips, as she gave an agreeing nod.

14

A short time later, they stood at the edge of the bank, looking out over the vast darkness of the lake. Owen made sure to steady her so that she wouldn't lose her balance.

Katiera inhaled long, and held more breath than any average person ever could. Without warning, she let loose with an ear-splitting call in a language that was mostly in high octaves. Owen winced at the unpleasant sound, but continued to still hold her steady. In a few short moments, she was finished. But the sound still echoed out over the open waters.

Owen's ears rang loudly from the high decibels, and he almost felt nauseated in its wake.

Katiera nearly passed out from expending all the air in her lungs, and he gripped her tighter to keep her steady.

"What was that?" Owen asked, still reeling from the repercussions in his ears.

"That's how we communicate over long distances." She breathlessly answered. We have an innate sense, almost like radar, that hones in on distinct tones, and tells us the location of the signal.

"I believe you succeeded. I think they probably heard you in California." He sarcastically answered.

She tried to walk on her own, but was too weak, and Owen had to catch her fall.

"Water! I need to be refreshed with water!" She pleaded.
"Okay, Katie!" He immediately scooped her up into his arms. "But I think we better do it this way."

In a residence, not too far away, Randy Gustafsson, better known by his nick name Bear, stormed into the living room where his thirty something son, Matty lazily slouched on the couch playing video games with another man about his age named Josh.

Randy was a tough, biker type in his mid-sixties with a large beer belly. He had crazy eyes, and a gray mohawk that tied into a small pony tail in the back.

"Get off your asses! We got a job to do."

"What kind of job, Pops?" Matty asked as he and the other equally rough looking individual rose to their feet."

"Your father's brother and his wife have been missing for a long time now, and we assume they're not coming back." His mother Myra, a tough looking plump woman with ratty looking blondish gray hair answered as she strolled in from another room.

"Kevin's cottage doesn't have much. But it's easy pickings." Randy smirked.

"We might find some goodies that we can peddle online or sell at the flea market." Myra arrogantly added.

"Do we have to do this right now?" Josh questioned. "I was just kicking your son's ass at Mortal Combat."

"If you want to sit here and play with yourself, go right ahead, Josh." Randy answered with a serious expression, and pointed finger. "But I'll have you know that I don't pay you to sit around and play games."
Myra proceeded ahead toward the door without further delay, and motioned as she barked out the order. "Let's roll!"

Back at the cottage, Owen peeked into the bathroom where he saw Katiera asleep, and immersed in the tub water. He walked in further, and left a robe alongside the towel he had left earlier. He paused to admire the beautiful Mermaid that laid

16

before him, complete with her tail, just as she was when he had found her. He quietly closed the door once again, and took a deep breath.

The temperature outside had dropped considerably after sunset, and the old cottage was getting cold. He strolled over to the fireplace to stoke the fire he had started earlier in the day, and realized that he had forgotten to buy more wood.

"Damn!" He whispered loudly to himself, before checking the time on his watch. He looked back toward the bathroom door for a moment, then pondered to himself. "Maybe I can get to the store before they close." He grabbed his keys from the kitchen counter, and hurried out the door.

The drive to the convenience store was only a few miles, but a short time after Owen left, the door to the cottage was kicked open. Randy and Myra strolled in and scanned the room with their eyes, as Matty and Josh sauntered in behind.

"Pretty nice place for a summer cottage." Randy stated, while Myra noticed the simmering embers in the fireplace.

"Look, Bear! Someone's been here."

"Squatters maybe?" Matty suggested as they all looked for other clues.

The noise had roused Katiera from her sleep, and she called out from behind the closed bathroom door. "Owen! Is that you?"
They all directed their attention to the closed door, and Randy signaled to Josh.

"Go check it out."

The long haired, lanky Josh slowly opened the door, and entered. When he came out, he was pulling along a now legged Katiera by the sleeve of her robe.

"Lookie here what I found. She's straight out of the bathtub, and damn, does she ever smell good."

Matty strutted forward with a chuckle. "Looks like old Owen has himself his own personal Barbie doll. What's your name, honey?"

Katiera refused to answer, and only stared at him with a scowl.

"Cat got your tongue, baby?" Josh taunted. "Maybe we can go in the other room, and I'll make you tell me."

He tried to pull her in closer, and she let loose with an ear piercing squeal that shook the cottage, and caused everyone to reel back, covering their ears.

"Son of a bitch! What the hell was that?" Matty roared, still protecting his ears from the reverb.

A bright light illuminated in the windows from the outside at that very moment, and what sounded like a generator hummed for a long, few seconds over the cottage, before it accelerated into a sonic type boom, that made everyone cower except for Katiera. It was over in no time at all, and everything was normal once again.

"What the hell is going on here?" Myra yelled.

Randy paced toward Katiera. "If you know what that was, you better start talking, girl."

"Step away from my daughter." An angry voice commanded, as everyone froze, and turned slowly.

In the open doorway stood a muscular man that looked to be in his early 50s. Behind him was a beautiful blonde woman that looked like an older version of Katiera. Although they were both heavily clothed for the weather, the man's enormous biceps bulged in the tight sleeves of his jacket. He also carried a large steel case with a handle. All stood anxiously silent, but Josh continued to hold his grip on Katiera's robe sleeve.

"I said, let her go." The man warned, as he paced further into room, and Josh wisely let loose of her.

Randy arrogantly stepped forward to confront him. "Who the hell are you?"

"Who I am is no concern of yours." He shot back with a challenging stare, while Katiera hurried to shield herself behind the broad frame of her father. "I demand that you tell me what's going on here."

"There's four of us, and we are all packing firearms." Randy sarcastically chuckled. "We're the ones who should be making the demands." He paced ever so closer, within inches of his face, but the man never flinched. "Now, why don't I just take that oversized brief case there, and you'll do as we say."

The man simply, and soberly stared at Randy, almost prodding him to make the first move.

"I don't think he understands the logic of the situation, Bear." Myra commented with a smirk.

The man glanced at Myra, then set his stare back on Randy.

Matty wandered over, and set his eyes on the man's wife.

"You are one hot mamma! I can see where your daughter gets her good looks." He remarked as he tried to brush his hand across her cheek, causing her to react with a repulsive sneer.

He turned to his father with a sarcastic laugh. "I think Josh and I should take them in the other room while you and Maw check out that metal briefcase."

"We deserve a little bit of fun." Josh added, as he lustfully eyed the two women.

Randy reached for the briefcase, and with lightning speed, the man gripped his thick neck with his free hand, lifting him off the ground.

"Why don't I just disembowel all of you, and toss your miserable carcasses in the lake?" He angrily countered, as Randy struggled to breathe.

Myra pulled a gun, and pointed it toward the man. "That's enough! Let him go!"

Katiera's mother calmly stepped forward, and with a swift move, seized hold of Myra's wrist. "You need to drop your gun first, sister."

Josh and Matty went to draw their guns as well, but Katiera surprised them with a loud, threatening roar that prompted them to back away.

"Don't make me hurt you." The woman warned a stubborn Myra, who continued to struggle.

With little effort, the woman gripped harder on her wrist until a loud crunch could be heard. Myra immediately dropped the gun, and howled in pain.

"Bitch! You broke my wrist."

"You're lucky that's all I broke." She sneered back, as she kicked the gun away across the floor.

Katiera's father also let loose of Randy, who reeled back, coughing, and gripping at his own throat. The man still held tight to the briefcase, refusing to set it down.

"What's going on here?" Owen loudly announced as he marched through the open door, dropping a cord of firewood in his wake.

All attention quickly shifted toward him.

He looked to Randy and Myra who were bent over in pain, then glanced to a slowly approaching Matty. Katiera quickly took safe refuge behind Owen.

He turned to her, never taking his eyes off of Matty. "Are you okay, Katie?"

She quickly nodded, and clutched at the back of his jacket.

"If any of you harmed her in any way, I will deal with you personally."

Katiera's parents gave each other a wide eyed glance, and an impressed nod.

Matty nervously chuckled at the threat. "Seems like you grew a set of nads since I last saw you, cousin Owen."

"I was twelve years old then, and you were an oversized bully. I think the odds are a bit more even now."

Matty grunted, turned to glance at Josh, then looked to his parents. Randy had somewhat recovered, and was now tending to Myra.

"Let's get out of here."

They all began to slowly file toward the door, casting hardened glares as they passed. Myra paused in front of Katiera's mother, and boiled over with contempt.

"You haven't seen the last of us."

"I certainly hope for your sake that isn't true." The blonde beauty sneered back at the wench.

Owen followed them to the door, and waited for them to drive away, while Katiera rushed to emotionally greet her parents. Owen paused to examine the broken lock mechanism on the door. "Looks like they did quite a number on my door."

"That's quite a lovely family you have there." Her father sarcastically remarked as he boldly stepped forward.

"I'm sorry about that." Owen sighed. "They're like a pack of jackals that I want nothing to do with." He then extended his hand. "I'm Owen."

The man stepped forward, and accepted the handshake. "My name is Xander, and this is my wife, Tabitha."

Owen nodded to them both.

"Owen is the one that saved me, daddy." Katiera spoke up. "I was trapped in a fishing net, and he cut me loose."

Xander glanced back at Owen. "I'm forever grateful to you." He then turned back to his daughter. "How many times have I warned you not to go swimming in the lake this time of year. You know how quick those storms can form."

"I'm sorry, daddy. I thought I could get one last swim in before winter."

"We can talk about that later, Xander." Tabitha lectured back as she comforted her daughter.

Xander took a deep breath, and turned his attention back to Owen. "I'm very protective of my daughter. She's our only child."

"I respect that. I never should have left her here alone." Owen sighed. "I only drove down the road for some firewood." Owen continued with much anxiety. "I never expected all of this to happen."

"Fortunately, we were able to diffuse the situation." Xander replied, as Tabitha strolled closer to Owen, looking him up and down in a calculating way, before glancing back at Katiera with a sly grin.
"He's quite rugged and handsome. Isn't he?" Katiera only responded with obvious embarrassment, and Owen tried to change the subject.

"Could I fix you both a cup of hot coffee?" He offered.

"That sir, would be heavenly." Xander enthusiastically replied. "But first, is there someplace we can converse with our daughter in private?"

"Of course! You can all go onto the porch, and I'll close the sliding glass doors." He gestured. "You should know that her rib is badly broken. I've done everything I can for her."

"I'm aware of that." Xander replied as he slightly lifted the steel case. "I came prepared."

The gesture, and comment baffled Owen, leaving him curious about what the mysterious steel case contained.

On a dark road, a short distance away, Randy slowed down his pickup truck, and pulled off to the side berm. The van following him also pulled up behind, and came to a stop.

"Something wrong, Bear?" Myra asked as she held her limp wrist with a pained expression.

"I just have to talk to the boys for a minute. Then I'll get you to the emergency room."

He got out of the vehicle, and marched with a purpose toward the van. Matty stayed behind the wheel, and rolled his window down.

"What's up pops?"

He paused for a moment in thought as he stood at the window. "I can't quit thinking that something wasn't quite right about those people back at my brother's cottage. I weigh 260 pounds, and that guy held me up like I was a 5 pound dumbbell."

"How about that tiny wife of his? How do you suppose she broke Maw's wrist so easily?" Matty questioned.

"And, that deafening squeal and roar that came out of their daughter." Josh added. "That didn't even sound human."

"Don't you boys also find it odd that her parents showed up shortly after we saw that bright light, and heard that loud hum over the cottage?"

"That was pretty weird." Matty replied. "What are you thinking, Paw?"

"I don't know." He stroked the white whiskers on his chin. "But I do have a hunch about something." He glanced back toward his pickup. "I may be a little late. But you boys go on home, and we'll talk more about this when I get back."

After a short while, Xander re-entered the cottage from the porch still holding onto the metal briefcase. He shook his head, and laughed.

"The women have a lot to talk about. They should be in shortly." He continued to stroll forward to where Owen sat at the dining room table. "That'll give you and I a few minutes to talk."

"Is everything alright?" Owen asked.

"You were right. She did have a broken rib, but it's fixed now." He poured himself a cup of coffee from the carafe that Owen had put on the table.
"Fixed? How can that be possible?"

"We have the advanced technology to fix injuries." He gestured toward the steel case with a grin.

Xander could read Owen's puzzled reaction to his answer.

"Let me try to explain. Do you have any old injuries that still give you a problem?"

"I have an old knee injury from when I played college football. Still hurts like hell. Especially in this cold weather."

"Would you mind if I took a look at it?"

25

Owen shook his head no, as he scooted his chair closer.

Xander carefully felt around the knee cap, and definitively nodded.

"You do have some cartilage damage, and a bit of arthritis."

"How can you determine that without an MRI?"

"I could read in my mind what I felt with my hands." He paused to take note of Owen's baffled expression. "I'm a physician in my world."

Owen showed a bit of enlightenment, but still had countless questions.

"Let's try something." Xander lifted the case onto the table and opened it, while Owen curiously watched.

He took out a device that looked like a large flat scanner device with a handle. He powered it up, and several infrared lights emitted energy as he was careful to hold it in the downward position.

"Now, I want you to close your eyes, and concentrate your energies on the injured area."

Owen did so, and could immediately feel the shock like force stimulating his knee from the laser's that Xander slowly ran over it. As he concentrated on the area, he could actually feel the tissue moving, and mending itself.

After a short while, Xander lifted away, and powered down the device.

"Okay. Now I want you to stand up, and tell me how it feels."

Owen cautiously stood up, and shook his leg. He bent both knees in a half squat, and stood back up.

"That's amazing! I haven't been able to bend it like that for years."

Xander only smiled with exuberance.

"You mentioned that you played football. Have you ever had a concussion?"

"As a matter of fact, I did have a few bell ringers back in the day."

Xander stood, and gave an all knowing nod.

"Have a seat, Owen. I can help you with that as well. Do the same as you did with your knee."
He began slowly running the scanner over his head, making sure not to miss an inch, while Owen clenched his eyes shut.

Owen could feel the energy, and it felt like his brain neurons were exploding to life as the pulses massaged them.

Xander lifted the device once again, and powered it down.

"How did that feel?"

"Like absolute nirvana. My mind feels so much clearer, and more powerful."

Xander only grinned as he placed the device back in its box.

"If we had more time, I'd work on some of the other blockages that the rigors of this life have caused."

"I'm totally awe stricken by your methods. How is it that you came across this technology?"

"We are far more advanced than your world. You are catching up slowly, but we probably have several centuries more knowledge about everything." He took a sip of his coffee.

"I don't know how to thank you. I feel better than I have in years."

"Consider it small payment for saving my precious daughter." He glanced back toward the still closed door to the porch. "You should know that she is quite fond of you."

Owen was careful with his words as Xander waited for a response. "I must say that I've grown quite fond of her as well in the short time we've known each other."

Xander could not help but smile exuberantly at his answer, before he looked off in the corner with thought. "She is quite special, you know." He paused. "Although, she has been a bit of a challenge for my wife and I."

Owen leaned into the conversation, as he continued. "In what way?"

"Even though she's extremely intelligent, she has a tough time concentrating on more than one thing at a time." He stood, holding his coffee cup, and began to pace as he talked. "She tends to wander off on her own, and daydream quite a bit."

"Sounds like she might have Attention Deficit Disorder. Surely you have advanced methods to treat that in your world."

Xander turned with raised brow, and nodded. "We've been able to somewhat master the science of genetics. But unfortunately, there are some defects that we've not been able to conquer."

"Excuse my indifference, but I don't find Katiera's issue to be much of a problem."

Xander turned with much surprise. "I'm quite impressed with that answer. Men generally tend to see it as a weakness, and look to other women instead."

"I guess I'm just a different breed of man. I see a beautiful, sensitive person who deserves to be loved by a good man."

Xander looked away, unable to contain a smile. "Unfortunately, in the world of the Oceanids, men have the advantage of choosing among many young women. It tends to lessen the chances for those like Katiera."

His eyes caught Owen's family pictures that adorned the wall in front of him, and he was quite surprised to see a familiar face.

"I know this man very well."

Owen strolled over to join him with an expression of extreme curiosity. "That man is my father."

"Your last name is Gustafsson?"

Still quite puzzled, Owen nodded yes.

"Your father is one of our trusted allies at NASA, and he's also a very good friend of mine." He turned his full attention to Owen. "Where is he now?"

"He, and my mother were taken in the rapture."

Xander reacted with an enlightened, and thought filled expression. "Yet, you were left behind."

As they conversed Tabitha and Katiera entered from the porch. Tabitha immediately spotted another photo, and quickened her pace, pointing toward it, shifting everyone's attention.

"I know that woman!" She exclaimed. "She's one of us."

"That's impossible!" Owen stated. "That's my great grandmother. She died in 1980."

"I'm quite certain that's Cynethea."

"My family did call her Gramma Thea."

"I remember I was just a young Mermaid when she left to be with a human on land."

Owen pointed to the picture of his great grandfather. "That would be the man in the picture next to hers." He then looked to Tabitha with a perplexed expression. "How could that be possible? If she had lived, she'd be well over a hundred years old."

Tabitha exchanged an amused glance with Xander, as she strolled closer. "I am 97 years old, Owen."

"And, I'm 93." Xander added as he put his arm around his wife. "I guess you can say she robbed the cradle when she captured my heart."

"An Oceanids average lifespan can be as much as 500 years."

Owen was flabbergasted by the revelation, and looked to Katiera for further information. "Then how old are you?"

Her eyes shyly drifted to the floor. "I'm 72. I'm considered to be a Mermaid well beyond my prime."

Owen's expression of caring and sympathy did not escape notice by her parents. He stumbled back, and fell into one of the dining room chairs, totally overwhelmed by what he had heard.

"Well, there is positive news from all of this." Tabitha paced over to where Owen was now sitting. "Owen, you're also one of us. You have Oceanid blood running through your veins."

Owen's attention was peaked, but he didn't know what to say. Katiera looked to her father with renewed vigor, and he responded with an assured wink.

Katiera then set her sights on a picture of Owen's father when he was a little boy.

"Is that your father when he was a little boy?"

"Yes, it is." Owen answered, as she then strolled over, and sat down next to him.

"I remember that little boy." She stated.

Owen only responded with wide eyed surprise, pleading for an explanation while everyone else moved in closer as well.

"When I was young, I snuck out one night with some other Mermaids. We gathered on the beach at the place your people call Eaglehurst. We wanted to watch the supply spacecrafts as they came and went from our world."

"I have no doubt that Angeline influenced you to do so." Her father sternly stated.

"That girl was always a bad influence." Her mother distressfully added, prompting a smirk from Owen.

"Anyway." Katiera continued. "That little boy saw us. The others scampered into the water, but I stopped to look. I'll never forget his face. He was so cute. "

"You were always the curious one, Katiera." Her mother replied, shaking her head.

"How old would you have been around that time?" Owen asked with further amazement.

"I don't know." She answered in deep thought. "Perhaps around 16."

"If we would've known she was out at that hour of the night, we would've grounded her for an entire year. Xander growled.

Owen was amused over the little family squabble, but decided to intervene.

"Are there any other surprises you'd like to reveal?"

All three exchanged glances, and shrugged.

"It's very late." Xander stated. "We should summon the craft to pick us up."

Katiera shot from her chair, and approached her father. "Oh daddy! Can't we stay at least until tomorrow?"

"We shouldn't inconvenience Owen any further, honey."

"I insist that you all stay." Owen stood. "You two can sleep in the Master Bedroom, Katiera can stay in the Spare Bedroom, and I'll sleep out here on the couch."

"Please, daddy!" Katiera pleaded.

Tabitha exchanged a quick pleading glance with her husband as well.

"Okay! Considering the revelation that came to light this evening, perhaps it would be good for us all to get better acquainted."

Katiera hugged and kissed her father on the cheek. "Thank you, daddy."
Xander sighed as Tabitha gave him a wink of approval.

"It's been a long day for all of us. Perhaps we could continue this conversation in the morning?" Xander concluded.

"That sounds good to me." Owen replied.

Katiera smiled at Owen with a gleam of excitement in her eyes that made his heart race.

3

A SHIFT OF DIRECTION

At Randy Gustafsson's house, a late night meeting was convening between him, his son Matty, and Josh. Randy pulled up a chair around the dimly lit dining room table, and leaned forward to converse.

"How's Maw?" Matty asked.

"She'll be in that cast for a while." He answered.

"We should track that bitch down, and make her pay for what she did." Josh angrily suggested.

"I have a better idea." Randy reasoned. "I think I know who those people were."

Matty and Josh straightened in their chairs as their interest peaked.

"Who do you think they are, Paw?"

"I believe they might be space aliens." He answered with a serious expression.

Josh burst into uncontrollable laughter, and Randy shot up from his seat in a fit of anger. He put a choke hold on him from behind with his large arms.

"You dare laugh at me boy?" He tightened the hold. "Don't you forget who took you in when those no good parents of yours kicked you to the curb." He let loose of the hold as Josh waved his hands in surrender.

Josh coughed and gasped for breath as Randy stomped victoriously back to his seat.

"Go on, Paw. What makes you think they're aliens?"

"When I was a kid." He began with a sigh. "My grandfather would take my brother down to the lakeshore in the middle of the night to watch the Lake Erie lights."

"I thought that was just an urban legend." Matty inserted.

"I thought it was for quite a few years as well. People would report them as a UFO sighting, claiming the lights disappeared into the lake, then glowed beneath the surface." He glanced at the other two men with suspense. "The Feds would come to town to investigate, and almost overnight those same folks came out, and denied everything they reported. The whole story ironically went away until another sighting took place."

"How come Grandpa Billy never took you to see those lights."

"He never had much to do with me after Gramma Thea noticed this here mark behind my right ear." He gestured to it.

"What is it, Paw? I never really noticed it."

"I don't know." He shrugged. "I assumed it was a birthmark. It's been there for as long as I can remember." He chuckled, and continued. "I always thought they were a couple of crazy old coots anyway. My parents thought the same thing, but they still allowed Kevin to spend time with them. He was their favorite." He looked away with slight resentment.

"What does all that have to do with those people we saw tonight?" Josh asked.

"I'm kind of wondering after all these years if there really was something about those lights." He paused in thought. "Maybe there's some connection with that light we saw before they showed up at the cottage."

"How does Owen figure into all this?" Matty asked.

"Good question." He nodded toward his son. "I'd also like to know what he's doing back here with winter coming up." He shook his head. "It don't make no sense."

"You thinking he knows something?" Josh probed.

"I wonder." He leaned back in his chair. "Before Grandpa Billy died, he gave Kevin an engraved steel box. He hid it somewhere in his room where I couldn't find it." He paused with intensity. "One day, I looked in his window, and he had the box open."

"What was in it?" Matty anxiously asked.

"It was some type of futuristic crystal that looked like a tuning fork."

"Did he do anything with it?" Matty further inquired.

"He noticed me in the window, and pulled the shade down." He paused to take a breath. "That was the last time I ever saw it. I'll never know where the hell he hid that thing."

"Since Kevin and his wife are no longer here, maybe Owen has it, and maybe it has some sort of connection to those people." Matty suggested.

"What are we gonna do?" Josh questioned.

"Let me think about it some more." Randy pondered. "In the meantime, I want you guys to keep an eye on that cottage."

At the cottage, everyone had settled in for the night. Owen turned off the table lamp near the couch, and pulled a blanket over himself. He stared at the ceiling in thought over the day's events. Suddenly he heard light footsteps across the wood floor, and looked off in that direction in the dark. He saw the white robed figure pacing toward him, and smiled to himself.

"Owen?" A soft voice whispered. "Can we talk?"

Without answering, he reached up, and turned the light back on. Katiera stood shyly at a safe distance. He could smell her fresh, pleasant scent, and was enraptured by her feminine beauty. He propped the upper portion of his body up, and directed all of his attention toward her. She could see the bare muscularity of his torso, and she trembled with penned up passion.

"Well, what would you like to talk about?"

"You called me Katie earlier in the evening."

"It kind of came out that way. If you were in my world, that's probably what people would call you for short."

She looked off in thought for a moment. "I kind of like the sound of it. You can call me that from now on, if you'd like."

Owen smiled with slight amusement. "Was there something else you wanted to talk about?"

She nervously fidgeted, and shrugged.

"You know, you don't have to stand over there. I don't bite."

His comment made her laugh, and he motioned for her to sit at the edge of the couch.

"Now, what's on your mind?"

She hesitated for a moment, almost afraid to make eye contact. "When you kissed me on the porch earlier, did you really mean to do that?"

Owen sighed, and looked her straight in the eyes. "I'll tell you the honest truth, Katie. I wanted to kiss you then, and I want nothing more than to kiss you right now."

Before he could say another word, Katiera leaned in, and initiated a long, passionate kiss. Her lips felt like soft velvet against his, and the warmth of the moment took away the late October chill in the room. As their kiss came to a subtle conclusion, both breathed heavy from the enraptured intensity. Owen wished he could just embrace her in his arms for the remainder of the night. It had been far too long since a woman had ignited his soul in that way. They stayed inches apart for what seemed like an eternity, staring dreamily into each other's eyes.

"How was that?" She breathlessly whispered.

"Unforgettable." He whispered back, still somewhat reeling.

"We should talk more about this tomorrow." She concluded as she stood, walking away with a happy grin. She paused, and looked over her shoulder in an almost flirting way. "Goodnight, Owen!"

"Goodnight, Katie!" He sighed, never taking his eyes off the beautiful woman until she was completely gone from his sight.

The morning sun streamed through the shuttered windows of the cottage as Owen awoke to the sound of activity in his kitchen. He sat up on the edge of the couch, and wiped the sleep from his eyes as he looked in that direction. He stood, grabbing his t-shirt from the back of the couch, and Tabitha peeked out from within the kitchen to catch a pleasing glance at his manly physique.

"Good morning, Owen."

"Good morning." He seemed somewhat embarrassed at being seen shirtless. "Where is everyone?"

"Xander is hydrating in the shower, and Katiera is still sleeping."

He wandered over and sat on one of the counter stools opposite Tabitha as she busied herself at the stove.

"I figured the least I could do is prepare breakfast." She grinned with pursed lips.

"I appreciate that, Tabitha." He yawned. "I didn't sleep long, but I slept more peaceful than I have in years."

"That must be from the scanner. Xander told me he treated you last night." She poured him a cup of coffee, and set it on the counter in front of him, pausing to carefully measure her next words. "I could see the caring in your eyes when you addressed Katiera last night."

"Was it that obvious?"

"Painfully." Tabitha could not contain an amused smile.

"I find myself being very sympathetic with her situation." Owen sipped his coffee. "I'm only in my early 30's, but I still feel I'm a bit behind on the curve."

"You're a good man, Owen." She patted his hand, and sighed. "The type we always hoped Katiera would find."

The comment made Owen's eyes widen as she turned back toward the stove, and dished a generous helping of scrambled eggs and spinach onto his plate.

She set it down in front of him, and handed him a fork. "Tell me how you like this." She leaned against the counter.

Owen scooped a fork full into his mouth, and reacted. "These are the most delicious eggs I've ever tasted."

"I energized, and purified them before cooking it." She smirked. "That is the way that eggs, and all food should taste in its true natural form."

"Amazing!"

"She sure is." Xander mused as he entered the room, kissing his wife on the cheek. "Hopefully she hasn't told you all of our secrets."

"Only half." She joked with him.

"Do you like to fish, Owen?" Xander asked as he also leaned against the counter.

"As a matter of fact, I do."

"Your father wouldn't happen to have a spare fishing rod around here, would he?"
"I think there might be one."

"You and I have quite a bit to talk about. The best conversations always take place while fishing."

"I know of a really sweet spot." Owen grinned. "We can go there after breakfast."

At the home of Randy Gustafsson, Myra strolled into the dining room where Randy was eating his breakfast. She held her car keys and a heavy jacket in her good hand.

"Can you help me get this damn thing on, Bear?" She huffed. "The last thing I need to do is get pneumonia on top of this broken wrist."

Randy got up from his chair, and began placing the jacket on her, making sure not to disturb the cast on her forearm.

"Where in the hell do you think you're going?"

"I'm going to get to the bottom of who those people are."

"You're not going back to that cottage, Myra. At least, not without me or one of the boys."

"I'll be fine, Bear. I'm just going to spy on them." She stated with purpose. "I'm taking my car, and I'll park down the road where no one will notice it." She looked toward the empty chairs at the table. "Where are the boys?"

"Still sleeping. You should sit down and have a cup of coffee, and wait for them."

"I may still be sitting there in the afternoon hours." She sarcastically replied. "Why don't you go with me?"
"I can't. I have an important meeting later this morning." He sighed. "Why can't you simply wait."

Myra stepped closer, challenging her husband. "That bitch broke my wrist. That was a big mistake, and I vow to stalk her until I get my revenge."

"Just be careful." He stepped aside to let his wife pass. "We both are well aware of what those people are capable of doing."

"True. But obviously they aren't aware of what we're capable of doing." She smirked.

Katiera stretched her arms upward, and yawned as she entered from her bedroom at the cottage.

"Well! Good morning, sunshine! Tabitha quipped, as she sat alone at the dining table. "I was beginning to think you'd be sleeping the day away."

"I slept so well, mother." She giddily responded as she took a seat at the table, and lowered her voice to a hush. "I think Owen is falling in love with me."

"There's no need to whisper. The men went fishing a short time ago." Tabitha reacted with a pursed smile, and a sigh. "I know you've waited a long time, sweetheart. But don't you think you're moving a bit too quick."

Katiera let out an exhilarating breath. "I've never had such strong feelings for a man. He's so handsome, and masculine. Yet he's also gentle and kind."

"He is a land dweller. That could be very complicated for the two of you."

"It worked for Cynethea."

"Cynethea had a much shorter life because of it, my dear."

"But I'm sure that short life was very happy for her."

Tabitha answered with a surrendering sigh. "You really do love him, don't you?"

"More than words could ever describe."

Her mother pondered in worried thought for a moment. "After I get you fed, we'll take a walk along the beach, and talk about this some more. I think the fresh morning air will do us both some good.

"That sounds wonderful." She smiled.

At the point where a large creek fed into Lake Erie, Owen and Xander chose a perfect place to cast their lines into the cold water. The foggy morning mist lingered thick in the air, and its moisture, coupled with a stiff northern wind chilled their exposed faces.

"According to this morning's fishing report, the water temperature is a chilly 55 degrees." Owen casually commented as he placed bait on the hook, and cast his line into the water. "I would imagine that's even cold for a water dweller. How do you ever survive the winters?"

"Fortunately, we're quite tolerant of the cold, and we're also fortunate that the lake only freezes on the surface. We're able to come up, and swim beneath the ice with the rest of the fish."

"Come up from where?" Owen questioned with a puzzled expression that amused Xander.

"We don't live in the water, Owen. We live beneath it."

"You're telling me that there's an unknown world out there beneath the lake?"

"One that would boggle your imagination." Xander smiled with an assured nod before changing the subject. "By the way, I never got to ask you what line of work you were in."

"I'm a marine scientist for the state of Florida."

"I'm impressed. Now I understand how you knew exactly what to do when you found Katiera."

Just the mention of her name made Owen's heart race, and Xander could sense it. "I shudder to think what might have happened if she had been found by someone else." He sighed. "She'd probably be dissected on a cold steel table in a research lab."

"That's the exact reason I distance myself from most of my peers." Owen's voice rose with a tinge of anger. "They're more interested in killing, and studying that which is different, rather than honoring its right to live."

Xander took in a deep breath of the crisp air, and pondered.

"I'm beginning to think there may have been divine intervention in the fact that you weren't taken with the others"

"I appreciate that you're a man of faith, Xander. But outside of being here to save your daughter, I can't understand how a loving God would take my friends and family, while leaving me here in this evil world to fend for myself."

"Sometimes we're blind to God's real purpose."

"I'd like to believe that was true." He paused in painful reflection. "After the rapture, I lost my house, and all my belongings in Hurricane Ian. Our research facility was wiped out as well. I then took a transfer to the east coast where I lived in my parent's primary residence. Then I got laid off when the economy went bad."

"And, here you are with us." Xander responded with raised brow, prompting Owen to ponder his situation further.

"I guess the most positive thing that's happened to me in a while is finding Katiera."

"I have to ask you this, Owen." He paused to measure his words. "Most men of your age would normally be settled with a wife and children. How is it that a bright, handsome young man like yourself is still single?"

"That's getting rather personal, but there was someone special at one time." He painfully recanted.

"What happened?"

"She grew tired of the long, unpredictable hours that I worked, and complained that the state didn't pay me enough." He grunted. "She took up with a rich, real estate investor that was twice her age. After that experience, I never really trusted anyone else."

Xander couldn't hold back an amused chuckle, which didn't settle well with Owen.

"What in the hell is so funny about that?"

"Owen! You may not realize it, but you were the luckiest man in the world when she walked out of your life. You were never meant to be with that materialistic woman. She never really loved you, and she would've brought nothing but a lifetime of misery."

Owen took time to consider what he had said, smiled, and then gestured toward his pole. "You may think I'm the luckiest man, but neither one of us are having much luck catching fish."

Xander simply peered out at the gray misty skies over the lake as though he never heard what he said. "Sometimes we're so busy looking back to our past failures that we fail to see the good fortune in front of us." He paused. "You already caught a very big fish in this lake, Owen." He smiled. "My daughter is very much in love with you, and if I can say so myself, she is the best catch you could ever hope to land."

"I think I already know that." Owen stated with a sigh.

"Why don't you come back to Station 37 with us?" He suggested. "I have a feeling you'd be very happy there."

Owen couldn't help but laugh. "I can't shape shift into a fish. How could I ever make it in your world?"

Xander chuckled, and glanced upward. "You have so much to learn about your own hidden abilities, my friend."

Owen looked out to where his bob was being bounced aimlessly by the waves. "I don't think we're going to catch anything. You want to call it a day?"

"Not just yet." Xander grinned as he stood, and held the palms of his hands out toward the lake. He then chanted an off key melody in his native tongue, and the sound echoed out over the surface of the water. Within seconds, a large school of fish were gathered in the waters in front of them, and they each immediately reeled in a catch.

"That's amazing!" Owen marveled. "How did you do that?"

"Sometimes when you have patience, and wait long enough, good things happen." He paused with a grin. "As I said before. You have much to learn. And if you wish, we can teach you everything you need to know."

On the blacktop road that led to the cottage, Myra pulled her weather worn Toyota off the berm a short distance from it, and grabbed hold of the binoculars that were lying on the seat beside her.

"Okay Owen! Let's see what you and your new friends are up to." She smirked.

A few moments after leaving her car, she managed to position herself in a hidden spot in the woods, just within sight of the cottage. She placed the binoculars up to her eyes to get a closer look.

"Looks like Owens' car is gone. I wonder if his alien friends are there." She conversed to herself.

Just then, Tabitha and Katiera exited the house, and made their way toward the cliff leading to the beach.

"There's the two barbie dolls." Myra sarcastically whispered to herself.

She waited for the two women to disappear below the cliff, before cautiously moving in for a closer look. She looked into the windows that she could see into, and was careful that no other eyes were watching her. After years of participating in home burglaries with her husband, she had become an old pro at this type of activity.

"Looks like Mr. Muscle isn't around either." She quipped.

She moved to the edge of the cliff, and watched the women on the beach joyfully conversing, and looking out over the lake.

As she observed, the two women surprisingly shed their clothes until they both were totally naked, and then proceeded to stroll into the cold waters.

"What in the hell are they doing?" Myra spoke out loud, as she put the binoculars to her eyes to get a better look. "They'll freeze to death."

She watched as they waded in just above their waists, then plunged their entire bodies below the surface. She drew an anxious, shocked breath at what she saw next. Two graceful tail fins flipped above the waves as they swam away.

"Bear and the boys are not going to believe this." She pondered for a moment at what she had just witnessed, before turning to glance back at the cottage. "I wonder if Kevin is hiding that key that Bear was telling me about? She thought a few moments more. "Maybe I'll take a quick look inside the cottage."

Meanwhile, Owen and Xander were now conversing on their way back with enough fish for a few good dinners.

"I still can't get over how you summoned those fish." Owen commented.

"I'm sure without even realizing it, you telepathically communicate in a similar way when you're aiding injured marine life. I have no doubt they understand that you're trying to help them, and they respond."

"When I think about it that way, I guess you're right."

Owen thought about a question he had wanted to ask Xander, but he was struggling with a way to phrase it. Xander could read his expression, and his silent pondering.

"I know you have a question for me, Owen. Get it out." Both men smiled with amusement.
"I was just wondering. Were my parents, and the others raptured to some different world, or did they just dissolve in the air, and they're all dead?"

Xander drew a deep breath before answering. "I can say with certainty that they aren't dead." Owen quickly glanced at him with surprise before he continued." They're all being held in safe places until the drama plays out on earth."

"Do you know where my mother and father might be?" He anxiously asked.

Xander sympathetically shook his head no. "I might be able to help you locate them. But it could take some time."

"As long as I know they're safe, and alive. That's all I care about."

"I can assure you they are, my friend." He sighed. "I'll speak with my contacts within the Nereid colonies, and the other Oceanid communities. Perhaps they may be able to help."

Owen responded with a thankful grin. Then set his sights to the Toyota on the berm of the road ahead.

"Looks like someone may have broken down." He quickly glanced at the car as they passed, before turning into his driveway."

"Inside the cottage, Myra had been rummaging through drawers and cabinets to see where Kevin might've hidden the mysterious key. As she made her way into the master bedroom, the first place she set her sights on was underneath the bed. She reached beneath it, and pulled out the steel case that Xander had been previously safe guarding.

"Well! Would you look what I found. This might even be better than the key."
She set it on the bed, and was preparing to open it when she heard Owens' car pull up outside.

"Oh shit!" I gotta get out of here."

In a quick panic, she grabbed the case with her good hand, and fled into the outer room. She alertly looked around, noticing the back door. She opened it with difficulty, and managed to escape into the nearby woods without either man seeing her.

Owen and Xander were occupied lifting the cooler of fresh caught fish from the back of the SUV, while Myra circled back to her car.

"We'll take these straight to the kitchen for cleaning." Owen ambitiously stated.

"Not just yet." Xander proclaimed. "First, we need to fill this cooler with water while the fish are still in it. Do you have an outside spigot?"

"Yes, there's one right at the front of the house. Luckily, I haven't shut them off yet."

After the men filled the cooler, Xander hovered the palms of his hands over it, closing his eyes in concentration. Within seconds, the clear water turned to a murky brownish black. Owen winced at the horrid smell it emitted.

"What's all that?"

As Xander opened his eyes, he calmly answered. "That is all the mercury, chemicals, and other pollutants that the fish ingested into their beings from the lake waters."

"That's disgusting!"

"What's even more disgusting is the fact that our bodies would've inherited those same pollutants had we not purified the fish." He nodded with assurance. "We'll repeat this process two more times, and I guarantee when we finally cook them up, they'll be the tastiest fish you've ever eaten."

"If they taste as good as the eggs that Tabitha made this morning, I can hardly wait."

On the beach below the cottage, the two women came ashore from their short swim, seemingly unshaken by the cold temperature.

"I certainly hope no one is watching." Katiera quipped as they put their clothes back on.

Tabitha casually scanned their surroundings with wide eyes. "If there is, they'll certainly get an eyeful of two very gorgeous Mermaids.

They both giggled.

Back at the cottage, the men hauled the cooler of fish into the kitchen.

"That's rather odd." Xander stated as he glanced around. "I wonder where the women went."

"Perhaps they're napping. There isn't much else to do around here."

Xander continued looking around the room suspiciously, noticing certain things had been disturbed. "Someone's been here."

Xander hurried toward the master bedroom, while Owen opened the door, and checked the spare. Finding that Katiera wasn't there, he swiftly headed to the master bedroom where he found Xander on the floor, checking under the bed.

"It's gone! They took the box."
"Do you think they took the women too?"

"They would've had quite a fight on their hands. My wife and daughter are both highly skilled in the fighting arts." He searched his surroundings with a distressful expression. "I should have never left the healing device unattended."

"We can assume with much certainty that my uncle and his gang have it."

Just then, the door opened, and the two women sauntered in.

"Where in the world have you two been?" Xander asked with heightened anxiety in his voice.

Tabitha stepped forward to aggressively answer her husband. "Since you two men went fishing, we thought we'd take a stroll, and a short swim."

"You took a swim?" Xander huffed. "What if someone saw you transform?"

"Oh really, Xander! There's barely a soul to be found this time of year around here."

"In the defense of the women, I have to say they're right. Most of these cottages are second homes, and rarely inhabited during the winter months." Owen spoke up, garnering only a stern glance from Xander.
"Neither one of you even thought about locking the door when you left?" He further questioned.

"Why should we, daddy? Katiera defiantly asked. "We don't use locks in our world."

"Both of you are so naïve to the ways of the land dwellers." He anxiously paced. "Someone broke into the cottage, and took the healing device while you two were out frolicking."

Both women reacted with surprise and shock.

"It had to be one of those despicable people from the other night." Tabitha suggested.

"That's what we're thinking." Owen answered. "But we can't be certain. These are desperate economic times, and it could be some drifter looking to pillage an uninhabited cottage."

Xander continued to pace, then turned to Owen. "That car that we saw on the side of the road. If we find it at your uncle's house, we'll know it was them for sure. We should go there now."

"Hold on, Xander." Owen warned. "You can't go there like a raging bull. They are heavily armed, and their bullets will kill you."
"Owen's right, sweetheart." Tabitha added. "We need to sit down, and think this thing over." She sighed. "Besides, I seriously doubt that any of them have the intelligence to figure out how that device works."

"Why are you so protective of the technology anyway?" Owen questioned. "A device such as that would revolutionize healthcare for humanity."

"You don't understand, Owen. It would be a disaster if that device was used for profit rather actual healing. Only the rich and elite of your society would be able to afford and benefit from it."

Tabitha sat down while Katiera remained standing in anxious thought.

"I'm sorry, daddy. This is all my fault."

Xander quickly moved to embrace and console his daughter. "Things like this happen, honey. You're certainly not to blame."

Owen approached her as well. "Your dad's right about that." He assured. "Besides, I would've never met all of you if none of this had ever taken place.

His caring eyes met hers, and she responded with a warm smile. For that one moment, everything else taking place in the room ceased. Katiera's heart raced as it always did while around Owen, and she wanted more than anything to embrace him. Owen felt the same way, but chose to move the conversation along.

"If there's anyone to blame, it's my bone headed uncle and his family." He vented, still not able to take amicable eyes off of Katiera. "They've been a thorn in the side of my family for years."

A very wise Xander took full notice of the magnetic energy that passed between the two, and exchanged a quick, enlightened grin with his wife. "Maybe we should all sit just down and discuss the situation at hand."

Myra Gustafsson anxiously entered her house, quickly placing the steel case on a table top. Carefully, she opened it, and examined the healing wand with a perplexed expression.

"What in the hell is this thing?" She whispered to herself.

"What you got there, Maw?" Matty questioned as he stumbled into the room, wiping sleep from his eyes.

"Don't tell me you're just getting up?"

"I was up for most of the night gaming on the internet."
He paced closer, and yawned. "Isn't that the steel box that alien
freak had?"

"I snuck into the cottage, and took it." Myra answered
with a smirk, while Matty closely examined the wand.

"What do you think it is? Some kind of scanner?"

"There's a power button here on the handle. Let's fire it
up, and find out."

She pressed the button, and the infra-red lasers shined
directly onto Matty's face, causing him to reel back. "Damn it,
Maw! Point that thing down."

He blinked his eyes to recover while his mother held it
down toward the table. "Hold this thing for a minute. I only have
one free hand." He carefully took hold of the device.

"Wave those lasers over the palm of my hand." She
ordered.

Matty carefully placed it over her open palm, and Myra's
eyes grew wide.

"That's amazing!" She marveled. "My hand is tingling.
It's like my blood is rushing warm, all the way into my fingers."
She clenched her fingers to her palm. "Turn it off."

Matty raised it away, and fired it down while his mother
stretched her fingers, then clenched them again.

"Look at that, Matty. I haven't been able to flex my
arthritic fingers like that in quite some time."

Both her and her son looked toward the device with
wonder. Then Myra had an enlightened thought.

"Let's try something." She told him with a sly grin as she settled her casted arm on the table. "Run that thing across my broken wrist."

At the cottage, Owen and his new friends pondered their dilemma.

"What do you think your useless uncle will do with that device?" Xander vented.

"My guess is he'll try to figure out what it is, and when he can't, he'll take it to someone who might know. Then, he'll no doubt sell it." Owen answered.

"At least that buys us some time." Tabitha suggested.

"That's a good thing." Xander replied, seriously eyeing everyone at the table. "I'll need to consult with others about this situation. Considering that they are heavily armed, we may need to bring in reinforcements."

"I sense there's something more to all of this." Owen countered, causing Xander to reply with a long sigh.

"When I held your uncle's throat at arms length, I noticed a distinct mark behind his right ear." He paused as Owen leaned into the conversation with heightened interest. "Do you know if he was ever a victim of alien abduction?"

"Not that I'm aware of." He cluelessly answered. "He's just been a social misfit his entire life."

Xander looked to the pictures on the wall in the other room.

"I noticed there's a generation missing from that wall. What's the story with your father and Randy's parents?"

"I never knew my grandparents, and all known pictures of them were destroyed in a fire."

"What fire?"

"They died when their house exploded and burned in the middle of the night. It was assumed there was a gas leak."

"And your father, and Randy survived this fire?"

"My father was away at college, and Randy wasn't home at the time."

"Conveniently, I suppose." Xander gave an enlightened nod.

"Are you saying that my uncle killed his own parents?"

"Owen, I think at some point your uncle was abducted by the evil aliens, as many others of his generation were." He stood and began to pace as he talked. "They would implant a chip at the base of their brain behind their right ear, gaining control over their thoughts and actions." He halted to address an astonished Owen directly. "They program these people to destroy all that is good, and to aid them in the takeover of this world."

"Wouldn't he be aware of all this? Surely, he'd remember being abducted."

"I'm certain they erased his memory of the event prior to returning him to earth."
"These evil aliens you speak of. Who exactly are they?"

Katiera finally spoke up with much disdain to answer his question. "They are the Draconians, the Reptilians, and the evil Grays. We are part of the Pleiadian Federation that have been battling them for centuries."

"They've infiltrated your world for at least that long. They're master shape shifters as we are, and have interbred with your people over the years to create hybrids." Xander finished her statement.

"They've gained control over all facets of your society, and brainwashed your people. They are the enemy that we are here to help you defeat." Tabitha added.

Owen was totally flabbergasted by the revelation. "So, I assume you're the white hats that my father often spoke about." He pondered. "I'm beginning to see the whole picture now, but I still don't see how my uncle, and the healing device fit into all of this."

"Your uncle is unconsciously under their control. If he takes that device to a person who is also allied with the evil aliens, they'll know that it is our technology." Xander answered with much anxiety.

"If they were to find out where our stations are located, they would attack with the misled element of your world, and destroy our civilization." Tabitha further stressed.

"And, they would falsely claim that we were the evil invaders in order to justify their acts." Xander sat back down with a thought filled sigh. "I'll need to leave here tonight to consult with the elders." He looked to his wife and daughter. "I'll leave you two off at station 37."

"But daddy!" Katiera protested. "I don't want to leave Owen. I'm in love with him." She declared in a frustrated huff. "There! I just said everything I know you already assumed."

Her parents mustered a grin, and glanced toward a surprised Owen for a response.

"Yes!" He set his focus on Katiera. "I'm in love with you as well. That's exactly why you can't stay. It's not safe here."

"Then come with us, Owen." She pleaded.

"How would I ever get to your world, Katie? I don't have the tolerance to cold water as you do, and I don't have the lung capacity, or ability to shape shift."

"There's another way to get there." Xander answered with a wink and a grin. "Come with us, and should you decide to return here, so be it."

Owen anxiously glanced toward Katiera, then back to her parents. "What will I need for the journey?"

"Just bring yourself, sweetie." Tabitha answered. "We have everything you'll need."

Xander stood once again, and gave a firm pat to Owen's shoulder. "With that settled, you and I have some fish to prepare. We'll all feast well before we depart."

"When will we leave?" Owen further questioned as he reached over, and took hold of Katiera's hand.

"Late. We have to go under the cover of night." Xander replied as he eyed the amorous couple. "I promise that Tabitha and I will give you two lovebirds some private time before we depart."

Meanwhile, Randy stormed into his house, tossing his jacket onto the back of a chair. Myra sat in the living room waiting for him, along with Matty and Josh. He looked toward all of them, not noticing the absence of Myra's cast, nor her lingering smirk.

"I see you two finally decided to get up." He grunted. "While you slept, I sold that furniture we stole last week. Got $200 for it."

Myra held up her arm, stretching her fingers out, and flexing her wrist.

"Notice anything different, Bear?"

His expression turned to one of surprise and amazement. "How'd you do that?"

She stood, and approached him. "Remember that steel case that the alien had the other night?"

"Yeah!" He stared back, begging for more info.

"I stole it, and figured out what it was."

"It's some sort of healing device, Paw." Matty exuberantly spoke up. "We used it to heal Maw's wrist."

"And it worked on my arthritic fingers as well." Myra added.

"How in the hell did you get in that cottage?"

"I waited until they left, and just walked right in." She paused with a grunt. "I was looking for that crystal key you were telling me about, and found this instead." She held up the steel case. "I got out of there just in time before Owen and the big guy returned."

"If that thing healed you, it could net us a fortune." Randy chuckled.

"There's more to the story, Bear." She continued to smirk. "I saw the women go down to the beach. They took off their clothes, and went into the cold water."

"That's crazy! Any normal human would've succumbed to hyperthermia within minutes."

"But they didn't." Myra paced the room. "I saw them transform into fish."

"Mermaids?" He questioned with disbelief.
"Tails and all."

"We should try to capture them, Paw." Matty suggested.

"You numb skull!" Randy balked back. "Those bitches could kick the shit out of all three of us." He stroked his whiskers. "I got a better idea."

"What are you thinking, Bear?"

"I need to make a few phone calls. I think we're onto something real big here."

As early evening set in, Owen stood on the enclosed porch, and looked out over the billowing gray clouds over the lake. Katiera entered the porch as well, carefully closing the sliding glass door behind her. Owen smiled to himself as she gently took hold of his bicep, and stood close to him.

"Those are snow clouds out over the lake. We might get a blizzard later tonight." Owen commented.

"It'll be alright." Katiera assured. "We'll get out well before the storm." She nudged closer. "Can we sit down and talk?"

Owen gave an obliging nod, as they both settled onto the porch swing.

"This is where we had our first kiss." She smiled giddily.

"That's a moment I certainly won't forget." Owen recanted as he looked out over the dark lake in thought. "I'm curious." He began. "You mentioned that you visited my world in the 1980's. Where did you go?"

"Some of my friends and I went to a place called The Peninsula Inn."

"I heard my father and mother speak of that place." He chuckled. "They tore it down sometime before I was born."

"It was a wonderful place, Owen. They had a live band, and we all danced barefoot in the sand." She paused in anxious remembrance. "I had this yummy drink called a wine cooler. Some guy bought it for me."

"I would imagine you girls garnered quite a bit of attention." Owen smirked.

"There were these really cute guys that talked to us. They wanted us to go home with them." She lowered her voice in a naughty tone. "I think they wanted to have sex with us."

"I certainly have no doubt about that." He chuckled. "Where else did you go?"

"We went to this amusement park named Waldameer."

"I used to go there when I was a kid." Owen spoke up with excitement.

"The midway lights were so wonderful. I can remember the pleasant smell of popcorn, candy apples, and cotton candy that lingered in the air."

Owen responded with a sentimental smile. "I remember that as well."

"I think we rode the carousel at least five times. I rode the same jumper the whole time, and remember the happy music that mingled with the joyful laughs of the children." She fondly remarked. "It's an experience I'll never forget."

"So, you don't have amusement parks or carousels in your world?"

"They do in Nereida, and other larger civilizations. But our station is way smaller. We only have a population of around 500."

"Where is this Nereida that you speak of?"

"It's the large city of the Nereid civilization that exists beneath the deepest part of the Atlantic Ocean. The Nereids are our closest ally here on earth."

Owen leaned back in wondrous thought.

"I'm quite curious. What did you girls use for money when you walked on land?"

"In our world, we have a money exchange. We have tokens that bind us to certain public service responsibilities, and they give us money from your world in return."

"Are you saying that there's no official currency in your world?"

She shook her head. "No banks either."

"How do you pay for things?"

"Through barter and exchange."

"So, there is no economic hierarchy?"

She giggled as she shook her head. "There is no poverty or elites. Everyone simply volunteers their own labor and unique talents for the benefit of all."

"Wow!" He exclaimed with amazement. "I have so many things to learn about you and your people."

Katiera's blue eyes glanced upward at his face, and she gave him a flirting smile as she drastically shifted the conversation.

"Would you like to make love to me, Owen?

Quite surprised by her question, Owen nervously cleared his throat. "Not here, Katie!" He lowered his voice. "Not with your parent's in the house."

"No, silly!" She laughed. "You'd have to commit to me first, then we'd have to wait for an appropriate time." She sighed. "Will you make a pledge to be my special someone?"

"Yes, Katie! I most certainly will, and I can't wait to share many special moments with you." He leaned in and gently kissed her.

After a few seconds, she pulled back, looking dreamily into his eyes. "Will you take me to Waldameer sometime?"
He kissed her on the forehead, and chuckled. "I promise we'll go there next summer, and we can ride the carousel as many times as you want."

She joyfully placed her hand against the side of his face, and kissed him again.

"I love you, Owen."

"I love you too, Katie."

Tabitha secretly peeked through the glass of the sliding doors at the two young lovers. "I'm so happy for you, sweetheart." She whispered to herself, before turning away with an emotional sigh.

Just then, Xander struggled against a strong gust of wind to enter the house. The large swell of cold north wind blew in, sending a lamp, and several other items crashing to the floor.

"Mercy!" Tabitha exclaimed. "I sure hope the transport craft will be able to hover over us in this wind."

"We can only hope." He answered, pausing to catch his breath. "We all must be outside the cottage by 10:00."

Owen and Katie swiftly entered from the porch to see what had happened. Xander motioned toward the broken lamp. "Sorry about the little mishap. There's quite a Canadian Clipper moving across the lake tonight."

"I noticed it was beginning to snow as well." Owen added as he looked up at the pictures of his family that were blown crooked. The picture of his great grandmother Thea was the only one that had crashed to the floor, revealing a large hole in the wall behind it. Owen paused to look at it with wonder.

Without saying another word, he grabbed a wooden dining room chair, and stood on it to investigate, while everyone else gathered to watch.

"What is it, Owen?" Katiera asked.

"Some sort of hidden compartment." He craned his neck to look inside. "Wait! There's something in here."

He reached inside, and pulled out a very old, ornate silver box.

"I recognize that box." Xander stated with much surprise, while Owen stepped down, and carried it to the nearby dining table. "It's from our world."

Owen opened the box, and slowly pulled out the crystal tuning key, while everyone else watched in amazement.

"I haven't seen one of those in years." Xander marveled, as he stepped closer to investigate.

"What is it?" Owen impatiently questioned.

"It's the key that opens the portal to our world." He paused with emphasis. "At least that's what it was used for at one time. We have a more modern method that we use now."

Tabitha reached down her shirt, and pulled out a chain with a platinum key on the end of it. It had a cluster of crystals imbedded into it.

"We use these now. They have a chip that sends an encoded signal to the portal." She explained, while Owen carefully handed the outdated relic to Xander.

"Surely, Cynethea must've brought it to this world." Katiera suggested.

"Yes." Her father answered. "They would give those keys to the Mermaids that chose to live on land in case they ever wanted to return. Even if it was discovered by an individual from this world, they would probably never know what it was used for."

"I'd have to guess that your great grandparents entrusted it with your father when they died, and he kept it hidden away for all these years." Tabitha asserted.

"We have to take this back to our world, where it belongs." Xander seriously stated as he placed it back in the box, and secured it.

"Why all the secrecy when no one in this world knows what its purpose is?" Owen further questioned, as Xander paced away in worried thought.

"There is one man who presently walks this earth who knows what it is." He turned back to address Owen directly. "If he were to get possession of it, he could destroy our civilization."

"Who is this man?"

Xander paused to anxiously glance at his wife and daughter before answering Owen. "He's the immortal enemy of our people. His name is Lucifer Morningstar."

"Wait a minute!" Owen shook his head in disbelief. "The same Lucifer Morningstar that we refer to as the Devil or Satan?"

"One and the same." Xander replied with certainty.

"If you recall from your Christian Bible, there is a seven year period following the rapture that is known as the tribulation." Tabitha explained. "It is during that time that Satan dwells among the people on the earth, and creates much mayhem and suffering. I do believe we may be in that period of time, Owen."

Xander looked up to the hole in the wall. "Surely, it was an act of divinity that helped us discover that key."

Katiera took hold of Owen's hand, and offered an expression of assurance. "Just as it was a divine act that enabled Owen to find me." She nodded.

"Our God is certainly in control." Tabitha concluded.

4

THE SECRET WORLD OF STATION 37

As evening dragged on, the blizzard outside grew with intensity. Wind gusts blew against the windows, and howled like a pack of wolves. Owen had busied himself the whole time securing the cottage for the long winter ahead, shutting the water off, and draining the pipes. He now sat pensively with the two women, occasionally glancing up at the clock which now read 9:52. Xander paced nervously, looking out the north window every few seconds at the snow swept sky.

"We really should go outside now. I expect the transporters' lights to break through the darkness any minute now." He stated firmly.

"We can tolerate the cold winds, but Owen can't." Katiera stressed with concern.

"I'll be fine, Katie." Owen responded as he stood, and fastened his winter jacket.

A low level rumble could now be heard above the wind. It was likened to the sound of approaching thunder.

"Hurry! It's time!" Xander exclaimed, as he opened the door, and herded the women outside.

Owen was the last to leave, and he took time to secure both dead bolt locks. "That should keep the place safe until spring." He muttered under his cold breath.

A moment of sentiment besieged him, before he turned to see an array of circular spotlights split through the dark sky above them. They illuminated off the falling snow that by now had accumulated quite considerably on the ground.

"Hurry, Owen!" Katiera desperately screamed above the loud hum of the transport, and the howling winds.

Owen hurried through snow, and took hold of Katiera's outreached hand just as a hatch opened on the underbelly of the craft. Before he could further react, a huge vacuum lifted them all off the ground, pulling them upward.

In no time at all, they were inside the craft, and the hatch closed behind them, yielding to a somewhat eerie silence. Katiera still held tight to Owen's hand as he nervously eyed the large cargo area around them.

"Are you okay?" She asked with deep concern, and Owen answered with an anxious nod.

Xander motioned for everyone to follow, as he moved toward an opened tubular compartment that led upward into another portion of the craft. They all stepped into the tight area, and the door slid closed. They were swiftly sucked upward through the tube, where they slid to a smooth stop, and the door slid open once again.

As they stepped out, Owen marveled at the complex circuit boards that surrounded him in the round room. An attractive brunette woman was the sole pilot at the flight console, and she paused to address everyone.

"Welcome aboard!" She said in a pleasant voice.

"Sela! It's good to see you again." Xander exuberantly replied.

The woman swiveled her chair around to get a good look at the group, as the craft hovered in place, tilting from side to side in the strong winds. "Well! In the process of Katiera getting lost, it appears she's found a very handsome man." She teased.

"This is Owen." Katiera responded. "Owen, this is Sela."

"It's a pleasure meeting you, Sela." Owen said, as she reacted with a cordial smile.

"Sela is one of our best pilots." Xander proudly proclaimed.

"So, they say." She chuckled. "Now, I need everyone to strap into their seats. It's going to be a rough ride until we rise above this storm.

Owen and Katiera sat facing her parents as they all secured their restraining belts.

"Will I need any oxygen?" Owen inquired. "I'm afraid my lungs aren't equipped to handle the speed and altitude that these crafts are capable of."

"Actually, we'll only be cruising at a mere 200 mph." Xander replied. "That's less than half the speed of a commercial airliner, and we'll only be travelling just above the clouds."

"We only use excess speed and altitude when our destination is space." Tabitha added.
"The craft also adjusts to the pressure variant when we go above the stratosphere or underwater." Xander concluded.

The vessel shook violently as it ascended through the brunt of the storm, then settled as it rose above it. Katiera squeezed Owen's hand as it then swiftly accelerated toward their destination. After only about 10 minutes, the craft slowed once again, coming to a hovering stop in the air.
"Hold on tight, everyone. We're going underwater." Sela announced.

The vessel shook once again as it descended through the storm, then with a loud thump, it entered the water.

Owen was sensitive to the pressure change. His ears popped as they descended to the depths, and he felt somewhat nauseated. He leaned back, closing his eyes, and held even tighter to Katiera's hand.

The craft settled lightly on the lake bottom, and a huge cloud of silt stirred up, obscuring the view out the large windows surrounding the pilot. A loud noise that sounded like an electric blender came from the bottom of the vessel, and it began slowly spinning in a clockwise manner.

Owen anxiously glanced at everyone else who appeared to be unusually calm. Xander caught his confused expression, and grinned.

"We're burrowing down to the portal."

Soon, they came to a complete stop, and Owen followed the lead of everyone else, releasing his seat belt restraint.

"We've arrived, ladies and gentlemen." Sela announced. "I hope you enjoyed tonight's flight."

"Before we disembark, I want to show you something we found on land." Xander smirked, as he reached into his satchel, pulled out the silver box, and opened it.

Sela swiveled her large pilot chair to get a closer look.

"Oh my!" She chuckled. "That relic belongs in a museum. I didn't think there were any still in operation."

"If there are, we can only hope our enemies don't get their hands on it." He turned to the others as he stashed the box back in his satchel. "Everyone grasp onto their keys."

Katiera had already removed hers from around her neck, and pressed it tightly between her hand, and Owen's. "Whatever you do, don't let go of my hand."

"Believe me, I won't." Owen anxiously replied.

There was a sudden flash of light, and a loud noise, as though a bolt of lightning had travelled through the craft. When the blinding light had receded, everyone was in an entirely different place.

Owen glanced around with amazement at the darkness around them. He could see that they were in a country setting just outside of a large town center, where lights lit up the night skyline.

"Where are we?"

"This is our home, Owen." Katiera proudly proclaimed. "This is Station 37."

"Is it always night time down here?"

"No." She giggled. "We turn off the artificial lighting at 10 PM every night, and bring it back up at 6 AM every morning?

"That way we can preserve our natural circadian rhythm." Xander added.

"How do you get light down here?" Owen further asked with amazement.

"We generate it." Xander grinned as he patted Owen's shoulder. "We'll show you everything tomorrow."

Owen was then startled by what appeared to be a hovering golf cart without a driver that silently pulled up from out of the darkness, and came to a halt in front of them. Sela placed her satchel in the back storage area, and climbed into the passenger seat.

"I need to go get some rest." Sela stated with a sigh. "It's been a long day."

"Sleep well, Sela." Tabitha bid to her as she departed.

She waved to all of them, as the cart rode back off into the darkness.

"Are we waiting for one of those to pick us up as well?" Owen anxiously asked.

"No, we'll all walk." Xander calmly replied. "Sela is staying in town for the night, but our house is just a short distance from here."

As Owen took hold of Katiera's hand once again, the couple followed the lead of Xander and Tabitha. His eyes wandered curiously to the darkness around them, and he filled his lungs with the fresh, oxygen rich night air.

"This is amazing!" He exclaimed as they strolled along. "This reminds me of the air we used to breathe when my parents and I would travel to the country."

Another thought occurred to him, and he came to a sudden halt.

"What's wrong?" Katiera asked.

"It just occurred to me that I don't even know your last name."

"Our last name is Torrance." She chuckled.

"Katie Torrance." He further paused in thought. "I like the sound of that."

"Come on!" She tugged on Owen's hand, and winked. "My mother and father will think we're purposely trying to lag behind."

Along the pleasant path, they came to a clearing where a magnificent, two-story Craftsman style house stood regally among the surrounding trees. The dim lighting that surrounded it created a comforting aura of a bygone era that Owen felt very attached to. Xander turned, toward the trailing couple with a cordial grin.

"Welcome to our home, Owen."

Katiera reacted with the excitement of a little girl, and paused her steps to savor the sight.

"Oh daddy! There were times when I thought I'd never see this place again."
Her eyes welled up with emotional tears, and Owen gave her hand a light, assuring squeeze.

The inside was just as welcoming with its hard wood floors, inlaid bookcases and cabinets shielded in beveled glass. There were grand wood pillars that separated rooms, a quaint fire place, and stain glass windows. It was like stepping back to a time when true craftsmanship went into every detail of building a home. The charm was further accented by the décor which could have been inspired by a classic copy of a Better Homes and Garden magazine. The three occupants of the home displayed prideful pleasure in Owens' reaction, as his eyes wandered wondrously to all parts of his surroundings.

"This isn't anything like I expected." Owen marveled. "I thought everything would be modern and sterile in this world."

"We adopted the old forgotten charm of your world, and replicated it with modern, advanced methods." Tabatha explained.

"I saw a place like this one time on a visit to your world when I was very young. It impressed me so much that I had to obtain the blueprints." Xander further stated.

"You'll see many replicas of classic architecture when we give you a tour tomorrow." Katiera added.

"I can hardly wait." Owen responded. "Like all of you, I cherish the things that once were, but hardly exist anymore. At least in my world."

"Such a shame that beautifully designed buildings were bulldozed, and replaced with ugly, and non-redeeming structures." Xander sadly continued. "Fortunately, some of our teams were able to salvage many of your cultural treasures before they were hauled off to a landfill." He motioned all around him. "Many were used in this house, and in the construction of other homes and buildings here."

Owen was impressed beyond words.

"It's getting very late, and we all have a full day tomorrow." Tabitha sighed as she turned to her daughter. "Would you show Owen to the guest room, and help him get settled in?"

"Yes, mother." She respectfully answered, before taking hold of his hand once again, and leading him up the stairway.

Her parents beamed with emotion as they watched the couple ascend. Owen paused to bid them a good night, and they cordially nodded in response.

"I'll ring a bell for breakfast." Tabitha called out. "Don't be late."

On land, Randy trudged into the house where his wife, son, and Josh were lounging in front of the television.

"I was beginning to think you weren't making it home tonight, Bear." Myra quipped.

"Did you get any takers on the device, Paw?" Matty anxiously asked.

Randy grinned as he strolled further into the room, and dropped into his recliner. "Got some fella traveling into town to talk with us tomorrow."

"How were you able to make contact with him?" Myra asked, as everyone sat forward to listen with interest.

"Remember that rich guy that we pawned those high end items off to a few months back?" All nodded. "He was real interested when I told him. Said he definitely had a buyer."

"We're all gonna be rich." Josh spurted out with enthusiasm.

"We'll just have to see." Randy answered as he stroked his whiskers, and pondered. "I sure ain't giving it away for next to nothing."

He reclined the chair back, and grunted. "Myra, would you mind fetching me a cold beer?"

She had already jumped up from her seat before he even finished the question. "Coming right up, Bear."

Owen laid awake in his comfortable bed that night, staring at the ceiling. The sound of birds, and creatures of the night mingled with the cool night air that wafted through the open window of the room. How were they able to simulate all these things from his world into a manufactured space below the lake? This, along with so many other questions flooded his mind as he laid there.

He also thought about the beautiful woman in the adjacent room, and longed to hold her in his arms. Just the thought of her brought peace to his mind. He smiled, closed his eyes, and drifted into a deep sleep.

Little did he realize that in that other room, Katiera also laid awake thinking about, and longing for him as well. She snuggled a pillow close to her body, finding comfort in those thoughts, as she also drifted into a peaceful slumber.

5

THE GALACTIC FEDERATION OF LIGHT

Owen waked to the ringing sound of a handbell. He sat straight up, startled, as he anxiously looked about the room. In those waking moments, he had almost forgot where he now was. He tossed the thin blanket aside, stretched his arms, and yawned. He took note of the light now streaming into his window, the mild temperature, and the crisp smell of the morning air.

A short time later, he made his way downstairs where a full breakfast banquet was already on the dining table. Xander and Tabitha had already settled, waiting for him and Katiera to arrive.

"Good morning, everyone." Owen cordially stated as he took his place at the table.

Katiera finally made her appearance as well, lightly bouncing down the stairs.

"My daughter." Xander sighed with humor. "Always the last to the table."

"Oh, daddy!" She exclaimed with visible embarrassment as she took her place next to Owen.

Owen smirked, and took hold of her hand under the table, gently squeezing it. Almost immediately, she calmed.

His three host's all bowed their heads reverently, and he followed suit with a moment of thankful silence, before Xander looked up, and glanced around the table.

"Let's eat. We all have a full day ahead of us."

Owen felt something softly breeze by his lower pant leg, and he lifted the table cloth to see that it was a beautiful caramel colored cat. The little creature looked up at him with wide eyes, and meowed, begging for attention.

"Well! Look what I found." He playfully stated as he hoisted the purring cat onto his lap.

"That's our little Pollyanna." Tabitha replied.

"I think she likes you, Owen." Katiera teasingly smirked.

"You're a beautiful little torti." Owen remarked to the cat, before addressing everyone else. "How old is she?"

"I think she's about 40 years old now." Tabitha nonchalantly answered.

Owen glanced around the table with wide eyed surprise. "You mean to tell me this cat is actually older than I am?"

"If we bring them here as a kitten, they can actually live to be a hundred years old." Xander replied with a chuckle.

"I have to say, I'm overwhelmed with amazement."

"You haven't seen anything yet." Katiera giggled, with an amorous sparkle in her eyes.

Xander raised his coffee cup in agreement. "She's right. Prepare yourself. You'll see things today that you would've never imagined could be possible."

After breakfast, Xander ushered Owen to a pristine, old carriage house behind the residence. Katiera anxiously followed along.

"Do you like the classic cars of your world?"

"I sure do." Owen answered with exuberance.

'You'll certainly enjoy this." Xander replied, pausing to exchange a wink with his daughter, before pulling the large sliding door open.

Housed within was a shiny two tone, blue and white 1957 Chevy Bel Air Convertible. It looked as though it was just driven off the show room floor.

"Wow!" Owen marveled as he eyed every detail of the classic. "This car would fetch over a hundred grand in my world today." He shook his head. "How did you ever get possession of it?"

"I rescued it from a junk yard back in your world, brought it here, and restored it with our more advanced technology." Xander proudly explained.

"We rescued quite a few others as well." Katiera added. "Daddy, and some of the other Oceanids get together in the town center from time to time to display their projects."

Owen looked inside at the intricate design of the console and dash. "They created works of art back in those days. Unlike the overpriced, disposable junk they build today." He paused as his eyes admiringly glanced over the beautiful machine one more time. "How could they ever have destroyed these beautiful classics?"

"The eyes of progress do not have the same appreciation of these things that we do, Owen." He paused with a sigh. "Their view of the world is a narrow one, that creates, then destroys, and regrets their actions later."

"Being that your world is an enclosed environment, how can it handle the carbon monoxide from these vehicles?"

"As I had mentioned before, I added a bit of advanced technology to the emission system, and we use alternative, clean burning fuel." He explained, before referencing to their surroundings. "We don't use these cars every day, but when we do, our advanced air filters and purifiers are equipped to handle any of the toxic fumes they might emit."

Owen took in a deep breath of air. "So, basically you're saying that the air we breathe here is totally free of toxins."

"Just as it once was in your world, Owen."

"Daddy and I will show you the facility that makes it all possible." Katiera further stated.

Owen was startled by the rapid arrival of a floating, driverless golf cart, similar to the one that picked up Sela the night before.

"How do these things appear out of virtually nowhere?" Owen inquired.

"We summon them by telepathy." Katiera answered with a sly grin, while gripping onto Owen's arm. "Stick with me, and I'll teach you everything."

"Hop aboard, Owen. We have much more to see." Xander concluded.

Back on land, a large stretch limo pulled to a stop outside of Randy and Myra's house. The driver got out, opened the back passenger door, and two well dressed men emerged.

Lucifer Morningstar paused to survey his surroundings with a critical eye. The other average built man with short cropped hair, and sun glasses paused in step with him.

"Is everything alright, Mr. Morningstar?"

"Let's make this quick." He commanded. "You examine this gadget, then I'll write the lowlife's a check, and we can get out of this cesspool of a town."

"Yes, sir!"

Randy stepped out of the house to greet the men, and Morningstar grunted.

"Just the sort of inbred moron I expected." He whispered to himself.

Randy ushered his two guests in while the rest of his family anxiously waited. "Welcome gentlemen! This is my wife Myra, my son Mattie, and his best friend Josh."

Morningstar coldly glanced at the all three, but never acknowledged them. The other man spoke for him.

"I'm Dr. Mark Foster, and this gentleman is Mr. Lucifer Morningstar."

"As in the Prince of Darkness?" Matty chuckled mockingly.

"I've been called that name, among others as well." Morningstar replied with a sober expression.
"Just don't let Ozzy Osbourne know you stole his title." Josh sarcastically quipped, which caused Morningstar to turn with a sneer.

"That's the sort of remark I'd expect from an illiterate ingrate such as yourself."

Josh boiled with anger, but a stern glance from Randy quickly calmed him.

"Enough with the small talk." Morningstar commanded. "Let's see the device you conveniently found."

"It's right here on the dining room table." Randy answered.

Dr, Foster moved in close to examine it, and Morningstar curiously watched over his shoulder.

"It's definitely not like any device I've ever seen." Foster remarked, turning to the couple. "You said you figured out how it works?"

"Yes!" Myra spoke up. "It healed my broken arm, and cured the arthritis in my hands."

"It took care of the arthritis in my knees as well." Randy added.

"Is that so?" Morningstar sternly asked as he pulled out a switch blade knife, and popped it open very close to Randy.

"Now wait just a minute." Randy stressfully stated, as he backed away. "I ain't letting you cut on me."

"No need." Morningstar smirked.

Josh had been leaning on the table, and with cat like reflexes, Morningstar suddenly plunged the knife into his hand, and quickly pulled it out.

"Ahh! You son of a bitch!" Josh wailed as he reeled back, and blood spurted like a fountain from his wounded hand.

"Let's see how it works, Dr. Foster. Fire that thing up." Morningstar commanded with a sinister grin.

"Put your hand on the table." The doctor ordered.

Josh painfully set his hand on the table top, as the blood quickly pooled around it.

Dr. Foster ran the device over it for a few seconds before the blood clotted, then the gaping wound miraculously closed, and healed over. Other than the residual blood, there was no evidence of a wound. Josh pulled his hand away, and looked at it with astonishment, while Foster turned to Morningstar.

"It definitely works as they said."

"I think I may know where the technology for this device originated." Morningstar stated. "Tell me how you came about possessing this."

"I stole it from his brother's cottage." She gestured toward Randy, who wasted no time in speaking up as well.

"Some big fella, along with his wife and daughter were there when we first broke in. They were guests of my nephew. The big guy held on to that there steel case like it was something real valuable. He wouldn't give it up for nothing."

"I snuck back in later when they were gone, and stole it." Myra concluded, while Morningstar's interest suddenly peaked
"Tell me more about this family."

"The women were gorgeous." Matty chimed in. "They had blonde hair, and large blue eyes."
"The man had the strength of an ox. He grabbed my throat, and held me up off the floor with one hand." Randy added.

"His puny little wife broke my arm with hardly any effort." Myra further added.

"How interesting." Morningstar paced in thought.

"It was just luck that I found that case." Myra continued. "I was actually looking for a crystal key that Randy said his brother might have."

Morningstar swung around with even more heightened interest. "Tell me more about this key."

"It's just something my grandparents gave to my brother after they both passed." Randy explained. "I was always curious about what it was."

"There's something else too." Myra further added. "I saw those two women strip down, and walk into 50 degree waters. Then they turned into fish, and swam away."

Morningstar's eyes grew wide, and he turned to Randy.

"I need you to take me to that cottage, right now." He demanded.

"Sure! Let me grab the keys to my truck."

Morningstar turned to Dr. Foster. "You and Bruce stay here with the car. I'll be back shortly."
"Yes sir."

Morningstar then handed a check to Myra. "This is for the device. It's not linked to BranchCoin, but it is backed by gold."

Myra took the check, and glanced at it. "Wait just a minute, Mister." She roared with sudden anger. "This is only 50K. That device is worth at least a million."

Morningstar marched within inches of her face. The boys moved to draw their weapons, and without even looking, Morningstar shot a bolt of electricity that struck them both, immediately sending them to the floor.

"You'll take what I offer, and if you refuse, I'll kill every one of you." He sneered. "Is that understood?"

"Yes sir!" Myra replied, backing away with fear in her eyes.

"If we find that key, I'll be taking that as well." He boldly declared as he motioned to a startled Randy. "Let's go. My time is way too valuable to waste on the likes of all of you."

Under the lake, the modified hover cart pulled to a stop near a humongous facility that covered at least 40 acres or more amidst an otherwise rural type countryside, complete with grazing cows. Owen raised himself from his seat, awe stricken by the sight.

"What is this place?"

"This is our power plant, and manufacturing facility." Xander announced. "We generate our energy here, cleanse our air, moderate our temperature, and make all the materials and products that we need to sustain life here in Station 37."

"We all play a part in its functioning. It's operated like a co-op." Katiera added.

Owens eyes wandered to two enormous storage tanks on one side of the building. "Is that your water supply?"

"No. Our water and treatment plant is near the town center." Xander replied. "Those tanks are where they store the energy that runs Station 37."

"How in the world is that energy produced without residual pollution?"

"Simple." He turned to animate the process to Owen. "We have a process where we smash hydrogen atoms with a fine tuned laser to create a reaction, that in turn creates an energy that is funneled, and stored in that front storage tank. Since energy is constant, the levels are monitored, and created as needed."

"I'm far from being a nuclear scientist, so it is a bit difficult to fathom." Owen chuckled. "What about the second tank?"

"That is our primary source." He grinned. "During sunny days, and lightning storms, we raise a device to the surface of the lake. The power that it captures from the sunlight and lightning strikes are contained within that tank. We are never short of energy in our world."

"Don't you worry that a passing ship or vessel might spot your device or accidentally strike it?"

"We keep it heavily camouflaged, just below the surface. Someone would have to be looking quite hard to find it, and we also have the situation constantly monitored to prevent such mishaps."

"That first tank you spoke about. Wouldn't the nuclear energy be quite a volatile threat to your world."

"Our method of creating it makes it far less dangerous, and leaves no residual waste for us to have to dispose." He further explained. "That second tank is the one you'd really have to worry about."

Xander then motioned for silence. "Listen. Can you hear that noise?"

Owen listened hard, and could hear the thumping sound of the energy bouncing against the inside walls of the container, and the loud humming sound that it produced.

"That is very volatile natural energy, my friend." Xander continued. We have to keep a constant watch on the readings in

87

that tank. If they get too high, we have to release some of the pressure into the ground containment unit."

"A single bolt of lightning packs enough power to supply one home for an entire day." Katiera stated.

"Imagine how much energy we're able to harness during the warm weather months in this region." Xander added. "During a given storm, we can capture and harness the power of hundreds of lightning strikes. The sun provides whatever more energy we might need. If our levels get too low during the long winters, we simply shift to our alternative power."

Owen was beyond amazement. "Why don't we have this technology in our world?"

His question raised a chuckle from Xander. "Because there's more benefit than there is profit from it. It would put all your major energy producing corporations out of business."

"I'm beginning to see how much our world is being held back by profiteering elites." Owen expressed. "Could I see the rest of the facility?"

"When we have more time, we'll give you a full tour." Katiera said with a warm smile. "It could take at least a day or more for you to see everything."

Xander diverted his attention, as though listening attentively to a silent conversation. Owen was quite puzzled by this.

"Is there something wrong, Xander?"

He motioned subtly to Owen as he closed his eyes in concentration for a few short minutes, before opening them again as though he had just wakened from a nap.

"Our guests are all here, and will meet with us at the Town Center shortly."

"How do you know that?"

"You have to remember, Owen. We communicate telepathically." Katiera replied.

"You don't have cell phones down here?"

The father and daughter shared a hearty chuckle at his question.

"Cell phones are an outdated antiquity in our world." Xander answered, still chuckling with amusement. "They are used as a control tool in your world. They can track your every move through its' signal. That's one of the many ways they maintain power over your lives."

"I have so much to teach you, Owen." Katiera amicably stated, as she affectionately pulled closer.

"I think we have just enough time to show Owen our archery range on the way into town." Xander stated.
"Oh, good!" Katiera exclaimed with excitement. "I'll get the chance to show off my skills."

On land, Randy and Morningstar arrived at the cottage, and found Owens' SUV parked in the driveway, completely covered in snow.

"That's my nephews' car. So, he must be here."

"We'll see about that." An expressionless Morningstar replied, as he pulled out his phone, dialed a number, and waited before he spoke again to the party on the other end. "I need you to track the phone of an Owen Gustafsson, who is presumably at a location just outside of Erie, Pennsylvania. He waited once more, and after a few moments, a sinister grin appeared on his otherwise sober face. "Well done." He stashed his phone beneath his jacket, and turned to Randy. "He's in there."

The two walked up to the door which was caked with ice and snow, and Randy gave a loud knock with his fist. They waited for a few moments, and Randy noticed the double locks.

"That extra lock wasn't there before." He stated. "You want me to go ahead, and kick the door in?"

"No need." Morningstar stepped forward, and with a point of his finger, the locks both popped open.

As they stepped inside, Morningstar immediately spotted Owens' phone on the dining room table. "That answers a lot. He's definitely not here. But why wouldn't he take his phone or his car?" He glanced around the cottage in deep thought. "I want you to tear this place apart until we find that damn key."

"What in the hell is so important about that key anyway?"

"Asking me questions can be a very dangerous practice, Mr. Gustafsson." Morningstar sternly warned in a threatening tone that made Randy's blood run cold. "Now, get to work."

Randy responded with a reluctant nod.

Back beneath the lake, the trio rode by a workout field where several individuals were practicing martial arts. Then they arrived at the archery range where several small children were honing their skills. When they saw Katiera, they all joyfully ran to greet and embrace her. It was a sight that brought a smile to Owen's face as he observed.

"The children are certainly quite fond of you." He mentioned as he and Xander hopped from the cart.

"Part of my responsibilities here are teaching, and watching over the children." She proudly replied while handing him a bow. "Let's see what you got."

"I haven't shot a bow since I was in high school." He answered as he readied an arrow on the string, and took aim at a target.

He cocked back, shot, and the arrow struck within the closest ring to the right of the bullseye."

"Not bad." She remarked, exchanging a quick glance with her father. "Try again."

Owen drew the bow, focused, and shot again. This time he hit the next furthest ring to the left of the bullseye. He rolled his eyes, and set the bow down with a bit of embarrassment that didn't escape the notice of Xander.

"You actually did quite well for an amateur, Owen." He spoke with encouragement.

Katiera picked up the bow, and took her turn. She drew back with a confident, steady glare, and struck the bullseye dead center. Owen was astonished by her accuracy, and all the children who were now behind them watching, cheered her on. She chose another arrow, and drew back once more. This time, the arrow split the first one right down the middle, and she observed her feat with a pleasing grin.

"Wow! That's unbelievable!" Owen marveled.

"She's one of our most accurate archers." Xander proclaimed with fatherly pride.

"With practice, I can help you improve your skills as well." She smiled as she entwined her arm with Owens', and kissed him on his cheek.

"There'll be more than enough time for that later." Xander mused. "Right now, we all have an important meeting to get to."

Back at the cottage, Randy had rummaged through every possible hiding spot, and created quite a mess in the process. He now stood amidst the clutter huffing and puffing, while Morningstar calmly relaxed in a nearby recliner.

"I've turned this place upside down." He spoke with frustration. "There's no way it's here. It has to be at their Florida home."

"Or, the Oceanids have it." Morningstar replied, as he rose from the chair, and glanced around with much concentration.

"The Oceanids?"

"Yes." Morningstar wryly answered. "I'm quite certain those were the aliens that you and your family encountered."
Morningstar paused to look at the pictures on the wall, and noticed the one with Cynethea had broken glass, and was hanging crooked. On a hunch, he immediately grabbed one of the dining room chairs, stood on it, and looked behind the picture.

"Well! Well!" He chuckled as he took note of the hole in the wall, and felt around inside. "Damn!" He exclaimed before stepping down from the chair. "That's where it was obviously hid. If he indeed, had it here."
"He could've moved it to his other home." Randy replied. "This was just their summer residence."

Morningstar stood for a moment in further thought.

"What's your brothers' name?"

"Kevin Gustafsson."

"What line of work was he in?"

"He worked for NASA. No idea what his duties were there. He and I haven't talked in years"

"So, he doesn't work there anymore?" Morningstar asked with peaked interest. "Did he retire?"

"He and his wife were taken in the rapture."

"They're being protected." Morningstar quipped angrily, before fiddling once more with his cell phone.

He scrolled down a list of names that he had accessed, and an expression of enlightenment graced his face. "He's definitely on our list. He must've held a very important position, and was obviously allied with our enemy." He stuffed his phone back into his coat, and turned his full attention to Randy. "Do you know his address in Florida?"

Randy shook his head. "All I know is that they lived in Cocoa Beach."

"That's all I need to know. I can find out the rest." Morningstar replied, as he motioned for them to leave. "You can also tell me everything you know about your nephew on the drive back to your place. I'm certainly interested in finding out what connection he has with the Oceanids."

At station 37, the trio arrived at the Hall of Advisors. It looked no different from the average meeting hall that you would see in most small cities. Owen was surprised by the simple appearance of the entire town center. Once again, he had somehow envisioned a space aged, ultra-modern place to match their advanced technologies. Instead, it looked more like the quaint, small town American scene, similar to that he had seen in pictures from the 1950's and 60's. It evoked a feeling of nostalgia and sentimentality.

The inside of the hall looked more like an early 20th century courthouse, with elaborate, ornate lighting, columned supports, as well as dark stained woodwork and furniture. Xander led the way through an arched doorway into the main hall. There was a long wooden desk that stretched across the front of the room, slightly elevated from the main floor, where four women and two men sat, along with one vacant chair.

"In case you're wondering, that vacant chair is mine." Xander whispered to Owen. "I'm one of the seven advisors here at Station 37."

With that said, he swiftly moved to take his place at the head table.

There was a gathering of people conversing on the lower level in front of the desk. They all ceased talking, and turned their full attention to Owen and Katiera. An attractive brunette woman who appeared to be in her mid forties, and chaired the center of the table, stood to speak first.

"Katiera, would you kindly introduce your companion to the room?"

"Everyone." Katiera paused as she took hold of Owens' hand. "This is Owen Gustafsson. The man who saved my life, and the man I have chosen to be my life partner."

Owen was quite startled by the public announcement since he hadn't formally proposed to her.

"I assume Mr. Gustafsson has agreed to this?" The woman further asked, with raised brow toward Owen."

"Yes, ma'am." Owen nervously answered, while the woman made her way down to the main floor, and proceeded to examine him with a critical eye. After a few moments, she turned to Katiera. "He has good genetics. A few flaws, but I'm sure your father can help him with that." She paused, glancing briefly at both of them, before speaking once more. "Congratulations to both of you."

She turned to the other board members. "Does the board approve of a union between the land dweller and our Katiera?"

Each took their turn to voice an "Aye." When it was Xander's turn, he answered "Absolutely!" while beaming with pride.

All the other guests on the lower level applauded the announcement, and moved in closer, while the other board members applauded as well, and came down to join them.

The woman smiled, and cordially nodded to Owen. "My name is Anna Pare'. I'm the head of the Council of Advisors here at Station 37."

"I'm pleased to meet you." He answered.

"I certainly hope we didn't put you on the spot?" she inquired with a smirk.

"Actually, in my world, the man customarily proposes first. That was something that I had fully intended on doing later."

"In our culture, the roles are reversed. The woman chooses, and it's up to the man to accept."

"It's official now, and I couldn't be happier." Katiera beamed with joy.

"If I must say so myself, you've chosen quite well, my dear." Anna replied.

Xander approached, and patted Owen on the back while also addressing Anna. "I've finally acquired a son."

"Don't Katiera and I have to apply for a license, and have an official marriage ceremony?"

All in attendance chuckled.

"I can join the two of you today without all that nonsense." She answered with a shrug, as she gestured to a man with long blonde hair, striking blue eyes, and a blue Neru waist jacket. "I can have our guest, Eno Calta help with the officiating. But first, we need to get important business out of the way."

"Should I leave the room?"

"Absolutely not, Owen. You're a major reason that we're all here." Anna replied much to his surprise.

Owen looked toward the man she had referred to, and he and his assumed wife stood out from all the rest. Like him, his female partner was equally radiant with her long blonde hair, and large blue cat like eyes that were almost hypnotizing. Their royal blue and gold trimmed uniforms with their names emblazoned on the breast, along with a symbol that looked like a six pointed star, were fashionably eye catching.

Eno took notice of Owen observing, and approached him to a close, uncomfortable distance, curiously gazing into his eyes for a long, few moments before turning to the others with surprise.

"He's one of us." He profoundly announced. "He's one of our Nordic star seeds."

Owen was flabbergasted and confused, and Xander also stepped forward with astonishment.

"How can that be?" Xander questioned. "Owen also has our people's blood running through his veins. His great grandmother was an Oceanid."

"I read the distinct markers in his eye fibers." Eno countered. "He's definitely one of our seeds as well. It's quite possible that he's a hybrid of our two races."

"Can someone please explain this to me?" Owen pleaded with frustration.

The two men continued to debate the issue, practically ignoring his pleas.

"Perhaps someone else in his lineage is also of direct descent to the Pleiadian Nordics." Eno suggested.

"He is of Swedish-American Heritage." Xander replied. "As we discussed prior to this, his father was a trusted ally within the space industry."

Eno finally swung his attention directly to Owen. "Yes, your father was a very honorable man and a good friend. He obviously was as secretive about his family as he was with our confidential information."

Owen was still somewhat perplexed. "My father never discussed his work with me. As far as space was concerned, he often said that we were not of this world. He would point to the stars in the night sky, and declare that our true home was somewhere out there." He paused. "I always thought he was simply making reference to our Christian belief."

"Perhaps he was making reference to both. None of us are originally of this earth." Xander proposed. "Though we're here, many of us do not take part in the evil practices that are regretfully dominant within this world."

Eno paced in deep thought for a few moments. "Perhaps it was your great grandfather that was our principal star seed. Kevin did mention on a few occasions that it was him that encouraged his interest in outer space." He then turned to both Xander and Anna. "Your assumptions were right. Owen has come to us through divine purpose. Even more so than you originally thought." He turned back to Owen. "Please excuse me for my ignorance. I never formally introduced myself." He asserted. "My name is Commander Eno Calta. I am a representative for the Galactic Federation of Light. The beautiful woman with me is my wife Nera." He gestured toward her with an amicable smile.

"The Galactic Federation of Light?" Owen cluelessly questioned.

"We are of the Alien races within the Pleiadian Star System. We have also been battling the same Dark Forces that your planet has suffered under for many centuries."

Xander motioned to the others in attendance. "We are what you'd call the White Hat Aliens."

"You all knew my father. Do any of you know where he and my mother might be?"

Eno sighed. "We do know that they were evacuated to a safe, and secretive place, along with all the others who were vulnerable targets of the Dark One."

"Who is this Dark One?" Owen asked with a slight sneer.

"He is none other than Satan." A young woman spoke up, as she strolled forward to address Owen, who responded with wide eyed surprise while she continued. "He goes by the name of Lucifer Morningstar, and is here on earth as we speak." Her defiant tone softened as she cordially nodded to Owen. "My name is Damaris. I am Sentry to the Atlantic region of the Nereid Empire." She paused to acknowledge Katiera as well. "It's good to see you again, my beautiful sister." She quickly shifted her attention back to Owen. "I sympathize with the loss of your parents. I was in love with a land dweller that was taken as well, and I too do not know where he is." Tears filled her eyes as she took a deep, emotional breath, and motioned for a tall, dark haired man among the guests to come forward.

He also cordially gestured to Owen as he approached. "My name is Guitierez. I was one of the uncompromised FBI agents who helped defeat the Secret Society in America. I am now the head agent of the newly formed Patriot Guard that President Chamberlain established to replace both the corrupt FBI and CIA agencies."

"For obvious reasons, Agent Guitierez is under heavy protection by our Federation." Eno commented. "As you well know, we are in the midst of very turbulent times that still threaten your unstable country."

"Have we entered into the Tribulation period that they speak of in the Bible?" Owen asked.

"None of us really know." Eno paced as he spoke. "It was supposed to have come in a more future time, but Satan hastened it by his presence. We had to evacuate those who we felt were threatened."

"We think Satan may have found a way to earth through one of the many worm holes in the universe." Damaris stated. "He killed the immortal gods Zeus and Poseidon, as well as Steven Spencer, and others that posed an immediate threat to his regime. They were all very good friends of mine."

"Steven Spencer?" Owen questioned. "Why does that name sound familiar to me?"

"He was one of the wealthiest men in the United States, and a valuable asset to our cause." Guitierez answered. "I'm sure you're aware of the new BranchCoin currency. He and a man by the name of Gerard LeRoux were behind its' creation. With our help, and with the aid of the gods, their company, Branch Consolidated Industries played a key role in bringing down the corrupt economy that the Secret Society and the Conglomerate Bank had built, and maintained since 1913."

"Where is this Gerard LeRoux now? Is he also dead?"

"We'd like Satan and his minions to believe he is." Eno smirked. "Actually, he's under our protection, and operating his company from a remote location."

A very beautiful dark skinned woman then confidently sashayed into the room along with Tabitha, who lagged a bit behind in her stride. Everyone's attention immediately shifted toward her. "Please forgive me for being tardy. The Lake Erie Portal is not very kind to travelers this time of year." The woman announced.

"Owen, this is Linda Sanchez." Eno announced. "She is the immortal Mermaid Queen of the Caribbean region."

Linda immediately moved to shake his hand. "There's no need for an introduction. Mr. Gustafsson's efforts in restoring our natural reefs is well known, and has greatly benefited the inhabitants of the Florida waters."

"I had a very dedicated team, Ms. Sanchez." Owen humbly answered.

"You always did have a flair for making grand entrances." Katiera teased, as the two Mermaids embraced.

Tabitha slipped her arm around Xander, and whispered. "I came as soon as I could after you summoned me."

Xander only answered with a pleasing grin.

Linda looked to all in attendance, and spoke emotionally. "It's good to see that you're all safe after the unexpected tirade of Lucifer Morningstar. I do believe we have quite a few challenges ahead of us." She looked to Damaris, Eno, and Guitierez. "Have you spoken about Branchview and Lockeport?" Both shook their head no.

"We only touched upon that." Eno responded.

"I spoke of the fate of the gods and Steven Spencer." Damaris added.

"As some of you might know, I am also marked for death." Linda paused emotionally. "Satan would've surely killed me had I not left Branchview a day early."

"He's also declared war on the Nereids." Damaris firmly stated. "We aided the gods and our American allies in defeating the Draconians and Minions of the Secret Society at Lockeport." She sighed before continuing. "We used the pulse weapon for the first time."

"Why wasn't the Federation made aware of this?" Eno posed sternly.

"It was a last minute decision. We had to save Branch Consolidated and the town of Lockeport from a hostile takeover. The United States would've been lost had we not taken action."

"It was a reckless decision that now endangers both of our societies." Anna scolded. "Not only is our enemy aware that we have such a weapon, but they will also be going to extreme measures to destroy us, and confiscate that technology to use on innocent humans."

Eno motioned for calm. "The Federation will make sure that doesn't happen. This I can promise you."

"Do we know what timeline, or realm that Lockeport and Branchview were banished to?" Linda asked.

"We haven't determined yet." Eno answered. "We do know that Satan destroyed them in this realm, changed the timelines, and erased all memory of their existence. The towns of Old Lyme, and Old Saybrook now exist with an alternative history, as though they had been there all along. Their inhabitants are as innocent and clueless as the ones they replaced."

"Wait just a minute." Owen intervened. "I know where Old Saybrook and Old Lyme are, but I've never heard of these other places. How can all of this be?"

"Satan destroyed all memory, history, and timelines of Lockeport and Branchview within this matrix." Eno explained.

"How can you say that the towns of Saybrook and Lyme just popped up out of nowhere?" Owen persisted. "I happen to know that they've always been there, and that they were a major part of our Colonial history."

"They indeed existed there all along. However, they were part of another reality or matrix." Eno replied to a still baffled Owen. "Satan simply reversed those realities. As your human brain advances in knowledge, I assure you that you'll better understand."

"We'll all try to bring him up to speed as we have with Agent Guitierez and his team." Linda assured. "The majority of the inhabitants that were evacuated from Branchview have been marked as safe, but there are still those who are missing, and are actively being pursued by Satan."

"Who are they?" Eno asked.

"Loraine Spencer, who was the wife of Steven is among those. The others are the Indian Shaman Stargazer, the immortal forest faire, Nebriana, and the immortal Green Man." Linda emotionally answered. "Nebriana's sister, Claudiana has been marked safe in the uncompromised North Land."

"Do you have any clue where they all might be?" Damaris inquired distressfully. "Perhaps my Tristan might be in the same place."

"We believe that Loraine and Stargazer may have escaped through the portal that existed in the Branchview Grand Ballroom." Linda paced as she spoke. "We also believe that Nebriana and the Green Man may be hiding somewhere in the remote regions of the Catskills with the other faire's, and the Woodspeople."

"The Catskills are a very mystical place. Many secret portals exist there." Eno stated.

As of right now, we can only assume that Satan believes they all perished when he set the woods ablaze that surrounded the estate." She heavily sighed as she glanced to everyone in attendance. "These people were our friends and allies. We'll never rest until they're all accounted for."

"I promise that the Federation will employ all of our resources to help." Eno assured.

"You can count on help from the Oceanids as well." Anna further assured, before turning back to Damaris with a wink. "Take that message back to the Nereids, and we'll also alert all of our other stations. As a unit, and with the energy of Almighty God, we will defeat Satan and his forces."

"What about Loraine Spencer, and Stargazer?" Guitierez inquired. "Does anyone have any idea where they might be?"

"They could be anywhere within the history and spectrum of time." Linda sighed. "We can only pray that they're in a safe place, and that they sought the help of myself, and the rest of the gods as we existed within that particular period of time."

Guitierez accepted the answer with great ponderance, as the room buzzed loudly with several conversations. He moved closer to Owen, and spoke in a low tone. "I know this is all a bit overwhelming, but just be glad they're on our side." He gave him an assuring pat on the shoulder.

Eno Calta then signaled for everyone's attention.

"I do believe we have a blessed union to officiate." He declared.

"Absolutely!" Anna joyfully exclaimed. "Then tomorrow, we'll celebrate with a great feast, and deliver the couple to their honeymoon love nest."

Owen was a bit puzzled over why they had to wait until tomorrow, and Eno read his expressions. He leaned in and whispered. "Sorry for making you wait. But tonight, we must pay your uncle a visit, and retrieve the healing device. We'll adjust the timelines to make it easier on the two of you." He winked at the couple.

Katiera took hold of Owen's hands, and looked straight into his eyes with much love, while her parents proudly flanked the couple on either side. All the others in the room moved in closer as well. "Are you ready to do this?" She sincerely asked.

"I've wished for this moment since the first time I laid eyes on you." He replied unwaveringly. "I'm more than ready."

On land, Morningstar had concluded his business with Randy and his family. He entered the back of his limo where Dr. Foster waited patiently. Without hesitation, he slid the partition window open to speak with his driver.

"I'll need you to send an execution squad to this house later tonight. Have them kill everyone, and burn the house to the ground. Can I trust you to do that, Bruce?"

"I'll see that it gets done, Mr. Morningstar."

He slid the door shut once again, and comfortably leaned back in his seat.

"Did you find what you were looking for at the cottage?"

"Unfortunately, I didn't." He answered in an almost annoyed manner.

"What would you like me to do with the device?"

Morningstar glanced down at the steel case that Foster cradled on the floor between his feet. "I want you to destroy it. That technology should never be available to the lowlife humans. Our mission is to destroy them. Not cure them of their earthly ailments."

"Wouldn't our elites benefit from it?"

Morningstar let out an arrogant grunt, followed by a smirk. He gripped onto the doctors' arm with his hand, and within seconds Foster grabbed at his heart, gasping for air. He let loose, and Foster slumped in his seat with a vacant stare.

"I'll take care of it myself. Your services are no longer needed, Dr. Foster." He coldly stated as he shifted his eyes to look out the window.

Inside the house, Randy stewed with anger as he sat at the table with his family.

"Something isn't setting right with all of this." He blurted out, while slamming his fist on the table. "I'd like to know why that arrogant bastard wants so much to get his hands on that key. He probably has someone rifling through my brothers' house in Florida as we speak."

"What do you think we should do, Bear?" Myra asked.

"I don't know. But I think he might be fixing to harm Owen. He picked my brain about him all the way back to the house." He paused to glance at everyone and shook his head. "I can't let that happen. We might not be close, but he is blood kin."

"You getting soft, Paw?" Matty sarcastically teased, causing his father to go into a boiling rage.

"You listen to me, boy." He pointed a finger of warning. "I played a role in bringing your sorry ass into this world, and I sure as hell have no problem in taking you out of it. You hear me?"

Matty answered with an uncomfortable nod, and everyone else at the table cowered a bit as well. Randy shot a quick glance toward Josh. "You know how to build one of those detonator bombs, don't you?

"Yeah! It's a piece of cake." He confidently answered. "What are you thinking on doing?"

"I'm still sorting that one out in my mind. I'll let you know when the time comes."

"What do you need me to do, Bear?" Myra queried.

Randy glanced down at the check that still laid on the table.

"Go over into Ohio, and get that, and all the alternative monies in the safe exchanged for BranchCoin, so the Conglomerate Bank can't track it. Have the Freedom Exchange put it in that small BC account I opened a few months back."

"BranchCoin?" Myra questioned. "That's only legal in the Patriot States."

"Exactly!" He grinned. "We've been using alternative cash to operate under the radar all along, and with great difficulty. I think Morningstar wants us to cash that check here in Pennsylvania, so the government here can confiscate it, and launder it back to him."

"We could just cash it in Ohio for Freedom currency, and spend it all before we come back across the border." Matty countered.

"True." Randy reasoned. "But then we wouldn't have secure backup funds. We'd be in the same position as everyone else that lives in the Socialist run states."

"I see your point, Bear." Myra expressed with confidence.

"So, are you saying that we're switching over to the Patriot system?" Josh further questioned.

"I'm saying that the Socialists lied to us in order to gain control." Randy glanced at everyone with a raised brow. "We all lost our jobs, and had to become thieves in order to maintain, and keep what we earned." He stood up and paced anxiously to vent his anger. "Globalist bastards like Morningstar now run every facet of our lives, and use our state governments to steal all they can from us."

"I know you all too well, Paw. There's got to be something else gnawing at you." Matty stated.

"You're right, Matty." He confronted his son. "I got this sick feeling in my gut that we aren't finished dealing with that pompous asshole that just left here, and I ain't about to back down."

6

A DASTARDLY PLAN REVEALED

After the ceremony uniting Owen and Katiera, they along with a small contingent that included Xander, Eno, Damaris, and Linda Sanchez all gathered in the field of wild flowers where Owen had first entered this hidden world. Three archers were chosen to accompany them as well for added protection. There were two women and one man. All donned heavier clothes, and insulated shoes to ward off the cold of the earth above them.

Xander assumed leadership in the group, and formed a circle in which they all held hands.

Before Owen could question in his mind what was taking place, a blinding light flashed, and all were taken up.

When he came back to his conscious state, they all were within the transport vessel. This time, it was a smaller unit specifically designed to transport groups of individuals, much like a commercial airliner. Sela, once again was seated at the controls, and she turned to greet her passengers with a smile.

"Welcome back everyone. Our weather on the surface is cold, with clear skies. Our destination trip should only encompass a few short minutes of earth time."

"Did you enter the coordinates I sent you?" Xander inquired.

"All entered, and ready to go." She confidently replied.

Everyone slipped on their safety belts as the vessel made its ascent from the lake bottom. Within seconds, it burst to the surface, and took off into the night skies. Owen was amazed as he viewed from his vantage point, the vessel streaking through the darkness outside the large observation window.

"How is it that it's now night time here, whereas we were still in daylight at Station 37?"

"As I mentioned to you earlier, we altered the spectrum of time so that you and Katiera would have more time to enjoy your celebration feast and honeymoon once we get back." Eno grinned with an assured wink.

"Approaching destination." Sela announced, as the vessel slowed considerably, and came to a hovering pause. "Prepare to disembark." She further ordered as everyone slid out of their seats, and gathered beneath the circular dome at the center of the craft. "I'll have to disappear into an alternate realm, so message me in a timely manner." She relayed to Xander, who saluted her in return.

All held their key pendant forward, and Katiera clenched tightly to Owens' hand. Once again, with the flash of light, all were transported. They all appeared in a small woods within sight of Randy's dark and silent household. When all had regained their bearings, Xander began handing out orders.

"It's shortly after 2AM earth time, so we'll assume that all the inhabitants are sleeping. I'll need you three archers to remain around the perimeter of the house to warn of any approaching danger." He turned to the rest. "I'll also need Katiera, Demaris, and Linda to have their bows readied in case they confront us in a hostile manner."

"What about the rest of us?" Eno asked.

"You, along with Owen and I will be the chief diplomats in trying to reason peacefully with these people."

"That should be a challenge in itself." Owen concluded as they all set their sights to the residence, and trudged toward it through the snowy underbrush.

A few moments later, the contingent marched onto the front landing, and kicked some of the snow off their boots.

"Here we go." Owen announced as he set to knock on the door.

After six loud knocks, the lights finally went on in the house, and Randy called out from the other side of the door with annoyance. "Who is it, and what in the hell do you want?"

"It's Owen. I need to talk with you."

"Are you kidding? At this late hour?" He peeked out the side window. "Who are all those people with you?"

"Look! We all come in peace. They just want to get their healing device back. Will you open the door?"

There was conversation taking place among the inhabitants of the house as they waited. After a few long minutes, Randy slowly opened the door, aiming a rifle at the group. Myra, Matty, and Josh stood behind him with their guns drawn as well.

"Would you put your damn guns down, Randy? I told you we're not here to cause trouble."
Owen said with aggravation.

"What about them girls with the bows and arrows?"

"They're just a precaution, in case you try to do something stupid." Xander assured.

"How do you suppose those tiny women are going to match up to our guns?" Matty arrogantly remarked.

"Those tiny women are expert archers, and highly trained warriors. Their bows are advanced weapons that shoot tempered steel arrows, capable of cutting straight through a body within split seconds of impact. Two arrows would take out all four of you." Xander firmly answered. "You'd all be dead before you got off your first shot."

The women cocked, and aimed just to drive home the point, while all four gave an anxious gulp.

"Any more questions?" Owen asked with a smirk.

Randy shook his head, lowered his rifle, and motioned them all in. The three men led the way, followed closely by the three women who closed the door behind them.

"We all know who the big guy is, and your Mermaid girlfriend there."

"She's now my wife." Owen remarked to Randy who responded with a raised brow of surprise.

"Okay. What about the rest of these folks?" Randy asked.

"Yeah! Who's the rock star dude with the cool threads?" Josh also inquired.

Eno was quite baffled by the question that was obviously directed to him, and Owen quickly explained. "I think he likes your uniform."

He reacted to Owens' explanation with an enlightened gesture, before turning his attention to the four members of the household.

"My name is Eno Calta. I represent the forces of the Galactic Federation of Light."

"Wow! He's a genuine space alien." Matty commented to Josh.

"The other two lovely warriors are Damaris and Linda." Xander concluded. "That's all you need to know." He further paused with emphasis. "Now, if you would all be kind enough to hand over our healing device, we'll gladly leave."

"We don't have it anymore." Myra answered.

"What do you mean you don't have it anymore?" Owen reacted with rising anger.

"We sold it to some rich son of a bitch by the name of Morningstar. Cheap bastard only gave us 50k for it."

All the aliens exchanged anxious glances, and Eno was quick to inquire further. "Lucifer Morningstar?"

"Yeah, that's him." Matty quickly replied. "The arrogant bastard actually thinks he's the devil."

"He really didn't give a damn about that device." Randy added. "He was more interested in that key I told him about."

"He knows about the key?" Xander blurted out.

Owen paced closer to Randy and Myra. "What else did you tell him?"

"We told him all about what the big guy and his family did at the cottage, and I told him all about your wife there, and her mother." Myra boasted.

"What about them?" Owen pressed.

"I saw the two of them turn into Mermaids, and swim away in the lake." Myra proclaimed.

Katiera let out a groan, and all the others expressed anxiety as well. Owen paced anxiously, like a kettle ready to boil over. He pointed to Myra and Randy.

"I can't believe you're related to me. How can you two be so stupid." He paced further, placing his hand to his forehead. "I wouldn't be surprised if you both voted for the Socialists in the last election."

"We did vote for the Socialist." Myra defiantly replied.

Owen swiftly turned to Xander with a sarcastic grin. "I rest my case."

Eno stepped forward to calm everyone down. "Everyone! Let's allow cooler heads to prevail." He curiously approached Randy. "What can you tell me about that scar behind your ear, Mr. Gustafsson."

"Hell! I don't know. It's been there for as long as I can remember." He narrowed his eyes. "Why?"

"We think you may have been abducted by aliens when you were younger, and they may have implanted a transmitter near the base of your brain." Eno explained.

Randy touched the scar, then broke out in laughter. The rest of his family laughed along with him, but Eno and the others remained quite serious.

"Have you ever heard voices in your head, telling you to do things?" Eno pressed.

Randy quit laughing, and took on a more serious demeanor as he thought over the question. "Maybe, once in a while."

"Were they the same voices that told you to burn down your parents' home while they slept?" Owen asked with great disdain that ignited Randy.

"Now you wait just a minute there, Owen. That's not fair." He trembled as he turned away.

Randy pondered for a moment before walking over to a cabinet, and pulling out a hunting knife. The archers all raised their bows, and Randy dangled the knife loosely in front of him. "You can put those things down. I'm not that stupid." He offered the knife to Xander. "Cut the damn thing out."

"Mr. Gustafsson, that is a very vulnerable area on your neck. I don't wish to harm you."

"Just do it!" He exclaimed with frustration.

"We don't have that device anymore, Bear. We won't be able to stop the bleeding."

"I can heal the wound." Eno intervened, as he nodded to Xander. "Do what he wishes you to do."

Xander reluctantly took the knife, and motioned for Randy to sit down. He turned to Myra with worried eyes. "I'll need some sort of alcohol, and towels for the bleeding."

Without hesitation she strolled to the nearby kitchen, and returned with a bottle of whiskey. She then turned to Matty. "Get a few towels from the linen closet."

Xander saturated the area around the scar, and Randy grabbed the bottle from his hand, taking down a large slug to dull the anticipated pain. Matty hurried in with the towels, and Xander delicately placed the knife over the scar, carefully carving around it with the sharp edge. Randy gripped tightly to the table, and endured the intense pain, while blood spurted onto the towels that Myra held close to the open wound. When the hole was opened wide enough, Xander reached in with two fingers, and pulled out the minute transmitter.

"Got it!" He exclaimed as he set it on the table, and Myra pressed the towel tightly on the wound.

Eno stepped forward, and took over for her. "I'll take it from here."

He clenched his eyes shut, concentrating as he pressed on the wound.

"Dammit! It's burning!" Randy yelled. "It feels like it's on fire."

Eno firmly placed his free hand on Randy's shoulder to calm him, then slowly lifted the towel away. The wound was completely healed over. Randy wiped the perspiration from his brow, then probed the area with his fingers before nodding to the benevolent alien. "Thank you."

Eno then shifted his attention to the bloody transmitter that laid on the table, while everyone else moved in close to inspect it as well. He picked it up, holding it between his finger and thumb, and inspected it more closely.

"This is old technology." He declared. "You must've been a carrier for quite a few years."

"Like I said before, I can't remember anything."

"They no doubt erased your memory of the abduction. It's a normal trait of the Greys." Eno stated.

"Who or what are the Greys?" Myra asked with a cynical expression.

"They're the odd looking creatures with the big eyes that you Earthlings generally relate to as space aliens. They're also the ones that crashed where Area 51 is now located." Eno answered.

"Are they good or bad?" Matty asked.

"I'd have to say this implant was done by evil Greys. Like humans, some are evil, while others cooperate for the good with the Federation." Eno further explained.

Xander took the butt of the knife, and crushed the transmitter. He then glanced up at Randy. "You won't have to worry about that anymore."

Both Eno and Xander suddenly paused as though listening to some unheard message.

"There's been an unexpected complication." Eno announced to those in the room.

A few seconds later the other archers entered, prodding an apprehended prisoner into the room.

"There were three armed assailants ready to move on the house." One of the archers explained. "We had to kill one of them, but we were able to capture this one."

"The third one got away." Another added. "But he's wounded."

Eno approached the captured mercenary who was a tough looking character with several tattoos that filled his arms, and portions of his neck.

"What are you looking at, pretty boy?" He smirked sarcastically.

"Did Lucifer Morningstar send you? Eno inquired, totally disregarding his question.

"I'm not telling you anything." He chuckled. "Why don't you fight me for the answer?" He asked arrogantly.

"Is that what you wish?" Eno calmly countered.

With a disrespectful grunt, he unexpectedly threw a quick jab punch that Eno easily blocked. With little effort, the Nordic flipped the man across the room, sending him crashing hard against the wall. Dazed, he tried to get up, but Xander shook a finger of warning.

"If you get up, you'll have to fight my friend here." Eno stated with amusement, while gesturing to Xander. "He's even tougher than I am."

Thinking for the better, the man stayed down. "I'm former Special Forces. Where in the hell did you learn how to fight like that?"

"We're all trained in highly advanced techniques of fighting." Eno answered, glancing to his entire team.

"Look! All I can tell you is that we were hired by the same unknown party that's hired us several times in the past." The man reluctantly answered as his eyes shot anxious glances between Eno and Xander. "We're always instructed to take photos to prove our targets are dead, and that the evidence was destroyed."

Myra and Randy exchanged looks of dread at his statement.

"Can you tell us anything else?"

"The person said there'd be airline tickets waiting for us at Buffalo/Niagara airport. We were to fly to New York where we'd be shuttled to the old Conglomerate Bank Building. We were then instructed to go the penthouse office to receive our payments. We go through that same scenario every time."

"Do you ever see the man that pays you?" Eno further probed.

The mercenary shook his head no. "There's always some big black guy that hands off an envelope to us when we get off the elevator. We're then instructed to leave."

"Now we know where Morningstar has his secret rat nest in this country." Eno quipped.

"When The Conglomerate Bank vacated the premises, he obviously took up residency." Xander added.

"The Conglamorate Bank still maintains power in the Socialist States." The man arrogantly remarked. "They just do it from somewhere in Europe."

"Yes. We already know." Eno answered confidently.

"What do you all plan to do with me anyway?" The mercenary desperately asked. "These people are very powerful. I'm sure they'll have me killed.

Eno pondered for a moment. "We can take you to a place far away from here. But you'll be required to serve time for your crimes."

"What about the one who got away?" Xander inquired to Eno. "I'm sure he'll tell Morningstar all about our archers."

Before Eno could answer, the mercenary began choking and coughing. Then his eyes rolled back as he slumped lifeless to the floor. Both Eno and Xander rushed to his side, and took notice of the foam around his mouth.

"He took a cyanide pill." Xander stated.

"He probably thought it was his easiest way out." Owen stated as he stepped forward to join them.

"We'll need to dispose of the bodies in a proper way." Eno concluded with a sigh while addressing the team.

"What about us?" Randy asked.

"You all need to leave here immediately." Xander ordered. "Destroy your cell phones so you can't be traced."

"Where will we go?" Myra countered.

"As far from here as possible, and you are never to tell anyone about us or what you saw here tonight." Xander answered. "Do you understand?"

All sheepishly nodded.

"You've already done enough damage in telling Morningstar everything you know." Owen scolded.

"Can't you take us with you?" Matty further inquired with high anxiety.

"I'm sorry." Eno answered. "We've already intervened in a way that was never intended, and in the process, we've put our own people in danger."

"We all really need to go." Damaris spoke up with urgency. "It's getting quite late."

"Even though we all brought water, we'll need to fully hydrate our bodies very soon." Linda spoke for the first time. "This dry, cold air isn't helping the situation."

Without further word, Xander picked up the dead mercenary, easily slinging him over his broad shoulders, and the group filed out the door. Eno and Owen were the last to exit, but before they had the chance, Randy halted them.

"Wait!" He called out, and they both paused. "Is this Morningstar fella really who he claims to be?"

Owen took a step back inside to answer. "You just had a room full of people from another galaxy in your home. Is it so impossible to believe that Satan also exists?"

His question left them all speechless.

"I suggest you obtain a Bible, and get caught up." Eno added in conclusion before they both departed.

After the door closed, Randy's family silently glanced at each other for a moment.

"What do we all do now, Paw?" Matty asked.

"We need to do just as they told us." Myra raced to answer.

There was another anxious pause of silence as everyone waited for Randy to speak.

"We'll do just that." He nodded rapidly, holding back a rush of rage. "But not before we kill that bastard Morningstar, and save our world from any further tirade he may stir up."

"Are you crazy! He's the devil!" Josh exclaimed.

A grin broke across Randy's face. "I have a plan that will finish him off for good." He stood and peeked outside through the curtains, feeling the spot with his fingers where the transmitter was removed. "It's the least I can do, and it might be the only damn good deed I've done in my entire life."

Meanwhile, across the globe in northern Ukraine, Morningstar continued his endless quest for world control. He arrived at a large manufacturing facility that was heavily guarded by a Neo-Nazi militia. He was greeted at the front desk by a mousy looking young woman with thick black rimmed glasses, and a white lab coat.

"Good morning, Mr. Morningstar. Dr. Podhadzny and Senator Rothstein are waiting for you on the factory observation landing."

Morningstar responded only with an insignificant grunt, and followed the woman as she led the way. As he was ushered onto the steel balcony overlook, he was immediately greeted by Dr. Podhadzny who was a short, balding man in his early sixties. "Welcome, Mr. Morningstar." He spoke in broken English.

Rothstein, a sharp dressed man in his fifties, simply nodded as a greeting.

"I hope it's well worth my time for you to have beckoned me here." He answered in an unenthused manor.

"It was well worth your time, Mr. Morningstar." Podhadzny flipped the power switch that lit up the darkened warehouse. "You're about to view the first batch of robot warriors that are well ahead of schedule." He proudly motioned toward the floor below that stretched as far as two football fields.

Packed in tight rows, the titanium figures stretched from end to end, with their blank eyes staring straight ahead. "All we need to do is insert their power chips, and they'll activate into indestructible killing machines. There are no modern armies or weapons on earth that can destroy them." He further proclaimed with pride while Rothstein was silent with amazement.

Morningstar broke into a slight smirk. "An army of terminators. Just how many are ready for action?"

"There's 2,000 here in the warehouse, and several more in the adjacent factory, being assembled as we speak.

"The aid package that we were able to pass through before the Patriots took control should provide enough laundered funds to move ahead with our agenda." Rothstein added.

"All made possible by the generosity of the U.S. taxpayer." Morningstar mockingly remarked.

There was an awkward pause as Morningstar further admired the sight.

"May I ask what your immediate intentions are for these remarkable creations?" Rothstein meekly asked.

"It is quite rude for a benefactor of my generosity to ask such a question, Senator. But if you must know, these are the soldiers who will eventually dispose the earth of all common, lowly human beings."

"I hope you specifically mean the Patriots in America." Rothstein added with a grin.

"My army along with our allies will crush them into oblivion." Morningstar sadistically chuckled before continuing. "We will eventually create enough AI units to destroy the majority of the human race, and those left will specifically function as servants to my chosen Elite Society."

The young woman's eyes grew wide at the revelation as she stood nearby, nervously clutching tight to her clip board.

"You do mean, The Secret Society?" Podhadzny asked.

"We're no secret anymore, doctor. I've renamed them The Elite Society to better portray who we really are." He proudly proclaimed.

"I have to ask this of both of you. Will I have a place in this Society of yours?" The doctor hesitantly asked.

"We'll always have a need for intelligent scientists like yourself, Dr. Podhadzny." The Senator stated, much to the relief of the doctor.

After all, you are a seed of the Draconians." Morningstar added with a subtle grunt. "At this moment, I'd have to say your position with us is quite secure."

Morningstar turned his attention back to the robots, and grinned ambitiously. "I've already managed to deceive most of the world population with lies, and brain manipulation." He bragged. "They'll follow along like naïve, blind sheep, not knowing of their imminent fate." His eyes grew maniacally wide. "I will cripple the eagle, and pierce its' heart so that the Socialist States can assume control of America. It will then become a part of my global empire."

"You can count on our complete cooperation." Rothstein confidently stated.

"Of course, Senator. After all, the Society does own you and your constituents."

"What happens after we conquer America?" Podhadzny asked with a tinge of dread.

"Then, my good doctor, we'll finally be able to destroy Israel. After that, my Elite Society will have sole possession of this planet." He quickly turned to Rothstein. "I hope that doesn't offend you, Senator. I do know that you're of Jewish descent."

"Not in the least. I only follow your doctrine, Master." He bowed.

"The young girl suddenly cleared her throat, and spoke up in a timid voice. "Excuse me, Dr. Podhadzny. I have a few urgent errands to run. Would you mind if I took an early lunch?"

Not at all, Miss Malasenko. Just make sure you're back by 1:00."
She gave a nervous nod, and swiftly departed.

"Kind of an odd little nerd. Isn't she?" Morningstar sarcastically quipped. "For her sake, I hope she can be trusted with the information she heard here today."

"Miss Malasenko is quite loyal. She's intelligent, does her job well, and has been thoroughly screened just as all of our other employees are." Podhadzny assured.

"I'm very pleased with the progress, gentlemen." Morningstar stated. "I'd like to linger a bit longer, but I need to be in Geneva, Switzerland tomorrow for the World Economic Forum."

"I happen to be attending that meeting as well." Rothstein replied. "You're quite welcome to travel there in my private jet."

"Under normal circumstances I'd decline, Senator. But I think it will give us a chance to converse in private."

"Absolutely, Mr. Morningstar. I'm eager for you to hear of the progress we're making in the Socialist States of America."

Miss Malasenko anxiously raced from the building, and into the parking lot. She fumbled for the key fob that was in her purse as she hurried to her car. She paused for a moment, and nervously scanned the lot, and then glanced back toward the building entrance where the Neo-Nazi's stood sentry. Feeling assured that no one was watching, she shapeshifted into her true form. The nerdy little book worm was now a tall, platinum blonde woman with larger than normal blue eyes that appeared almost cat like.

As she crawled into the drivers' seat of her SUV, she drew a heavy, anxious breath. She then clenched her eyes shut, and concentrated deeply in her efforts to communicate telepathically with an unseen force. Her thoughts were rapid, desperate, and to the point.

"Lavender to mothership. Mayday! Mayday! Please beam me out of here now."

A single emotional tear escaped from the corner of one eye, and trickled down her cheek.

7

A UNION OF DESTINY

The allied contingent returned to Station 37 in what would have been the early morning hours. The Nordic commander as promised, adjusted the time lines so that it was now mid-morning. A much larger passenger cart arrived to pick them all up for transport. Katiera snuggled close to Owen as they settled into their seats, and set out for their next destination.

"Now we can finally celebrate." She proclaimed. "Today is our special day."

"Yes, it is." Owen smiled, as all the others turned to glance at the loving couple with expressions of bursting joy.

In short time, the group arrived at a large, ornate building that had many distinct features of art deco design. A group of young maidens ushered the group to small dressing rooms where a fresh set of clothes awaited them. As they all prepared to enter the large hall, they all made sure that Owen and Katiera went before them. A loud ovation and cheers greeted the happy newlyweds. It was obvious that the entire population of Station 37 was in attendance. Owens' jaw dropped as he marveled at the lavish celebration that was prepared especially for them.

"How in the world did they prepare all of this in such a short period of time?" He asked.

"Everyone in Station 37 pitched in, and did everything. Each person was assigned a specific task." Katiera answered.

"This is wonderful! Do they do this for everyone who gets married?"

"It's a very special rite of passage when a Mermaid chooses her life mate." She answered with a nod. "I just had to wait a bit longer than everyone else."

"Which makes it all the better to savor." Owen smiled.

Those in attendance congratulated the couple as they made their way through. A woman with light brown hair, confidently toting along a handsome man, pushed through the crowd to reach them. With a fake smile, she gave Katiera a half hug.

"Oh Katiera, dear! I'm so happy you finally found your man." She looked Owen up and down with a critical eye. "And to think you had to go on land to find him." She gloated while pulling her own man closer.

Owen could sense the tension between the women, and quickly spoke up. "I'd have to say she did quite a fine job in choosing, and it was well worth the wait for both of us." He replied with an equally manufactured smile, prompting sarcastic grins to change to speechless expressions as Katiera carted Owen ahead through the crowd.

"That was a priceless encounter." He joked, "I guess they have those types in every society."

"To think that she was actually my best friend at one time." Katiera vented.

"I sense she was the friend who stole your man."

Katiera swung around, and planted a kiss on Owens' lips. "I got the better deal." She grinned.

Tabitha and Nera greeted the couple with hugs.
"Follow us to the main table." Tabitha said with great excitement.

As Owen made his way, he took amused notice of the band on the main stage that consisted of all women musicians, except for a male drummer.

As everyone settled, Nera and Eno Calta seated themselves across from the newlyweds. Owen eyed the couple with fascination.

"I'm so interested in hearing about your home planet." Owen expressed. "Where exactly is it located in the Pleiades Star Cluster?"

Eno gave a yielding glance to his wife who seemed eager to answer.

"We now hail from the planet Erra in the Taygeta system. It's quite similar in appearance to earth, but somewhat smaller in size."

"We originally came from the Lyran race. We fled our planet after the last great Galactic War." Eno added. "Those are your roots as well, Owen."

"Are you saying that I lived in a past lifetime on a different planet?"

"You've lived many lifetimes. You're what we refer to as an old soul." Eno answered with a grin.
"Your beautiful wife and her race were also close relatives of our people. We simply migrated to different planets."

"As you can see, my genetics are quite close to theirs." Katiera chimed in. "We were once of the Lyran bloodline as well."

Owen directly addressed Nera. "I can't help but notice how beautiful your eyes are. They almost look like giant cat eyes."

"That's because I have feline genetics from my mother." She blushed. "Like a cat, I'm able to see in the dark, and can also see great distances."

"She also has a keen sense of hearing. So, mind your whispers." Eno joked.

"Eno also has large eyes of solid blue, but prefers to wear lenses with a dark pupil to better fit in when visiting here on earth." She stated, while lovingly nudging close to her husband.

Owen was awe stricken. "There are so many questions I have about your part of the universe. I only wish I could visit there someday."

"Perhaps, someday you will." Nera smiled.

"We look forward to a day when all the members of The Galactic Federation are welcomed here on earth. We have so much knowledge and technology that we're eager to share with your people." Eno concluded with emotional tears welling in his eyes.

"I hope that day comes soon." Owen answered as he raised his water glass toward the couple.

Meanwhile, aboard Senator Rothstein's private jet, he and Morningstar casually sipped cocktails as they conversed.

"How familiar are you with Lake Erie, Senator?"

"Quite well, actually. I was born and raised just outside of Buffalo. Why?"

Morningstar countered his question with another of his own. "Have you ever heard of the Oceanids from Greek mythology?"

"Kind of." Rothstein answered with a perplexed expression. "Aren't they supposed to be Mermaids?"

"You might say that." Morningstar replied with a chuckle. "There are Mermen as well. They came here centuries ago from the planet Aquis in the Pleiadian star cluster."

"You're not saying they actually exist?" Rothstein mockingly chuckled.

"Indeed, I am." He answered with a serious stare. "What would you say if I told you they have a colony below Lake Erie?"

"If it was coming from anyone else, I'd have to question their sanity." Rothstein paused. "Do you know exactly where?"

Morningstar pondered before answering. "I'm not exactly sure. But I do believe it may be in the region between Erie, Pennsylvania and Long Point, Canada."

"Obviously, they live a peaceful existence there. Why did you even bring this up?"

"Because they, and their allies The Nereids are our sworn enemy, Senator."

Rothstein only replied with a perplexed expression before Morningstar continued.

"When the Draconians, and our hired terrorists attempted to gain control of Branch Consolidated and the town of Lockeport Connecticut, they were soundly defeated when the Nereids and immortal gods intervened on behalf of the Patriots. They overstepped their bounds, and used a pulse weapon that decimated my troops. Now the Oceanids appear to have entered the fray."

"Why wasn't I aware of this? I had no idea that such a town even existed."

"That's because I wiped it from the memory of all humans, including the members of The Society." Morningstar explained with a sly grin. "When they failed, I destroyed the town myself. I also killed the gods and Steven Spencer while I was at it."

"How did you destroy the town?"

"I banished it and the Branchview Estate to another matrix from where it never can return. I replaced it with the town of Old Saybrook that also existed in a parallel matrix."

"What are your plans for the Oceanids?"

"I need to locate exactly where their colony is in the lake." He pondered in thought for a moment. "Would you happen to know any mariners who may have a thermal sonar unit that can read heat pockets at the lake bottom?"

"There's an environmental firm that works out of Buffalo that may have one, but it might prove to be a difficult task this time of year. The lake waters tend to be quite rough, and they could possibly be frozen by mid January."

"Then we'll need to work fast, Senator. I need you to make sure the area I mentioned earlier is carefully scanned, and mapped out. Spare no costs."

"I'll get right on it." Rothstein assured, still appearing quite baffled. "I have to ask, Master. What do you plan to do when you locate their colony?"

Morningstar clasped his hands together, taking on a sinister expression. "I will drop a remote hydrogen bomb over the area. When it detonates, it will destroy their portal, and the power of the blast will also destroy the colony as well."

"But that would cause a catastrophe!" Rothstein exclaimed with panic in his voice. "Not only for the ecology of the lake, but it would also wipe out the entire shorelines on both the Canadian and American sides. Several innocent lives would be lost."

"We're at war, Senator. In every war there are casualties. Human life and ecology mean nothing to me." He grunted indignantly, before facing him once again. "I'd suggest that you warn your friends and family to seek higher ground when the time draws near."

Rothstein sunk down in his seat with great anxiety. "Yes sir."

In Pennsylvania, Randy sat at his dining table in pondering thought. Myra strolled into the room, sat down next to him, and took hold of his hand.

"What's wrong, Bear?"

"Nothing actually. I'm thinking clearer than I have in my entire life since they removed that damn device from my head." He gave an assured squeeze to her hand. "I spoke with Morningstar's assistant today."

"What did you tell him?"

"I told him I had information about the Oceanids, and that I'd like to arrange a meeting."

"I don't know if that's a very good idea. The bastard tried to kill us." Myra replied with high anxiety.

"Trust me on this, Myra. Me and the boys have a plan to destroy Morningstar once and for all." He confidently chuckled.

"What then?"

"Then I hope to join my nephew and the Oceanids in defeating the damn globalist, and making this country a better place. I've followed the evil path way too long." He glanced up. "Are you with me?"

"I'm with you all the way, Cuddle Bear." She replied with a smile.

At Station 37, Katiera and Owen were showered with applause and well wishes as they exited the reception venue. A flowered levitation cart waited for them, and the couple climbed aboard. As the cart picked up speed, and darted away, Owen looked lovingly into Katiera's eyes.

"Where are we off to now?"

"Our honeymoon suite, of course." She giggled. "It should be just a few minutes of your time to get there."

"I have a feeling I'm going to have a wonderful life with you."

"Beyond your wildest dreams." She confidently replied before they kissed.

Within a few short moments, the cart slowed once again as it approached a vintage log cottage, situated in a grove of shade trees, willows, and flowering bushes. It was on the shore of a peaceful sparkling body of water, that was fed by a gentle waterfall. The cottage had a large patio that extended out over the water, and below it was a wooden row boat. It looked like a postcard from paradise.

"Here we are." Katiera joyfully proclaimed. "This is where we'll stay until our house is finished."

"Our house?"

"All newlyweds receive their own house fashioned from their own thoughts and personality. Ours will be on a plot of land near my parents' property, and it should only take about a month or so for the community to build it for us." She explained.

Owen was flabbergasted, and further questioned. "You mentioned that they fashioned it from our thoughts and personality. How exactly can that be?"

"You have so much to learn." She giggled, as Owen disembarked, and lifted her down from the cart. "We can telepathically read each other's random thoughts, and shut out anything that shouldn't be heard."

"I hope they're not listening to my thoughts at this very moment. They're very private." He stated as he embraced, and pulled her closer.

"I can read them, and they are the same exact thoughts as mine."

They strolled hand in hand onto the front porch, and approached the rustic wooden front door. Owen paused in thought for a moment as he opened the door.

"You and I have had this scenario a few times. Let's keep the tradition going."

Owen easily swooped a giggling Katiera into his arms, and carried her over the threshold. He gently nudged the door closed with his foot, and proceeded to a couch in the great room, where he laid Katiera down, and gently kissed her.

"Wait!" She exclaimed while pushing herself up to a sitting position. "We must do something else first."

Owen sighed with disappointment, as he settled next to her. "We're married, and it's our honeymoon. Why do we have to wait."

"Trust me on this. "She assured as she placed both her hands to the sides of Owens' head. "Place your hands on the sides of my head like this."

Owen did as she said. "What is this all about?"

"We're connecting our minds so that we can be permanently joined." She nodded. "Now, close your eyes, and concentrate on me."

Once again, Owen complied, and Katiera closed her eyes as well. Both began to tremble as electricity passed between them. Their minds raced with a fast forward vision of each other's lives from birth to present. Sounds and colors convulsed their brain cells, in a nirvanic kind of ecstasy. In a short while it was over, leaving them both breathless.

"That was the most exhilarating experience I've ever had." Owen stated.

"You and I are now officially connected." Katiera replied as she stood and took hold of his hand. "Now we can move on to the good part." She remarked with a sly smirk.
Nothing more was said as Owen eagerly stood with renewed energy, and his new bride boldly led him from the room.

While the two newlyweds celebrated their marital bliss in a Utopian setting, Lucifer Morningstar held a late night meeting with the upper echelon of the Elite Society in Geneva, Switzerland. All attention was focused on him as he stood at the podium to address his followers in the darkened hall.

A dignified man in a tuxedo entered the hall virtually unnoticed, and silently strolled along the back aisle until he attained a good vantage point. He then leaned against the wall, and listened with great interest.

"My fellow members of the Society." He began. "I'm here to share the news that our long delayed conquest of the United States is now within our grasp."

All stood to applaud, and Morningstar paused with a pleasing smirk until it settled.

"All assets are in place to aid the Socialist States in defeating the Free States."

"But it appears that their economy is working much better than ours, and they've ably countered every obstacle we've put in their way." A man in the audience countered, causing Morningstar to react with a slight sneer.

"He's right, and people have been leaving the Socialist States for a better life in the Free States." A woman with a German accent also countered.

Morningstar motioned to silence the crowd. "I've taken all that into careful thought, and I assure you that we have a plan to destroy them forever." He paused to listen to the loud whispers being exchanged before continuing. "As I speak, an army of killer robots is being prepared in Northern Ukraine, and we'll soon restrict those who wish to leave the Socialist States." He paced. "We're also working on a new virus that's sure to wreak havoc in all corners of the earth. Israel will be the first country to feel the wrath. And yes, my friends, only we have the true vaccine."

"What about the loyal inhabitants of our states?" Rothstein inquired from his front row seat.

Morningstar chuckled lightly before answering. "The fools who follow us will eventually become our slaves." He paused with a matter of fact grin before turning his attention to the whole congregation. "We'll have control of all the farms to provide our food, and all the minerals and natural resources in the ground. No one will own a house, or have any assets. We'll control all the facets of the government, media, and commerce." He paused again to emphasize his point. "We will all be emperors of this earth, and no one will dare to challenge us."

His comments brought another round of applause, and he hesitated before continuing.

"I also have a personal agenda to carry out. I've declared war on the Nereids and Oceanids." He nodded confidently. "I've located a colony in Lake Erie that I plan to terminate very soon." He gestured toward a Tall Grey Alien who stood sentry on the stage behind them. "I've also recruited our Grey allies to exterminate the pesky Black Mermaids of the Caribbean. No longer will they hinder our drug and human trafficking operations. They've assured that when they kill Linda Sanchez, they'll personally deliver her remains to me." He smirked as another round of applause erupted.

"What will they do to accomplish this?" A voice in the audience loudly asked.

The Grey Alien stepped forward, and Morningstar yielded to it.

"We will send poison into their waters, and kill every living thing that exist there. We will also alter the weather to destroy their ecosystem." It stated in a gravel tinged voice that had no emotion.

"In doing so, they'll all but destroy the Free State of Florida as well." Morningstar added.

"With the aid of The Greys, The Reptilians, The Draconians, and our global allies, we will batter the Patriots and their forces into total submission." He further declared, which caused a wild, rowdy ovation to explode within the hall.

He waited for the commotion to settle before continuing.

"We'll conclude the mission we started way back in 1913 when our esteemed Conglomerate Bank seized control of the world economy." He proudly gestured to the dignitaries in the audience. "Since then, we've caused World Wars, and started smaller wars. We created the Great Depression, assassinated leaders, and instigated countless calamities. We orchestrated 9/11 to steal the St. Germaine Funds, and destroy the quantum computer of The Galactic Federation of Light. In the process, we also helped our allies in the Military Industrial Complex to reap a fortune from a seemingly endless war in The Middle East." He paused to arrogantly grunt. "All the while, we've used the media to deceive the multitudes. Even the idealistic twits that passionately support us fell for the great lie." He mockingly chuckled. "This is our time! We will kill the majority of the world population, and inherit the earth as our own. Nothing, and no one can stop us."

Maniacal chants of "kill, kill, kill" arose among the wild eyed congregation.

The mysterious man who stood at the back of the room, quietly, and calmly slipped out the exit door, casually bidding the sentries a good night as he passed. Once he was outside, he hurried his pace until he was at a safe distance, and was able to duck into the shadows. Without breaking stride, he shapeshifted into his true form of a handsome Nordic Alien. He then looked to the dark skies with his solid blue eyes, almost in desperation.

"My mission is complete. Beam me out of here."

At that request, there was a flash of light, and his being promptly vaporized. In the aftermath, everything was still and silent, with the exception of a barking dog somewhere in the distance.

8

A NEW MISSION

Owen woke up from a peaceful sleep to the sound of chirping birds. The early morning light peeked through the sheer curtains that lifted slightly from a gentle breeze. As he gathered his senses, he realized that Katiera was not there. Without hesitation, he threw the covers aside, and slipped on a pair of gym shorts.

"Katie!" He called out before departing the room. He paused, but there was no answer.

He walked out onto the balcony deck, and leaned against the railing.

"Katie!" He called out once more. This time, he saw a green finned tail pop to the surface of the water, before the beautiful young woman fully emerged as well.

A smile graced his face, as he watched his wife wave back at him.

"Come in and join me, Owen. The water is heavenly."

Without hesitation, he hurried to the bottom of the stairs, and dove head first into the crystal waters. The giant splash he created made Katiera giggle. He popped to the surface, and swam to her, where they embraced in a romantic kiss. They were so involved in the moment that they failed to notice someone watching from shore.

Linda Sanchez cleared her throat to get their attention. "I hate to be the one to intrude on such a private moment, but I drew the short straw."

The couple swam to the shore and curiously emerged as Linda stood firm with her arms crossed. She eyed the couple admirably as they stepped forward. Katiera appeared to be unaffected by her total nudity, and Owen rushed to retrieve a towel to somewhat cover her up.

"You two do make quite an adorable couple." She smirked.

"You mentioned that you were sent by the others. Is there anything wrong?" Owen inquired as he slipped his arm around his wife.

"Quite a bit has transpired since last night." Linda sighed. "The Nordics need to leave right away, and they wanted to brief us before they departed."

"Can you tell us what's going on?" Katiera further questioned.

"Let's just say that Satan and the Elite Society have been quite busy preparing a counterattack, and it's time for us all to unite against them. I'm sure they'll cover everything in the meeting."

"Just give us enough time to get dressed." Owen replied with a nod.

"Very well. Just hurry! They're patiently waiting for us right now at the town meeting hall."

A short time later, the trio breezed into the meeting room to be greeted with very serious glances from those in attendance. They wasted no time in sitting down at the seats allotted to them at the large meeting table. Eno nodded to the couple as they settled in.

"Please accept our apologies for interrupting your honeymoon, but this is a very urgent matter." He stressed.

"I understand that fact. But I can't see where there's anything Katie and I can do in this matter." Owen answered.

At that, Eno yielded to Linda Sanchez who began with a deep sigh.

"As you're well aware, we're already dealing with red tide, and deterioration of the coral reef in the Florida and Caribbean waters. That lunatic Morningstar is enlisting help from the Grey Aliens to further poison waters to create an ecological catastrophe." She took a stressful pause. "We need someone with your expertise to help us in the case we aren't able to stop them in time."

"What method do the Greys plan to use?" Owen questioned.

"We don't know for sure." Eno answered. "But we've been granted permission from our allies in Florida to guard the main portals in both the Atlantic and the Gulf. If the Greys try to enter that airspace, our starships will blast them into oblivion."

"Unfortunately, the US Military doesn't have the advanced technology to handle an alien invasion." Xander commented.

"We have no choice, but to intervene on the earth's behalf. We can't stand idle, and allow such an event to take place." Eno further added.

"Morningstar, and the Elites have ignited what could become a universal war." Agent Guitierez stated after being a somewhat silent observer for much of his visit.

"You can count on my help." Owen eagerly replied.

"I'm going with you then." Katiera defiantly spoke, causing all at the table to exchange concerned glances.

"Absolutely not!" Owen quickly answered. "It's much too dangerous."

"He's right, sweetheart." Xander reasoned. "We are at war, and you know as well as I do, what a ruthless lot those Greys are."

"I can't let my husband go without me. Wherever he goes, I go too. If we die, we die together."

"We can't stay at my parent's old residence." Owen huffed. "I'm sure Morningstar's people have ransacked it, and have it under surveillance."

"I have a safe place where you can both stay." Linda replied. "It's a large estate on the Gulf Coast." She exchanged a quick glance with Guitierez. "Agent Guitierez and his team are stationed there as well."

"We must move onto other things." Eno intervened. "Time is definitely not our ally."

"Our agents have delivered other troubling news as well." Nera Calta announced. "The Elites have built an army of killer robots that they plan to unleash on the world. Their factory is located in a remote area of Northern Ukraine."

Eno glanced toward Damaris. "We understand that your people in Nereida have perfected the technology for the aqua pulse weapon. Do you have a large enough version that could obliterate a huge building and its' contents?"

"We sure do." Damaris answered. We have large panels positioned at the entry portal to our city that protects us from potential attacks. Fortunately, we've never had to use them."

"Could one of those repeater panels possibly be mounted onto one of our starships?" Eno further probed.

"I think we can do it." Damaris replied. "We'd need to tap into the starships water reserve to create a large enough percussion."

"Good! One of our ships is waiting to transport you and I back to Nereida." Nera stated. "I can work alongside your technicians to make this possible."

"Now for the last bit of intelligence we've gathered." Eno glanced to Anna Pare' and Xander. "It appears that Morningstar is currently scanning the lake bottom for heat signatures. He plans on dropping two hydrogen bombs when he locates your settlement."

"What can we do to counter such an act?" Anna inquired.

"I'm sure he's paying big money for someone outside of The Elite Society to handle the task for him." Eno replied. "I'm afraid we won't be able to engage them directly without loss of innocent life, and thus dragging The Federation into a full scale Earth War."

"Morningstar would like nothing more than to have that happen." Nera added.

"I have an idea." Xander announced as he stood and brought up a hieroglyphic screen of the lake bottom. "As you can see, the large heat signature is Station 37." He pointed to a smaller signature. "This small blip just off the tip of Presque Isle is something entirely different." He moved his finger to another location. "This other large area over near Cleveland is the underground salt mines that extend under the lake."

"What is that smaller signature?" Owen inquired.

"Have you ever heard of the Lake Erie Monster, and the Storm Hag?" Xander replied.

"Those are tales we heard about as kids." Owen chuckled. "I'm sure they're both just urban legends."

Xander countered with a smirk. "They do exist, and that's where they live."

"We've kept peace with them for years, and they've generally remained in their place other than an occasional random sighting. But if they were violently disturbed, I'm sure they would retaliate with brute force." Anna stated.

"That would further complicate things." Xander declared as he thoughtfully paced for a moment, before turning to Guitierez. "Agent Guitierez! Would you possibly be able to spare a few of your agents."

"I think I might be able to arrange that. What do you have planned?"

"We'll have our people seek out every large exploration boat between Buffalo and Cleveland." Xander explained. "When we locate the one that is carrying the bombs, we'll have the ability to remotely disable the explosives without them knowing."

"Why not also stop the vessel before it leaves port? We could arrest those on board, and get valuable information." Guitierez countered.

"We have to let this play out." Xander seriously answered. "My theory is that they'll drop the bombs on the areas they believe are part of Station 37" He paused. "My guess is that they'll detonate the explosions when the ship and crew are back in port, and well out of harms' way."

Guitierez gave an agreeing nod. "But what about the monsters? If they were disturbed, they could raise further havoc. Shouldn't we take defensive measures there as well?"

"We'll be able to calm them through telepathy." Xander answered. "Those beasts survived the ice age. The lake is also their home, and they deserve the right to peacefully coexist there for as long as they wish."

"There is one more issue to address before we go." Nera stated. "It appears the Elite's are poised to release another pandemic on the world very soon."

"We don't know where their lab is located. But I think we have a way to counter their plans before they have a chance to launch them." Eno further added.

"How can we do that?" Anna inquired.

"We'll have to check with my superiors. But perhaps it's time to permanently purge the world of the evil players." He sighed. "We'll unleash the Angels of Death, just as they did in the Bible during the Passover."

Everyone drew a deep breath of dread, followed by an uncomfortable silence.

"We'll just have to take things as they come." Eno concluded. "Right now, I must leave, and join my forces. Time is of the essence." He stood, along with Nera, and the two Nordics embraced in a kiss. "Good luck with your mission, sweetheart. I'll see you when this is over."

Nera gave him a nod of confidence before he evanesced completely from the room.

Nera then motioned for Damaris to join her at the front of the room.

"It's time for us to leave as well. Hopefully, we'll see you all again when this is over and done." Nera firmly stated.

The two women then held hands, and within seconds, they too, vaporized from the room. In the moments after, there was a dull silence from all that remained, as they processed the situation.

Linda then exchanged glances with Owen, Katiera, and Agent Guitierez. "I guess it's our turn."

"There's a cart waiting for all of you outside." Xander replied in a worried tone. "Sela is waiting on the outskirts of town. She'll transport you all to Florida."

He then turned to Owen, and firmly shook his hand. "Take care of my baby girl."

Owen replied with an assured nod.

"Please tell mother that I'm sorry I couldn't say goodbye." Katiera emotionally hugged her father, until he regretfully cut it short.

"You all need to go now. We're operating on earth time, and we have very little of it to work with."

In Midtown Manhattan, Lucifer Morningstar materialized in the penthouse suite of the former Conglomerate Bank Building. His chauffer and bodyguard Bruce, quickly roused from a cat nap.

"Welcome back, Mr. Morningstar. I trust your travels proved to be worthwhile."

"Quite!" He abruptly answered, while taking a seat next to him on the couch. "Hopefully, I can enjoy a little leisure time now that I'm back."

"About that." Bruce began with a sigh. "A lot happened since you've been gone."

"Such as…?"

"Those three assassins you sent to kill the Gustafsson's failed. Only one came back to tell the story." He chuckled. "Claimed there was a trio of archers that ambushed them, and he was the only one that got away. Had a pretty nasty wound on his bicep."

"Interesting!" Morningstar responded with great thought. "Where is this man now?"

"I killed him, and properly disposed of the body." He bit his upper lip. "I guessed that's what you would've wanted."

"Yes." He replied with a nod. "You did well, Bruce."

"There's more." He continued with a deep breath. "Randy Gustafsson got in touch with us. Said he's got some important information about what his nephew and those aliens are up to. Also said he'd travel here to meet with you in person."

"Is that so?" Morningstar smirked. "And just where is this vile vermin willing to meet?"

"In the parking lot of an abandoned building over in Queens."

"When?"

149

"Two o'clock this afternoon." He answered with a pause. "That's why I left the limo parked out front."

Morningstar rolled his eyes to the ceiling. "Now I know what they mean in saying, no rest for the wicked."

A moment of silent thought fell between the two men before Morningstar shifted his attention back to Bruce.

"Why did you choose to be in my employ, Bruce?"

He sat forward to answer. "Where I come from, I could never make as much money doing the things I'd be forced to do there just to survive."

"It doesn't bother you that The Elite Society, and their political leaders have kept Black people in oppression for centuries, and continually lied to them about it?"

Bruce shrugged, and gave an answer he felt Morningstar wanted to hear, although his expression displayed the indifference churning inside. "There always has to be winners and losers. A man's gotta do what he has to do to get through." He abruptly changed the subject. "You want some lunch before we go?"

"I think I'd like a pastrami sandwich from that little deli on 5th Avenue." He smiled in response.

"I'll get that ordered up." The large framed man answered as he rose from the couch.

Just outside of Sarasota Florida, the contingent of Linda Sanchez, Agent G., Owen and Katiera were ferried by a large dinghy onto shore from the Gulf. All sported oxygen masks to fend off the lethal stench of the red tide. As they disembarked onto the beach, and plodded through a multitude of dead and

150

decaying fish, Owen and Katiera paused to marvel at the spectacular house that stood ahead of them.

"What is this place?" Owen asked through his mask in a muffled tone.

"We call it Branchview South." Agent G. answered.

The group was greeted at the entrance by a housekeeper, who quickly ushered all of them in. They all pulled off their masks, and took a deep breath of the interior fresh air.

"Katiera and I desperately need to rehydrate." Linda announced before turning to Agent G. "Could you help by familiarizing Owen with his surroundings?"

Agent G. gave an assuring nod to Linda, and Katiera kissed Owen before the two women departed.

"Your wife is very lovely, Owen. You're a lucky man." Agent G. smiled.

"Are you married, Agent Guitierez?"

"I had a fiance'." He answered with a lump in his throat. "She was also my agency partner." He paused with difficulty before continuing. "Her name was Davika Banerjee."

"What happened?" Owen asked with sympathetic interest.

"After we defeated The Secret Society in this country, we foolishly thought we were finally safe." He paused. "Lucifer Morningstar sent a hit squad to my secret residence. I had gone out to get a pizza, and was only gone for about 20 minutes." He emotionally sighed. "When I returned, Davika was dead, and the house had been ransacked for information."

"I'm sorry." Owen solemnly replied.

"That's why my team and I are all in one place here at Branchview South. Mr. Spencer had a state of the art security system installed that makes this place as safe as a fort. Hopefully, we can operate securely from here for the time being."

"Can we ever defeat Morningstar, and what remains of The Elites?"

"With the cooperation of Katiera and Linda's people, the Galactic Federation, and Patriots like you and I, I'd like to believe that we can."

Owen responded with an optimistic, yet dubious expression.

Just then, a dignified, middle aged Black man breezed into the room.

"Excuse me, Agent G. I didn't know we had company."

"No problem, Gerard." He gestured to Owen. "This is Owen Gustafsson. He's one of us, and he's here with his Oceanid wife." He hesitantly looked to Owen. "This man's identity is highly classified, and should never be mentioned outside of these walls."

At that, the man firmly gripped Owen's hand, and identified himself. "I'm Gerard LeRoux."

"The President and CEO of Branch Consolidated?"

"As Agent G said, only to the ears within this house." He expressed with a smile.

"Owen's in a similar predicament with his family." Agent G stated. "When we have more time, you'll need to hear how he and his wife met. It's quite a story."

"I can't wait to hear it." Gerard said with a grin. "If you gentlemen would excuse me, I was just on the way to my study for a meeting with Alton Sinclair." He shook Owen's hand once more. "It was a pleasure meeting you, Owen."

As he departed, Owen looked to Agent G. with wonder. "Who is Alton Sinclair?"

"Mr. Sinclair is his right hand man, and is also being kept here." He continued with a sigh. "He is also the step father of the heirs to the Branch Consolidated Empire."

"Are they in hiding as well?"

"They were taken up to an undisclosed safe place."

"In other words, they're among the missing."

Agent G. simply concluded with a nod before moving ahead to another subject.

"You and Katiera will be spending most of the remainder of your time offsite with Linda. Like Gerard, I have to remain here at the safe house, and secretly communicate with my team on the outside."

"Considering the stench from the dead fish and the red tide that's prevalent outside, that might be fortunate. At least for the time being" Owen quipped.

"All kidding aside." he seriously stared at Owen. "Along with Mr. LeRoux, be sure to never mention my name, Alton Sinclair, nor the location of this house. Morningstar has spies planted everywhere. No one outside of our inner circle can be trusted."

"You have my word." Owen assured.

In the deepest waters of The Atlantic Ocean, Nera and Damaris arrived to find engineers from both Nereida and The Galactic Federation already hard at work, mounting the eliminator shield onto the Federation's war ship within a large bubble enclosure at the oceans bottom.

"Ready to get your hands dirty?" Damarus quipped.

"I trained most of our technicians. I better be." Nera answered with a friendly smirk. "I'm not sure we have enough water supply to cool our engines when it's time to go back through the portal. We'll need an ample supply to operate the shield as well."

"Then we'll just have to build an auxiliary tank inside your operations room." Damarus stated.

"How long will that take?" We're working on a very tight schedule."

"If we get everyone to pitch in, we'll get it done well ahead of launch time."

"I like the way you think, Mermaid." Nera grinned.

Meanwhile in Queens, Randy and Myra waited in an empty parking lot for Morningstar to arrive. Randy talked nervously into the open speaker of his cell phone with his son Matty, and Josh who were in a van on the far side of the lot.

"Are you sure you and Josh placed that bomb securely under Morningstar's limo?"

"No worries, Paw. It's placed, and ready to go."

"It was a piece of cake." Josh chimed in. "His driver had it parked outside the building all day."

Just then, the limo entered the vacant lot that was strewn with garbage.

"It's time, guys." Randy announced with determination.

The limo pulled to a complete stop several feet away, and there was a long pause before the back door opened, and Morningstar began to step out.

"Now!" Randy urgently ordered.

Josh hit the remote button that he held tight in his hand, and the limo exploded into a huge fireball, sending debris flying everywhere. Morningstar was propelled several feet through the air, landing hard on the asphalt in front of Randy's truck. His motionless body burned as they watched.

"So long, you evil bastard." Randy chuckled.

"We did it, Bear. We killed Satan. Myra exuberantly chimed in.

Suddenly, the burning body in front of them began to slowly rise to one knee. It transformed into a hideous beast that set its eyes on the truck. Matty and Josh watched in horror from the van.

"Holy shit!" Josh cried. "Let's get the hell out of here."

The van accelerated in its attempt to escape, but lightning shot from the beasts' hoof, instantly exploding the vehicle into a raging inferno. Randy and Myra observed with shock as the beast turned his determined attention back toward them.

"What the...."

Before Randy could put the truck in gear, and accelerate, the beast leapt onto the hood. With one swift move, its' hoof crashed through the windshield, impaling Myra where she sat. In fearful horror, Randy tried to flee the truck, but the beast was on him in a flash. As it pinned him to the asphalt, it brandished a sharp blade.

"Tell me what you know about Owen Gustafsson and the Oceanids." The beast groveled.

Randy responded by spitting in its face. "Go to hell!"

Satan sneered in anger, and with a quick maneuver of the blade, the beast lopped Randy's head completely from his body.

The beast then stood, and transformed into Morningstar, who stared down at the terror-stricken face of the severed head that rested in a pool of blood.

"Fools!" He scoffed. "You actually believed you could kill me."

He glanced across the lot at the flaming van, and grunted. He then paced back toward the burning limo, pausing for a moment to watch in reflective thought.

"I'm sorry, Bruce." He mumbled in an uncharacteristic gesture of remorse, before casually strolling away from the carnage.

9

THE GALACTIC FEDERATION STRIKES BACK

In a seemingly vacant building outside of Sarasota, the trio of Linda, Owen, and Katiera arrived, and parked near a back entrance. They were far enough away from the Gulf that their protective oxygen masks were no longer needed.

"What is this place?" Owen inquired. "It looks like it's been vacant for a while."

"Looks can be deceiving, Owen." Linda replied as she entered a code to open the door.

Inside, there was a bustle of activity within a modern medical facility, complete with research labs, doctors, scientists, and attendants all wearing white lab coats. Linda took one of the white coats from a nearby hook, examined the label, then handed it to Owen.

"This is an XL. This should fit you." She stated.

"You never did answer Owens' question. What exactly is this facility?" Katiera pressed.

"This is where your husband will be working." She replied with a sly grin. "We desperately need his oceanographic expertise." She motioned to them both. "Follow me."

They passed by several large containment tubs that contained sick dolphins, sea turtles, and manatees. They then entered into a secure area where much to Owen and Katiera's surprise, at least a dozen critically ill Mermaids hydrated within nearly full tubs of water. Both reacted with sympathetic expressions. Owen couldn't help but think of the first time he laid eyes on Katiera. She too had been in a similar state.

"What happened to these poor souls?" Owen painfully inquired.

"These are my people, Owen. The Black Mermaids of the Caribbean." She continued. "We are small in number because many of us have left the water, and taken earth mates over the years. Mermen, as in other species of Water People are very rare. As mentioned, a good bit of them have left the colony to live on land as well." She gestured toward two tubs that contained men. "These are among the few young Mermen that are left."

Owen and Katiera paced among the tubs, glancing at each face that looked back at them with desperate and pained expressions.

"We mostly evacuated the waters several months ago. But these are among the ones that didn't escape in time. They are suffering from environmental poisoning." She distressfully sighed. "Many didn't survive."

"Don't the Caribbeans have their own sanctuary beneath the waters?" Katiera asked.

"We never established one." She answered. "When the Tall Greys invaded our planet over two thousand years ago, our small group were the among the few to escape slaughter. We were never able to establish an advanced technological society like you have in the larger Oceanid and Nereid civilizations." She paused. "Poseidon and Zeus made me an immortal goddess all those years ago, and my people chose to jointly live on land and in the sea. We swore an oath to patrol, and keep these beautiful waters safe and clean. With our species numbers dwindling to just a few hundred in recent years, that task has become increasingly difficult.

"What can I do, Linda? Other than nursing Katiera back to health, I have no experience with your species.

"You have quite a reputation at doctoring manatee and dolphins back to health. As you've no doubt learned from the Oceanids, we do share similar genetics with those sea mammals."

"Besides, you have other healing powers as well." Katiera grinned, while she affectionately squeezed his hand. "You have so much love in your heart, Owen. That is the most powerful medicine in the universe."

"I'd have to agree with the pretty lady on that one." A booming voice chimed out as a rather imposing, muscle bound figure entered the room. He stood close to seven feet tall, had the head and fur of a lion, and the body of a human. His eyes were the mellow color of emerald green, and he also wore the traditional blue uniform of the Galactic Federation. His enormous biceps showed prominently beneath his long sleeve sweater, and his bare feet were similar to that of the large cat he portrayed.

All looked toward him with wide eyed, speechless awe. None had ever seen such a being.

"I'm sorry if my presence startled you." He cordially nodded. "My name is Mhakta Sandovar. I am originally from the feline planet Achta, and I am a physician with the Galactic Federation. Eno Calta sent me here to help." He gave another respectful nod to all three, as he set his large satchel on a nearby table, and pulled out a small, flat sided device.

"We're pleased to meet you Mhakta." Linda replied, still marveling at his appearance. "I'm Linda Sanchez, and this is Owen Gustafsson, and his Oceanid wife, Katiera."

159

"That looks similar to the healing device that my people have." Katiera remarked.

"You're right about that as well. It's a bit more advanced than the Oceanid model however." He looked to all three. "Eno filled me in on your situation here. I'm rather unfamiliar with your species as well, but hopefully I can be of assistance."

"We certainly need all the help we can get." Linda stressed. "My people are on the doorstep of death."

"We'll bring them back." Mhakta confidently assured. "I'll also look forward to getting better acquainted with each of you during the process. This is my first actual visit to Earth."

"We all welcome you, and look forward to finding out more about you, and your planet as well." Linda smiled.

"They're all in a lot of pain." Owen finally spoke, still somewhat fascinated by the appearance of the newcomer he was addressing. "Before we set them on a dry table for detox and scanning, I think it might be a good idea to mildly sedate them so they don't succumb to shock."

"I agree, Owen." Mhakta mildly replied as he rolled up the sleeves of his uniform. "Let's get this process started immediately."

At his penthouse office in Manhattan, Lucifer Morningstar sat in his large, plush office chair mulling over the events the day. All the shades were closed, and the room was void of hardly any light. He glanced down at his cell phone as though expecting it to ring at any moment. After a few frustrating moments, he grabbed it, and dialed a number.

"Rothstein! I want you to escalate the timing on all our planned events." He paused to listen. "I don't give a damn how you do it. I just want it done."

He abruptly ended the call, and entwined his fingers before speaking out to the darkness with a sarcastic smirk.

"You failed to show after the third trumpet blast." He grunted. "You've forsaken your people as I expected. This is my world now." He stood, and paced around his desk, continuing his boast. "I have destroyed the gods, the world of Branchview, and nearly all that's good. I will totally destroy the free states of America, kill the majority of the worlds' population, and enslave whatever is left." He let out a maniacal laugh, before yelling into the corners of the room.

"Where have you been Son of God?"

A blinding white light filled the room, and Morningstar, filled with surprise, shielded his eyes against it, while a mellow voice bellowed out.

"I've been here all along Satan, watching and countering all your wretched moves."

"Why don't you physically show yourself, and try to put a stop to my carnage?" Morningstar taunted.

"No one knows of the day or time I will strike, and reveal my presence."

Morningstar mockingly laughed. "I've heard that promise for centuries." He scoffed. "Come down in your human form so that I can have you killed once again."

"I will not be mocked, Satan." The voice roared back with a tinge of anger. "Your reign has ended. A new era of enlightenment is about to rise, and there's nothing you can do to stop it." The voice precisely concluded as the light quickly exited the room, leaving a noticeably worried Morningstar anxiously searching all corners of the dark room for more.

"No!" He angrily yelled. "I will not be defeated."

Back at the medical facility, Owen and Mhakta worked at detoxing a very sick Merman that was fully immersed in a large tub. Owen supported its body while Mhakta carefully ran the detoxifying unit over every inch of its body. The water had started to turn a murky black as the environmental toxins exited the sedated body, and the stench was almost unbearable. Owen winced at the unpleasant aroma, and Mhakta reacted with a subtle grin.

"You can only imagine how unpleasant it is for me. My sense of smell is at least fourteen times stronger than yours."

"I've only seen this one time before when my father in law drew the toxins from some fish we had caught in Lake Erie. He actually did it with his bare hands."

"I've heard that Xander is a very gifted healer." Mhakta answered with raised brow. "I hope that someday he and I have the opportunity to work together. Perhaps we can help your planet fully cleanse of its toxicity."

Owen took notice of Mhakta's large hand that steadily gripped the device.

"You have seven fingers."

"And you have five." Mhakta answered with sober amusement.

"Owen took notice of the unique expressions displayed on Mhakta's lion face as they conversed. It was like that of a wise old sage.

"I didn't mean to be rude." Owen explained. "I've just never witnessed any being quite like you."

"I'm equally intrigued by humans, and these shapeshifting mammals as well." Mhakta replied as he set the device aside, and helped Owen lift the Merman from the carcinogenic water. "This one is ready for rinsing." He added as they carefully transferred him to a nearby clean tub.

Both men drew a deep breath as they immersed the Merman, positioning its head above the water line. Mhakta continued conversing as he checked the vitals of their patient.

"Whereas your hearts are muscles that beat in rhythm, and your blood is the color of red." He continued. "You might be surprised to know that my heart is a crystalline orb that generates energy, and my blood is the color of green. Yet, despite our genetic differences, there are so many other ways that we are similar."

His statement brought an enlightened smile to Owens face.

"I'm quite intrigued. What can you tell me about your planet?" Owen eagerly asked.

"It's a beautiful planet of green vegetation, and very colorful plants. We have a moderate to cold temperature year round because of its distance from the sun. We rarely go above 55 degrees or below freezing."

"I'd imagine our weather here in Florida would seem quite warm to you."

"I know I can't chance being seen in public. But I do wish I could experience it."

"Well! When we're finished here, maybe I could sneak you out the back door for a few minutes of our earthly temperatures." Owen answered with a quick wink that prompted a warm smile from the lion.

Meanwhile, as darkness fell on the shores of Lake Erie, Xander led a small contingent of four Oceanid warriors, and two of Agent Guitierez' most trusted troops to a marina, surrounded by a high cyclone fence. A German Shepherd dog emerged on the other side of the locked fence, and began barking ferociously. Xander held an open hand toward the dog, and stared at him with immense concentration. Within seconds, the dog calmed, heeled, and whimpered like a puppy. The two agents looked at each other with puzzled expressions, and Xander replied with amusement.

"It's an ancient Oceanid method used to calm beasts."

He then pointed his finger at the heavy padlock on the gate, and focused on it with eyes closed. Within seconds, it popped open.

As they entered the enclosure, Xander gestured for his warriors to scatter, and whispered loudly to the two agents. "The vessel is docked over there."

The trio proceeded cautiously. The two agents were following Xander with their weapons on the ready for any unexpected trouble. Suddenly rapid footsteps were heard in the dark, and they found themselves surrounded by two guards toting assault rifles. The guards were dressed in all black, and sported Nazi swastika arm bands. It was a standoff.

"Put your weapons down, and no one gets hurt." One of the guards ordered.

Just then, two titanium arrows whizzed through the air, striking both guards in a vulnerable area outside of their body armor, immediately sending them to the ground. Xander quickly moved in to check on them.

"They're both dead." He announced, as he looked to the two archers that emerged from the dark. "Good shots."

"We had your back all along." One of the confident young warriors answered as she pulled a weapon from her belt, and aimed it at the fallen bodies. Within seconds, the bodies were vaporized.

The two agents, once again looked to each other with silent amazement before they all proceeded toward the research ship.

On the forward deck, there were two torpedo like bombs mounted, and awaiting their intended mission. Xander boarded the ship while the others observed. He brandished an odd looking weapon from his belt, and pointed it toward the detonator head of one of the bombs. A slight, prolonged zinging sound could be heard as he fired it, and a bright laser beam of light passed into the war head. He followed suit with the second bomb, then looked confidently to the others. "Mission accomplished."

Somewhere in the depths of the Atlantic Ocean, another mission was about to take place. The Galactic Warship, now mounted with the Nereid hydro vaporizing shield was set to emerge from the oceans bottom. Nera was at the helm, directing orders to her Nordic crew while Damarus observed.

"Fire up the generators." She urgently commanded as she worked the navigation controls.

The Starship creaked and groaned as it lifted from the bottom, and maneuvered to an upright position.

"Hang on tight, Mermaid. Things might get a bit bumpy."

As the quantum thrusters kicked into full mode, the starship accelerated roughly at an increasing speed as it shot upward against the weight of the ocean waters. Nera alertly eyed the temperature gauge as she anxiously steadied the ship. When the gauge hit the red line, she barked out the orders to the main control room.

"Activate the hydro coolers before we break apart."

Both women held their breath, never taking an eye off the gauge until it began to recede from the red zone.

"Hold on everyone!" Nera yelled to all within the main deck area.

Damarus closed her eyes against the pressure as the ship broke through the surface of the ocean with a loud thump.

The ship steadied as it righted itself, and shot with a steady climb toward the thermosphere, where it would cruise without being detected. Damarus could feel the temperature and air pressure adjustments in the main cabin area, and marveled at the advanced technology that she had only previously read about.

Nera let out a sigh of relief as she settled back in her chair. "With all that extra weight, that was quite a ride."

"How long will it take for us to reach our target?" Damarus asked.

Nera never took her eyes off the controls as she answered. "I estimate we'll reach the skies over northern Ukraine at approximately 2:23 AM adjusted earth time."

"That's only four minutes from now!" Damarus exclaimed with surprise.

"We're moving a bit slower with the weight of the shield." She grinned, glancing quickly to Damarus. "Lean back in your seat, and enjoy the show."

Damarus looked ahead through the large navigation window, and saw only darkness as the ship raced through the upper echelons of the atmosphere. It was like having tunnel vision. Suddenly the ship tilted its position, and the thrusters kicked into high gear as it ascended downward at an angle, then steadied to a mere cruising speed. She could feel the ship power down, as Nera controlled the navigation system, and brought it to a hovering stop over a sprawling industrial complex on the ground below.

"There's our target. Lock in." She ordered the crew as she quickly glanced up at the digital clock, and grinned. "We're actually one minute earlier than I anticipated."

Damarus leaned forward toward a control module that had only been constructed hours earlier, and saw the entire complex framed within a box on the screen in front of her.

"Activate the shield." Nera ordered to the main control room before looking to Damarus, and motioning to the red button in front of her. "You do the honors, Mermaid. On three, two, one, fire."

Damarus pressed the button, and the whole ship shook from the enormous shock wave that emitted from the shield. Within seconds, the complex, and everything within its vicinity evaporated before their eyes. Not even a shred of evidence remained of what was once there.

Both women paused with awe at the devastation they had just witnessed.

"We did it, Damarus." Nera proclaimed with a relieved sigh. "That's quite a powerful weapon your people have devised."

"That's the first time I've seen the devastation from it." Damarus answered, still staring ahead in disbelief. "Before this, all I've witnessed is what the handheld weapon could do."

"Maybe when this is over, our people can share the technology with each other. Hopefully, we'll have a period of peace where we'll never have to use it again."

Nera suddenly paused as if listening to an unheard conversation.

"What is it Nera?"

"That was Eno." She sighed after a few moments. "We're needed for another mission in the South Atlantic."

Without further word, Nera pulled back on the navigating wheel of the main console, shifting the ship upward, as it accelerated once again into the heavenly realms.

In another time zone, Owen, Katiera, and Linda returned to their sanctuary at Branchview South after an exhausting day of work. As they entered the house, they were greeted by Gerard LeRoux, Alton Sinclair, and Agent Guitierez who were having a relaxing discussion in the Great Room.

"The three of you look like you had quite a productive day." Gerard commented as he stood.

"We lost another one of our Mermaids." Linda lamented as she sunk into a nearby comfortable chair. "But thanks to Owen and Katiera here, the others are holding their own."

"The Galactic Federation also sent us some unexpected help." Owen added.

"Yes! In the form a very large cat." Linda continued, while the three men exchanged puzzled expressions. "I'll explain it all later."

Alton stood, and gestured a cordial nod toward Owen and Katiera. "Gerard told me all about you two. It's quite a story." He paused with a smile. "I'm Alton Sinclair."

"It's a pleasure meeting you, sir." Owen replied, while Katiera also responded with a respectful nod.

"Would you two please join us?" Alton offered. "We were waiting on Linda here to give us an update on things."

"And we'd sure like you to add some of your oceanographic expertise to the conversation as well, Owen." Agent G added.

"I'm sorry, but I'll have to pass." Katiera answered weakly. "I'm not feeling very well, and I really do need to immerse myself in water."

The three men then looked to Owen for a response.

"I suppose I can sit in for a short time." Owen stated before turning to his wife with a concerned expression as he kissed her. "I'll be along shortly, sweetheart."

All paused to observe as the lovely young woman departed before settling back in their places. Owen then scooted a side chair closer to the conversation, and settled in himself.

"It's good to see you again, Alton." Linda began. "How are things in North Dakota?"

"We've managed to set up an impressive new headquarters for Branch Consolidated, and so far, Morningstar and The Elites have not been able to penetrate our network of companies. Thanks to Agent G and his crew." He answered.

"I'm sure their burning the midnight oil trying to find a way of getting around your fire walls." Linda grunted with sarcasm.

"Our team of cyber experts have set up a shield that zaps the circuitry of any unknown IP address that tries to gain illegal access to our system." Agent G replied with much pride.

"It's a constant strategic battle." Gerard added. "But so far, we're winning."

"I'm sure those pompous windbags are pulling their hair out over that." Linda jokingly remarked, prompting a chorus of chuckles from the others.

"Not to hurry things along. But why exactly do you need to tap into my knowledge of oceanography?" Owen pressed. "Has anything else happened in the Gulf?"

All glanced to Linda to answer the question.

"As you're quite aware, Owen. Morningstar and his cast of evil aliens have done all they can to destroy our beautiful Caribbean Waters." Linda began. "Eno has intelligence reports that they plan to heat the waters to a boil, and deposit more carcinogenic substances into it."

"That would be an ecological disaster both on sea and land." Owen answered with great alarm.

All three exchanged quick, anxious glances before Gerard spoke. "You and Linda know these Caribbean waters better than any of us, Owen." He leaned further into the conversation. "What would be the consequences of freezing the Gulf and South Atlantic waters?"

"In the first place, that would be impossible to do." Owen quipped. "There's no science available on earth that can control the weather in such a way."

"We don't have that capability here on earth. But the Galactic Federation has such a technology." Linda replied, prompting a raised eyebrow from Owen.

"If the waters were frozen solid, that would also be an ecological catastrophe." Owen stressed. "It would kill every living being and organism inhabiting those otherwise warm waters. Even a short term deep freeze would affect the weather and ecology on the land as well."

"What if we simply froze the surface enough to kill the invasive flora and bacteria that the Elites and their alien allies have placed there?" Alton offered.

Owen sat back in great thought. "It might work. But the cooling and rewarming of the waters needs to be precisely monitored." He stood and paced in further thought. "All life can survive in the depths, beneath the freezing cold surface as long as those waters below remain above the freezing point."

"Kind of like how fish survive in the freezing northern waters?" Alton inquired.

"Precisely!" Owen answered. "But we have to remember that these are warm water fish." He stressed. "As I mentioned before, it's important that the cooling and warming periods are not done too fast or too slow. It could cause the warm water inhabitants to go into shock and die, and possibly spurn a hurricane as well."

"That's exactly why Eno Calta suggested that you oversee the operation." Linda announced. "Of course, you'd have to be aboard his starship to do it."

Owen was flabbergasted. "When do they intend to do this?"

"Tonight. They'll need you to be ready by 22:00 hours earth time." She answered.

"Tonight!" Owen exclaimed as he looked anxiously toward the stairs. "What about Katie? She said she wasn't feeling well."

"She'll be in safe keeping here with us." Gerard assured.

"I'll attend to her if needed." Linda further assured.

"In that case, I better get myself prepared." Owen hesitantly answered as he turned and began to walk away. Suddenly, he turned with great thought, and returned to the group. "I need to make sense of this. What would Morningstar and the Elites hope to achieve by destroying these waters anyway?"

"I know it's hard to understand, Owen. But they want to destroy me and my people. It's a personal vendetta." Linda firmly answered. If they were able to locate The Oceanids and Nereids, as well as all the other underwater civilizations, they'd do the same to them." She sighed. "You should also know that human life on earth is their next target."

"We're dealing with a self absorbed group of people who have no regard for any sort of life beyond that of their own." Agent G added.

"It's insanity." He voiced in disgust as he turned once again to depart. "I'll be ready by 10 PM."

After Owen ascended the stairs, the remaining group continued.

"He's right, you know. All this death and destruction is pure insanity." Alton voiced with equal disgust.

"And all for the principal purpose of power." Gerard vented with a tinge of anger.

"Well gentlemen!" Linda concluded. "We are dealing with Satan and his demons. Hopefully, we can all hold our own, and continue to pray that divine intervention entirely prevails."

After a short pause of deep thought, Alton inquired with much sincerity.

"Do you really think Eno Calta will be able to locate our families?"

Linda took a deep breath before answering. "I can only say that unlike us, he knows where to look."

"I don't intend to change the subject, or conjure up any unpleasant memories. But what exactly took place that day in Lockeport?" Agent G curiously inquired of both Alton and Gerard. "I do realize that we haven't really discussed it up until this point."

Both men took their time, still stinging from their losses.

"First, I witnessed the terrible event of Steven Spencer's death." Alton began. "Then all mayhem broke loose. There was a flash of light, and the next thing I knew, I was waking up under a tree in Old Saybrook. I have no idea how I got there, or how I was spared from the destruction."

Agent G's eyes wandered to Gerard next for his response.

"I was in the car with my family, driving south on I-95. There were two other cars that were traveling with us from

Branchview." Gerard emotionally sighed, "I saw that same flash of light. When my eyes opened again, I was still in my car which was now idling in the median strip. My family was gone, and there were no signs of the others either." Tears escaped his eyes as he concluded. "It was the worst day since the death of my son."

"I'm sorry." Agent G replied with much sympathy before continuing. "I find it very hard to imagine how an entire town and its population could just disappear."

"Everything is possible where the supernatural is concerned." Linda answered.

"Do you think the people of Lockeport were spared?" Agent G further questioned.

"I certainly hope so." Gerard replied. "There were many good people there."

"We'll find them all, and we will get through this. I'm confident of that." Linda stated firmly.

Without another word, she stood, and swiftly walked away as the remaining three men could only exchange uncertain glances amongst themselves.

Meanwhile, several miles north, Rothstein accompanied Captain Hennesey and the crew of the Odyssey Research Vessel as they ventured into the dark, icy waters of Lake Erie.

"I can't understand why Morningstar insisted on doing this tonight." Hennesey protested. "It's way too cold and dangerous for me and my crew to be out here after dark."

"Quit complaining." Rothstein countered as he winced against the frigid air that came through the partially open window of the wheelhouse. "You're all getting paid quite well for this. Besides, I'm not crazy about being out here myself."

"What do you suppose happened to those security guards back at port?" Hennesey asked.

"Bastards probably abandoned their post." Rothstein answered sharply. "Nothing seemed to be disturbed onboard, so I assume everything is okay."

Hennesey casually glanced at the nautical grid in front of him while firmly gripping the wheel. "We have roughly 85 nautical miles to our first drop site just off the tip of Presque Isle. We should be there in a little less than an hour with the calm conditions." He glanced quickly at Rothstein. "You may as well make yourself comfortable in that chair over there."

"Could we close that damn window in the meantime?" Rothstein quipped sarcastically as he shivered.

Only answering with a look of annoyance, Hennesey slid the window shut.

Back at Branchview South, Linda knocked on the open bedroom door where Owen was now sitting on the edge of the bed, tending to his ill wife.

"Is she feeling any better?"

"She's still rather nauseated, but she doesn't seem to have a fever." Owen answered.

"Would you mind if I had a few words with her in private?"

"No. Not at all. I really should prepare for my departure."

Linda gave him a caring smile as he walked past her and departed the room.

"Now tell me all you can about this sudden illness, young lady." Linda stated as she strolled further into the room.

"I felt rather nauseated this morning when I first woke up. But I felt better as the day progressed. It wasn't until this evening that I started to get sick again."

Linda gave an enlightened nod as she settled at the bedside, and took hold of Katiera's hand. "Have you ever ventured any further than The Great Lakes region?"

"No. That's the only part of the world I've ever known." Katiera nervously stammered.

"I never considered that fact previously." Linda answered with an enlightened nod.

"What? What is it?" She asked with great alarm.

"Your body chemistry is very delicate to your new surroundings, Katiera." She sighed. "Whereas I'm acclimated to the warmer climates, and salt air of this region, you're more equipped for the colder climates, and fresh waters of the Lake. The sudden change of air and barometric pressures could also be playing a part."

"Will those changes harm me in any way?"

"Other than making you exhausted and a bit nauseated, I don't think so. But perhaps we should send you home to Station 37 as soon as possible."

"I can't leave Owen." She protested.

"Let's do this." Linda suggested with much thought. "In the morning we'll have Mahkta examine you. Perhaps he has some suggestions, and perhaps a cure."

"He is quite intelligent. I have no problem with that, as long as we get some answers.

Linda replied with a warm smile as she brushed a lock of Katiera's blonde hair back away from her face. "Now, get some rest, my beautiful friend. Morning will be here before we know it"

"Will Owen be safe with the Nordic Aliens?"

"Owen will be fine, sweetie. He'll be back in a few days, and the two of you can then share some quality time together." She gave an assuring wink. "Okay?"

She answered with a nod as Linda stood up, and began strolling toward the door. Linda then switched the light off, and paused to glance back at the young Mermaid. "Goodnight Katie!"

Aboard the Federation Warship, Nera and Damarus sat anxiously silent at the main helm while the vast darkness of space whizzed by in a tunnel vision through the observation window in front of them.

"I hope we can get there in time." Nera sighed. "Having the added weight of the shield has slowed our progress considerably."

"May I ask what this mission entails?" Damarus inquired.

"Eno and the Federation Starship are on a special mission to cleanse the Caribbean Waters." She quickly glanced to Damarus. "I've received a message that the Draconians have somehow learned of that mission, and are planning a counter attack."

"The Caribbean is quite a vast area? How do we know where they might attack?"

"We don't. The Draconians are masters of surprise. They could suddenly strike from virtually nowhere."

"Then what's our strategy to counter it?" Damarus further questioned. "Shouldn't we alert our earth allies at The Space Force."

"Absolutely not! The Space Force does not yet have the advanced weaponry to use against the Draconians." Nera firmly stated. "We need to link up with the Starship to accompany it on its mission. Should the Draconians burst through the stratosphere, we'll blast their entire war fleet with the shield."

"What if we get there too late?"

"We can only pray that isn't the case." Nera nervously answered. "I've already telepathically communicated with Eno on the situation. I'm afraid that beyond our wishes, The Galaxy Wars have officially extended to earth."

Back in the icy waters of Lake Erie, Captain Hennesey and his crew approached their first target site. Though the air and the water were frigid cold, the night was calm with little to no wind or turbulence. The night sky was lit by a canopy of stars without a cloud in sight. Nevertheless, Captain Hennesey stepped from the cabin, and ordered his crew to drop anchor directly over the site.

As he strolled upon the deck, he continued to bark out orders.
"Prepare to drop the first bomb to the bottom."

Meanwhile at the lake bottom, the anchor struck a solid object, and created a percussive thud that could even be felt at the surface. The crew paused momentarily, rather puzzled by the sound.

"I think the anchor struck something, captain!" One of the crewmen yelled.

"Probably the remnants of an old shipwreck. These waters are riddled with them." He replied with little regard.

They proceeded to unstrap the first warhead, and maneuvered it into place for the drop.

Suddenly an entrancing woman's voice echoed up from the depths, and mingled in the still air. It was likened to the sweet voice of an opera singer. All paused with their activity to listen with hypnotic wonder. It even prompted Rothstein to wander out into the cold air, and take a curious stance next to the captain.

"Where in the hell is that coming from? Is that the wind?" He inquired.

"There is no wind tonight, you idiot." The captain quipped with annoyance. "It sounds more like we're being serenaded by some sort of mythical nymph from the depths."

"Perhaps it's the Oceanids that Morningstar spoke about."

Just then, the wind did stir, and the waters became a bit uneasy. Without warning, from beneath the depths, a large entity resembling a twenty foot wall of water with eyes, and an enormous mouth appeared just off the stern of the ship. The surrounding waters quickly turned violent, and the wind howled with a harrowing ferocity. The beast before them roared in a loud shriek that split the eardrums of the men while they struggled to keep their sea legs. Much to their horror, the giant entity smashed down onto the deck like an enormous fist. The ship immediately split in two pieces, and shattered upon the violent waters like a fragile toy. The frightening screams of the men could be heard over the fury as the vessel quickly sank amongst the high waves. Within just a few minutes, the icy lake had sucked down another victim, and then there was no sound at all, as both the water and wind calmed once again. Only a trail of debris bobbing on the surface remained in the silent aftermath.

Several miles to the north, under the lake, the Oceanids could hear the reverberated shrieks of the Storm Hag as it echoed along the lake bottom. It was as though the Hag was openly boasting of its conquest. It was a terrible sound not heard for over a century.

Xander and Tabitha stepped out of their residence to listen.

"Something disturbed the Storm Hag." Xander stated.

"Do you suppose it had anything to do with those bombs?"

"I have to believe it had some sort of connection."

"If so, I don't envy those that were caught in her wrath." Tabitha declared.

"We have to calm the beast, or else it will destroy everything in its wake. Including us." Xander spoke with dread.

"It very well could ignite the wrath of the Lake Erie Monster as well." Tabitha added.

"I'll gather a party of warriors, and we'll set out into the waters immediately."

"I want to go with you."

"You can't." He gently embraced his wife at the waist. "It's a dangerous mission, And I couldn't fathom the thought of anything tragic happening to you."

"I love you, Xander." She pulled him closer. "You are my life mate, and I refuse to let you go on this mission without me."

Xander knew there was little time to argue the matter, and reluctantly agreed.

10

THE DIVINE PLAN TAKES SHAPE

Just as Linda had instructed, Owen had donned his oxygen mask, and now stood on the Gulf beach near Branchview South. He looked out over the dark skies above the Gulf for any sign of an approaching starship. There was nothing. Only a pleasant sea breeze, and silence. He hated the feel of the mask against his face, but he knew he couldn't remove it. Suddenly, there was a loud whoosh sound, and in its wake, Owen disappeared, and was nowhere in sight.

Onboard the Federation Starship just seconds later, Owen materialized in the large tube of the transport room. Eno and two crew members quickly stepped forward as the tube raised away into the high ceiling, and they helped a somewhat stunned Owen to his feet. He awkwardly pulled the mask from his face, and unstrapped the oxygen tank.

"I'm glad to be rid of that clumsy thing."

"Welcome aboard, Owen." Eno spoke in a pleasant tone. "Hopefully, you won't need it once we're finished with this mission."

"It's good to see you again, Eno." He sighed. "I never expected to be taken up in such a way. I always thought that method was only something from an old Star Trek Episode."

"Quite the contrary." Eno grinned. "I'm sure before this is over, you'll witness a lot of things that you once thought were only science fiction."

Owen tried to step forward, but his legs buckled. The crew members swiftly caught his fall.

"It'll take a few minutes for you to get your bearings." Eno explained. "Then we need to get you to the bridge as soon as possible so we can get started."

In a bar in New York City, Lucifer Morningstar sat in a dark corner listening to a jazz ensemble while he cradled a glass of brandy in his hand. His mind drifted away with the music, and for the time, he was totally oblivious to the fact that all of his best laid sinister plans were being foiled all over the world. Suddenly, he was startled out of his far away thoughts by his cell phone. He glanced at the international number that flashed across the screen, and answered with a sneer.

"Talk to me."

He soberly listened to the Dutch accent that spoke on the opposite end, and his expression quickly turned to fiery rage. He ended the call abruptly, and fumed for a few long seconds before entering another number in the phone. He listened as a recorded voice announced that his call could not be connected. He expressed his frustration out loud to himself.

"Damn it! Why can't I connect with Rothstein?"

He stood up, and angrily threw his drink against a wall. The sound of shattering glass made the musicians abruptly quit playing, and the few patrons in the establishment paused their activity as well to quietly stare at the raging man. Morningstar glanced back at all of them with furious eyes.

"What are you pitiful morons looking at?"

No one dared to answer.

You can all go to hell!" He roared loudly before departing.

He continued speaking out his rage to himself as he exited onto the dark street.

"As usual, it's time for me to take matters into my own hands."

As the drama played out on earth, another scenario was being initiated in the far away constellation where the paradise planet of Lyra is located. Sonja Christos was interrupted during her daily routine as the librarian of time by a surprise visitor. She gasped anxiously as the large framed man with perfect shoulder length hair stepped from the shadows, and into the light.

"Poseidon!"

"Hello Sonja." He smiled "I simply go by the name of Philip now."

"We all thought Satan had killed you."

"He did. In body, but not spirit." Poseidon acknowledged while glancing around at the volumes of books within the old library before turning his attention back to Sonja. "The Supreme Power granted me my wish to be one of the Warrior Angels of Paradeisos."

"That's quite an honor." She paused with a bit of unease before continuing. "Unfortunately, Andreas is away with our son. I'm sure he'd be quite surprised to see you as well."

"Hopefully, he's still not angry with me for trying to win over your heart way back when."

"I'm sure he got over that episode years ago. As have I." She grinned.

"I assure you that I transformed my arrogant self into a more loving, and humble person before my life ended on earth."

"I believe that. It's written so in the Book of Time."

"Mommy!" A child's voice interrupted, calling out from within the endless book rows.

A young girl about the age of seven shyly stepped forward from among the archives. She looked just like a miniature version of Sonja.

"This is our daughter, Gianna." She turned to address the child. "This is my old friend, Philip."

"Pleased to meet you, sir." She respectfully nodded.

"You're just as pretty as your mother." Philip remarked, prompting the child to blush, and hide behind Sonja's long Victorian style dress.

Both adults exchanged an amused glance.

"Could you go and prepare some tea for our guest, sweetheart?"

"Yes, mother." She answered before rushing from the room.

"She's very cute." Philip mused.

"As you can see, like me, she's a child of the summer moon."

"Raven hair and bright blue eyes. No doubt, she'll one day attract quite an audience of young men." He whimsically quipped, which brought a full smile to Sonja's face.

185

"I'm training her to be a next generation librarian. She'll succeed me when my time is through."

There was an awkward silence, while Poseidon pondered what to say next.

"I'm sure you're wondering what prompted my visit." He paused. "I was sent here hoping to find answers."

"I know." She replied. "It's about your Branchview family. Isn't it?"

Philip reacted with surprise at her response.

"Do you know where they are?"

"They're all here in Lyra." She enthusiastically announced much to Philip's surprise. "I made sure they were brought here when they were evacuated from the Earth."

"What about my son, Dimitri?" He emotionally inquired. "Is he here with them?"

"Yes! As a matter of fact, both of your sons are." She answered. "Triton and his wife Andrea adopted Dimitri into their own family. He's six years old now."

"How time goes by." He shook his head. "Does he remember his mother and I?"

Sonja answered with a teary nod. "You're his heroes. We told him how you both died, and that your souls now dwell together in Paradeisos."

"Could I possibly visit with all of them?"

She answered with an enthusiastic nod. "Absolutely! I'll take you to them. But first, I'll need to arrange for my mother to watch over Gianna and the library."

"That's fine." He responded as uncharacteristic tears welled in his eyes. "I've waited a very long time for this reunion. I suppose I can wait a bit longer."

At that very moment, a menagerie of chaos was taking place all over the earth at a rapid fire pace. In the dark depths of Lake Erie, a dramatic showdown was about to take place between the beast known as the Storm Hag, and a group of Oceanid warriors led by Xander. Out of practically nowhere, the transparent beast, which looked like a large cluster of jelly fish raced through the waters toward them.

It let out an angry roar that shook the lake bottom, and drove the warriors reeling back several feet. Another loud roar came from the west as a large prehistoric, dragon like creature known as The Lake Erie Monster swam toward them as well.

Xander bravely swam forward to within feet of the beasts. He could almost feel the warmth of their hostile breath as he raised his palm toward them, and closed his eyes to communicate. The beasts held their place to telepathically listen.

"We come in peace." He began. "There were evil men who disturbed your lair. They disregarded the permanent buoys we had set into place many years ago to protect your territory. We had no part in this hostility."

The beasts calmed a bit as they continued to listen.

"We continue to honor the peace treaty we made several years ago. Be aware that a battle for earth is taking place at this moment. I assure you that the positive transition from evil to good is almost complete. I will soon walk on land as a human, and renew the pact we all have with the salt miners in the western end of the lake, so that they never intrude into the fragile caverns that you both call your home. Be assured that this lake will always be yours, as it is ours. Please go now in peace, and with trust of my words.

The beasts let out a shallow, gravelly grunt, and appeared to nod their agreement. Without further incident, both beasts abruptly turned, and swam off into the dark waters.

Xander opened his eyes, and appeared to breathe a sigh of relief, while Tabitha and the others surrounded him with great joy. He embraced his Mermaid wife, and spoke to her and the other warriors in their native tongue. "Let's all go home."

The group paused for a moment to listen to the haunting voice of the Sea Hag as it echoed away through the lake waters like the lament of an operatic soprano. A loud, but unthreatening roar also came from The Lake Monster as it retreated to the west. Peace had once again been instilled among the inhabitants of the Great Lake.

Over the Caribbean waters, the large Galactic Federation starship cruised slowly along the Thermosphere of the earth. Owen sat in a plush chair in the control center next to Eno, and concentrated on the panel screen in front of him that showed the topography of the earth below. He couldn't resist briefly glancing through the large window before them where he could see the lights of land that illuminated the coastlines. It was an amazing sight.

"Beautiful, isn't it?" Eno asked, prompting a smile and nod from a still nervous Owen.

"It's very difficult holding the temperature of the rays steady between 28 and 31 degrees." Owen commented. "We have to be sure that it doesn't go above or below that range."

"The worst effect that they'll be getting on earth right now should be one whopper of a storm."

Eno remarked. "We can only hope that the majority of people are sheltered, and not out in it."

"So, this invisible ray can cover all the expanse of the affected waters?"

"Up to 500 square miles as we move along." Eno replied.

"Amazing technology!"

"What would you say if I told you that your government has possessed this technology since World War II, and has kept it a secret from the people?"

"I'd have to say that the individuals in charge must be overwhelmingly evil."

"There's some truth to that. But it's also been concealed to keep evil people from gaining control of it." Eno's comment prompted a confused glance from Owen before he continued. "Imagine if those evil individuals were able to control the weather. The population would be at their mercy."

"How is it used within the planets of the Federation?"

"In a positive way that benefits all." Eno stressed. "Imagine holding back the essential rains until the populace is sleeping, and making the weather beautiful for their waking hours."

"It's a pleasant thought." Owen smiled. "Can it prevent catastrophic weather from taking place as well?"

"Absolutely, my friend."

The cordial conversation between the two men was interrupted by another crew member on the bridge who was alertly watching the radar.

"Excuse me, commander. I'm detecting a large craft that just entered the earth's atmosphere over the Bermuda Triangle."

"Can you get a make on it?"

"Not yet. I just know it's not one of ours, and it's very big."

"It very well could be a Draconian warship that's intruding earths air space."

"We have a definite read now." The crew member voiced. "By all markings, it is indicative of being Draconian."

"They must've illegally entered through an unfinished portion of the stargate." Eno sighed.

A befuddled Owen couldn't help but briefly glance up at the Nordics before quickly resuming his task of balancing the temperature controls. He had no idea what the men were talking about.

"Prepare to raise the shields in case they try to engage." Eno commanded.

"What's going on?" Owen anxiously inquired.

"It appears that the Draconians may have officially brought the Galactic Wars to earth." Eno answered. "We'll just have to halt our progress, observe, and determine what they're up to."

Simultaneously, the Draconian craft was experiencing heavy turbulence as a result of the violent storm that raged over the ocean. A conversation was taking place between the captain and his second in charge while the large vessel was being tossed about.

"Captain! The air temperature over the ocean has dropped to 30 degrees fahrenheit. The seeds we're dropping cannot survive those extreme conditions."

"That's impossible for the Caribbean this time of year. Someone must be countering our efforts."

"If that's the case, it's being done from outer space. We aren't detecting anything within the earth's atmosphere or surface."

The ship rocked violently in the unstable air conditions, nearly knocking the two Dracs from their commander's chairs.

"We need to abort. We can't hold steady in this turbulence."

"Should we retreat to our earth base, or head for space?"

The captain pondered before answering. "Take it up! We'll hold steady in the troposphere until this storm breaks."

The Draconian ship shifted position, and accelerated upward in a speed so fast, the Nordic Ship that unknowingly hovered in its path had no time to react. As the Dracs broke the troposphere, the ship collided with the Nordics, striking the outer netting of their protective shield. The impact was strong enough to violently shake both vessels. The Draconians sustained the most damage and casualties. Even still, the Drac commander immediately called for the fighter pods to be deployed for an attack on the Nordic craft.

Within seconds, the swift moving pods were attacking their shield from all sides. Sirens sounded aboard the craft as the crew rushed to deploy their own defense weapons.

"Take the ship up toward space so we can better counter the attack." Eno ordered.

Owen pushed himself up from the floor with a groan.

"Are you ok, Owen?"

"I hit my head pretty hard. But I think I'm all right."

"Strap yourself in your seat. Things might get rough."

"Commander! The power thrusters aren't functioning properly with our shield employed." A crew member yelled.

"We have to do something. These pods are going to pound us until they penetrate our shield."

Aboard the Draconian craft, another unidentified starship was detected on their radar, approaching from the northeast.

"There's another Nordic vessel coming straight at us, captain." He paused. "It looks as though they have some sort of strange contraption attached to the lower front of the ship."

The captain thought for a quick moment before giving the next order.

"Have a squadron of our pods split from the others, and blast them into oblivion." He angrily groveled.

Aboard the smaller Nordic starship, Nera and her crew quickly identified the huge Draconian craft.

"There they are!" Nera announced. "Get ready to blast away, Mermaid."

One of the other crew chimed in. "We have company. Fighter pods coming at us from the rear."

"How many?"

"At least twenty. Maybe more."

"Hang on tight!"

Nera shifted upward, avoiding the barrage of pod lasers, then quickly turned the ship sharply into the opposite direction. The shift caused many of the crew members to tumble about in the main flight deck. The pods were now straight in front, and below them in line with the pulse weapon. Damarus instinctively fired a pulse beam that obliterated all the pods into dust.

"Good shot, but we're not done yet." Nera declared as she turned the ship sharply in the opposite direction.

The Draconian crew were still in shock and awe at what they had just witnessed. The hydro pulse weapon was like nothing they had ever seen. Before they could further react, Damarus fired the pulse beam directly at them. All they could do was scream as the pulse wave struck their enormous vessel, blasting it into dust particles within seconds.

The fighter pods that had been attacking the warship, turned their attention to the smaller starship as it shifted into their vicinity.

"Come to mama!" Damarus comically quipped as the pods bunched together, heading straight for them.

Eno could see what was taking place, and ordered the shields to be dropped.

Before the pods could split off, Damarus fired another pulse, blasting most of them away.

A few pods were able to escape, and were now trying to maneuver around the rear of the Starship.

"Blast those Drac pods into oblivion." Eno ordered.

The larger Nordic Warship swiftly rose up, and above the smaller Starship, and blasted the pods away with precision before they could even maneuver for attack. The members of both ships drew a sigh of relief as the pods vaporized in space.

"Who are they, and what sort of weapon do they have?" Owen excitedly inquired.

"That was my wife's starship" He proudly proclaimed. "And that devastation was done with the Nereid pulse weapon."

"Is everyone okay?" A voice echoed, as the blurred images of Nera and Damarus appeared onto the communication screen.

"We're all fine. Thanks to you sweetheart." Eno smiled.

"We could've never done it without our Mermaid, and her awesome weapon."

"Thank you both!" Owen exclaimed.

"We'll see you in a few days on the ground, sweetie." Nera concluded with a wink.

"Yes, you will." Eno replied as the signal faded away on the screen. He then turned to Owen who was still awe stricken by what he had witnessed. "Let's thaw the Caribbean to its' natural state, and get you back home."

Aboard the Starship, Nera turned to Damarus with a grin. "That was unbelievable teamwork." She chuckled. "Now, let's take this weapon back to its permanent home."

Without words, an exhausted Damarus answered only with a weary, yet definitive nod.

11

THE REUNION

On the distant planet of Lyra, Philip was being led by Sonja through a veil of sea mist that opened to a wooded path as they made their way toward a long awaited reunion.

"This greatly reminds me of the pathway that once existed at Branchview." Philip remarked.

"Wait until you see what lies around the next bend." Sonja answered with a clever smirk.

As they walked forward, the path became wider, and as they turned the next curve, Philip could hardly believe his eyes. There before him was an identical image of the Branchview House.

"How in the world did you manage to do this?" He asked with an amazed expression.

"You should know better than anyone that all things are possible if you just imagine it." She smiled.

Philip stood for a moment soaking in the grandeur of the Great House that he thought he'd never see again. Then they both continued onward, up the stone path to the large oak door with the familiar lion's head knocker. Philip fondly ran his hand across the rough brass while Sonja opened the door. She then rang the spirit bell to alert everyone that they had arrived as they stepped into The Grand Foyer.

Almost on cue, a group consisting of the Branchview children, all older now, Tony and Andrea Freeman, Sharie LeRoux, and Mary Wallace all filed into the Grand Foyer. Dimitri broke from the group, and ran into his father's arms.

"Father! I can't believe it's really you." The child proclaimed.

Tears welled in Philip's eyes as he embraced the child he hadn't seen since he was an infant. He then set eyes on the others.

Tony stepped forward first to also embrace his father.

"I wasn't sure I'd ever see you again in this life." He smiled as his son Michael, and the two Spencer twins shyly stepped forward to greet him as well. "As you can see, Andrea and I took all the children in, and raised them as our own.

"We could have never done it without the help of our Branchview family." Andrea mused.

"We all pitched in, and did the best we could." Sharie added.

"Where is Loraine Spencer?" Philip asked in a confused manner. "I assumed she'd be here as well."

"Her and that Stargazer fella escaped into the mirror portal of The Grand Ballroom that day Satan destroyed everything." Mary answered.

"You were there?"

"Yes sir! I refused to leave Ms. Loraine alone at the house. But I sure wouldn't go back into that portal either." She paused to stress her point. "I stood my ground against that devil, and the good Lord spared me in the nick of time."

197

"Why didn't she leave with the rest of you?"

"She would not leave without Steven." Sharie emotionally answered. "None of us had any idea that Satan had already killed him."

An expression of horror came across Philip's face. "That means her and Stargazer could be anywhere within the spectrum of time." He turned to Sonja in desperation. "Is there any way of knowing where they might be?"

"I haven't received any indications. They may be existing under an alias."

"We all assumed that wherever they were in the past, they'd surely consult you and Ezekiel for help." Sharie suggested.

"Unless they're somewhere in the future where we no longer exist." Philip stressfully countered. "I'll definitely see what I can find out when I return to Paradesios." He looked around the room at each face. "Where are all the others?"

"They're all here in Lyra." Sharie assured. "We just weren't able to round them all up with such short notice." She paused in pensive thought for a moment. "Have you seen my husband, and Alton Sinclair?"

"I have not. But I do know that they are safe, and are working hard behind the scenes to preserve Branch Consolidated Industries, and to make the world a better place."

Sharie forced a smile through the tears, as Philip continued, turning his attention toward everyone.

"There's a positive change happening on the earth. The evil ones are being purged, and very soon will no longer exist." He smiled benevolently. "When that process is complete, I'll come back to take you all home."

There was an uneasy pause, as everyone exchanged a quick glance.

"With all due respect, father. We don't want to leave. This is our home now." Tony proclaimed.

"Some of the others feel the same way we do." Andrea added.

"Of course, I'll be going back." Sharie anxiously spoke up. "Audrey and the Branch siblings will as well. I'm not really sure about the others."

Philip's eyes wandered to Mary next, and she shook her head from side to side.

"This old house has always been my home, and it no longer exist on earth. Right here is where I want to spend the rest of my days."

Philip next glanced at Sonja seeking her thoughts on the matter. She simply responded with a shrug.

"They've all adapted quite well to life here on Lyra. They're all welcome to stay if they wish."

Olivia confronted Philip with sober boldness. "Can you find my mommy, and bring her home?"

"I'll certainly try." Philip answered, as he went to one knee to address the child.

London confronted him next. "When you see our father, will you tell him that we love him, and think of him every day?"

"I most certainly will do that as well." Philip emotionally answered.

At that, his attention was suddenly diverted. He looked upward as though listening to an inaudible voice.

"What is it, Philip?" Sonja inquired.

"I'm being summoned to earth. I must leave immediately." He turned his full attention back toward the others. "I promise you all that I'll stay a bit longer when I return." He then turned to Sonja with a quick wink. "Thank you for making this all possible."

After exchanging emotional hugs with everyone, Philip stepped away, closed his eyes, and vanished into thin air.

As people on earth were beginning a new day, another unexpected confrontation was about to take place. At the medical laboratory, Mhakta escorted Katiera from one of the exam rooms to an outer area where Linda Sanchez paced impatiently.

"It's just as you surmised." The smiling lion announced. "It appears that our Oceanid friend here is simply having an adverse reaction to her new surroundings."

"That sounds like it could be rather serious." Linda countered.

"Not at all." Mahkta replied. "We'll simply treat her in the same method that we've treated your people." He gestured to the large tubs that still contained patients. "She needs to get acclimated to the salt water, warmer temperatures, and I'll also have to purge the environmental toxins that she's breathed in."

"Why haven't those air toxins affected the rest of us in the same way?" She asked.

"The people who dwell on the earth have developed a resistance to those toxins." Mahkta explained. "Katiera's world is basically toxin free. Any substantial amount of time spent on land would shock her system."

"Much like having an allergic reaction." She assumed.

"Precisely!" The gentle Lion answered.

Linda then looked to Katiera with much concern. "I still think it would be best to send you back home to Station 37."

"No, Linda! I refuse to go." She defiantly stated.

"Go where?" Owen questioned as he unexpectedly walked into the lab with Eno at that very moment.

With great surprise, Katiera ran to embrace her husband, and greeted him with a passionate kiss. "Oh Owen!" She exclaimed. "They say I'm sick because I'm not used to the earths' environment, and they want to send me home."

"In that case we'll go together." He simply replied.

"But they need you here." She countered.

"Owen has completed the bulk of his mission here." Eno intervened. "I'm certain we can continue on without him."

Before another word could be said, Morningstar also unexpectedly stepped from the shadows of the room.

"No one is going anywhere." He arrogantly announced, as he slowly paced closer.

"Let's see now. We have a room full of smelly fish, a cowardly lion, a meddling Galactic alien, and a disgusting excuse of a human being."

"You're just as repulsive as ever. How were you able to find this place?" Linda asked with trembling voice.

"I have eyes watching all over this world, my dear." He sarcastically laughed. "I am the supreme leader of this earth after all."

"Not for long, Satan." Eno sneered with a tinge of anger in his voice.

In response, Satan paced closer. "And, what exactly prompted you to break the Galactic Treaty, and meddle with my affairs on earth?"

"You made that treaty null and void when you violated the timelines."

"I only sped up the inevitable." He answered, coming menacingly within inches of Eno's face, before turning a hardened gaze toward Owen.

As he and Katiera huddled close, Morningstar smirked.

"I wish you could've seen the fear in the eyes of your uncle and his family when I methodically killed them." He strolled closer, and ran his finger across Katiera's chin. She winced with disgust, and buried her head into Owen's shoulder.

"It's the same fear I hope to recapture when I systematically kill you and your little Oceanid wife." He turned away quickly, and without warning, turned to his true likeness. His repulsive, beastly appearance took everyone by surprise, as he reached out with his large hoof, and pinned Linda against the wall. "I'll kill you first, Black Mermaid." He snarled. "Oh, I've waited a long time for this revenge."

"You'll have to wait even longer, Satan." Another new voice chimed in, as Philip casually strolled into the room. "Let her go, now!" He further commanded.

"Poseidon!" The surprised beast exclaimed as he turned his attention to the newcomer. "I beheaded you. You're supposed to be dead."

"A much higher power than yourself had other plans for me." He chuckled, while boldly moving toward the beast. "You need to address me as Philip from now on. I am an Angel Warrior in the army of Paradeisos."

The beast sneered angrily.

"You forget that I was once among that legion."

"No. I'll never forget." Philip snapped back as a sword materialized in his hand. "It's time for you to leave this earth."

With cat like reflexes, the beast leapt toward Philip, causing all others in the room to gasp. His hoof also transformed into a sharp blade, and he swung it wildly as he pounced. Philip seized the arm of the beast, tearing it from his torso. The beast reeled back, and howled in pain.

Much to everyone's further surprise, the beast turned back into the likeness of Morningstar, and its severed limb regenerated into a new one.

"Is that the best you have, Philip?" He quipped. "You can't defeat me."

"You make the next move." He taunted.

Morningstar leaped across the room at Philip once again. He sidestepped his advance, grabbed his arm, and slung him hard against a wall with ease, shattering the fragile drywall in the process, and collapsing part of the ceiling. Morningstar looked up in somewhat of a daze from his crumpled position on the floor, while Philip held him at bay with his sword.

"How…?"

"I warned you before you killed me that I would be a hundred times more powerful in spirit than I was in life."

"It's too late Warrior Angel." Morningstar laughed. "As we speak, there is a worldwide army of my disciples and demons marching against the forces of good on the plains of Megeddon. Unlike what was originally written, we will win! Even without our killer robots." He maniacally proclaimed.

"You will overwhelmingly be defeated." Eno confidently countered as he stepped forward, and alongside Philip. "Just as it was originally written in the Book of Revelations."

Morningstar's expression turned to one of panic.

"If you, and your demons can manipulate the timelines, and change history. We can as well." Philip further stated. "All is fair in concerns of war."

"You may have won this round." He grunted. "But if you plan on defeating me, you'll have to catch, and kill me first." Morningstar boldly smirked.

Morningstar moved his hands in an attempt to disappear. But much to his dismay, it didn't work. An expression of anxious worry then appeared on his face, followed by a quick fit of rage.

"Why can't I disappear?" He cried out.

"Perhaps you've lost those powers you once had." Eno calmly answered.

Morningstar looked to Philip in last ditch desperation, and taunted him. "Go ahead! Finish me off, Angel Warrior. I know that's what you wish to do"

"As much as I'd like to, that's not my job." Philip simply replied, which angered Morningstar even further.

"I suppose you think removing me from this earth will defeat me." He once again smirked. "I'll find my way back through the portals." He snarled. "In the meantime, whatever is left of my demon army, and The Elite Society will carry on with my work." He held his hands forward as if mockingly surrendering. His actions only caused both Philip and Eno to scoff in amusement.

"The newly constructed Stargate will keep you and any other alien predators from entering this earth ever again." Eno commented.

Morningstar's expression turned serious.

"The time of dimensional advance and renewal has arrived." Philip added. "All your demons will be expelled from this earth along with you, and you'll all be sent to a place that only illuminates below the 3D realm."

"That would simply make it easy for me to rule on this other planet." Satan smirked.

"I think it will be more of a power grab." Eno boldly proclaimed. "Without your previous powers, you'll be a floundering nobody. All of the pompous egos on that planet will surely lead to self-destruction."

"You're wrong!" Morningstar sneered. "I'll always be more powerful than the average human."

His comments only drew humorous laughs from Philip and Eno.

Out of frustration, Morningstar once again attempted to surrender himself.

"Let's get it over with."

"I already told you that it's not our job to remove you from this earth." Philip reasoned with a sigh.

"Then tell me who it is that will remove me to this other planet?" He angrily growled.

"I think you already know that answer, Satan." Philip chuckled

At those words, the room began to fill with a blinding light, and a deafening sound likened to that of a multitude of approaching jet engines roaring loudly. It shook the walls with its power. Philip and Eno quickly herded all the others from the room, while Morningstar cowered into a corner in complete terror.

Philip slammed the door shut as Eno shuttled the group to safety at the far end of the adjacent exam room. They all listened in horror at the screams of Satan that cried out amongst the deafening fury. They continued listening while those screams faded away as the unseen energy carried him from the room. Soon all the noise dissipated to a peaceful silence, and the intense light that permeated through the closed door began to recede.

Philip and the others huddled close until it was sure that all had returned to normal. They all drew a sigh of relief, as they tried to gather themselves from the ordeal.

"My people were out there during that fury." Linda frantically expressed.

"I assure you that the energy did them no harm." Philip answered in a confident voice.

"I'll go check on the patients just to be sure." Mahkta replied as he cautiously opened the door once again.

"I think that's the last we'll see of Lucifer Morningstar for quite some time." Eno commented.

"At least here on Earth." Philip sighed.

Linda coughed, and felt the area of her throat that Morningstar had gripped.

"As usual, you have an uncanny knack of showing up just in the nick of time, Philip." She expressed with humor.

"Are you okay?" He asked with great concern.

"I've survived much worse." She answered breathlessly.

Eno confronted Philip, and offered a handshake

"It's good to see you again, Philip." He stated. "It's been a long time since we last crossed paths."

"As you can see, much has changed since then." Philip smiled.

Eno gestured toward the outer room. That enormous Lion out there is Mahkta, our Galactic practitioner."

Eno then made reference to Owen and Katiera. "This lovely lady is our Oceanid representative, Katiera. The handsome guy with her is her human husband, Owen."

They all cordially nodded.

"Thank you, for saving our lives." Owen soberly stated as he also shook his hand.

You mentioned that the others will be removed as well. Does that mean that this nightmare with the Globalist Elites is finally over?" Linda inquired.

"Almost." Philip sighed. "The next 24 hours will see the earth be cleansed in a way that has never been witnessed since the Passover, or the Great Flood in Noah's time. I will say that it won't be a pleasant experience for them."

"Will all of us be safe?" Katiera sincerely asked.

"Yes. Only those that have been previously warned, and remain impure souls will be removed."

"As it is rather a customary practice for those of earth, perhaps we should break for a cup of coffee, and discuss this situation further. Eno suggested.

"My good friend, I can never turn down an offer for coffee." Philip smiled as he gave a friendly pat to Eno's shoulder.

As they all exited the room, Philip and Linda exchanged friendly nods and an assured wink.

"I missed you, old friend." She expressed sentimentally.

"I've missed you all." He fondly smiled. "I have much news to share with you and the others."

12

THE PURGE BEGINS

In another part of the world, two other Angel Warriors were in the process of crashing a gathering of The Elite Society at a meeting hall in Switzerland.

The master of ceremonies, Klaus Schultz had just taken the stage to address the audience. There were Draconian sentries flanking him on either side of the room as he began to speak.

"Fellow members of The Elite Society, I welcome you all here tonight." He paused as the audience applauded. "I'd like to direct your attention to the live cam screen at the center of the stage." He motioned as the screen dropped down. "This is a live scene of the battle taking place in Israel as I speak."

As the live feed appeared on the screen, a silent pall fell upon the crowd. The only scene was not of an active war, but of total death, destruction, and morbid silence.

"I don't understand." Schultz stammered.

The angels Miklos and Andreas stepped from the shadows at the back of the stage.

"It appears that your demon army has been defeated, Mr. Schultz." Miklos spoke.

"And not a single white hat perished." Andreas added.

"I demand you tell me who you are." Schultz spat out angrily.

"Who we are is no concern of yours. We're simply messengers." Miklos answered.

"Where is Morningstar?" He further demanded.

"Mr. Morningstar won't be able to attend tonight." Andreas answered while they strode further to the front of the stage.

A visibly frustrated Schultz pointed to the control room. "Turn off that despicable feed." He ordered.

The screen went blank once again, and he then turned toward the sentries. "Kill these intruders." He boldly ordered.

As the sentries advanced, the angels aimed their swords toward them. Much to everyone's shock, lightning bolts shot from the tips of their weapons, striking the Draconians, and incinerating them instantly. The action stalled any further advance of the other sentries that were stationed at the back of the hall.

"Now, if I may talk." Miklos requested to Schultz who reluctantly yielded the center of the stage. "After tonight, The Elite Society will no longer exist."

"That statement is total insanity." Schultz interrupted. The Society has existed almost since the beginning of time."

Overwhelming boo's and negative comments directed toward the angel's rose amongst the audience.

Schultz motioned for silence. "Let the fools speak."

"As I was saying." Miklos continued. "You'll all be removed from this world just as your leader, Lucifer Morningstar already has."

A few muffled gasps echoed through the hall as the angel paused, then continued.

"Once that happens, you'll never be able to return again."

His comments were met by silence, and blank stares.

Schultz chugged down the remaining contents of his champaign, and broke the silence by belching in a loud, mocking manner. His actions prompted a chorus of equally taunting laughter from the audience that bordered on total chaos.

The two angels could only exchange a fleeting glance of disbelief.

"You, nor anyone else can have us removed. We own all the wealth in this world, and have all the power." Schultz arrogantly chuckled.

Miklos raised his hand to silence the crowd once again. "Neither one of us can, but there is a power much greater that can."

"You speak of your God?" Schultz laughed. "Your God gave up on this world long ago."

"That's what you were led to believe. The energy of God will move, and send an angel of death among you." Andreas warned. "He will sweep through this world like a mighty wind, destroying everything that's evil."

"Ooh! I'm so scared!" Schultz mockingly exclaimed before Miklos calmly continued the conversation.

"Because we're merciful messengers, we'd like to put out a call for anyone who wishes to seek forgiveness to come forward. We'll take you safely from this hall, but you will have to account for your shortcomings within the realms of the justice system." He paused with emphasis. "However, on a positive note, you will be spared the wrath of God."

"That's preposterous!" Schultz boasted. "We own the world justice system."

"Not for long, Mr. Schultz."

There was an uneasy chatter in the aftermath of his words. Several seconds passed before a middle-aged woman and man rapidly stood, and moved forward toward the stage. "Save us, please!" The woman screamed.

Schultz pulled a revolver from his suit jacket, and shot both of them dead before they reached their destination. "Fools!" He arrogantly scoffed.

"You'll regret those actions, Mr. Schultz." Miklos charged.

He only responded by aiming his gun toward the angels, and proceeded emptying the remaining four shots from the barrel. Much to his surprise, the bullets had no effect whatsoever on the celestial beings.

"You've all sealed your fate." Miklos concluded as the angels made their way from the stage, and headed toward the exit at the rear of the building.

As they departed through a sea of slurs, and angry taunts, a chilling draft stirred within the large hall, and along with it came a mournful droning sound that could've stricken even the bravest individual with terror. Everyone became silent, and started to look around in confusion and fear. Total panic and chaos ensued in the wake of Miklos and Andreas leaving the building. People suddenly rushed for the exits, but the doors were now locked.

The two angels paused outside the meeting hall at a safe distance, and listened to the muffled, horrifying screams that came from the inside.

"So, it begins." Miklos stated with remorse.

"Our work is definitely finished here." Andreas added conclusively.

Back in America, Philip and Eno were preparing everyone for what was about to take place as they all conversed in the breakroom of the rehab hospital.

"As I had previously mentioned, the angel of death will pass over all the earth in the next 24 hours, and remove all that are not pure of soul." Philip explained.

"How can we be sheltered from the wrath?" Katiera asked with concern as she huddled close to Owen.

"I would encourage you all to stay safe and secure in your houses. Though you will be spared, it will definitely not be a pleasant time to be out in the elements."

"Philip and I will stay with all of you until the deathly purge passes." Eno assured.

"I'll stay here with my people, and the creatures of the sea." Linda stated firmly.

"I'll stay as well." Owen added before looking to Katiera. "You should go back to Branchview South. You'll be safe there."

"I'm not leaving you, Owen. I'm staying!" Katiera protested, causing Eno and Philip to exchange amused smirks.

"Very well." Philip declared. "Eno and I will retreat to Branchview South, and alert every one there of the happenings.

Eno looked to Mahkta with a smile. "What about you, big guy?"

"I will stay here with my new friends." He answered.

"What will happen in the aftermath?" Owen asked.

"There will be a couple of days to adjust, and then the new world will commence." He answered with vigor. "At that time, all that were evacuated from the earth will be rounded up for their return."

"Including my mother and father?" He further inquired.

"As promised, I'll make it my mission to find them." Eno assured.

"In the appropriate time, contact with the Galactic Federation will also officially be established." Philip expressed.

"It will be a wondrous time of unity for us all." Eno further established.

Philip looked to Linda, and motioned her off to the side.

"Are there any more of us that are still here on earth?" He asked in a lower tone.

"I believe that Nebriana and Green Man might still among us." She answered. "If they indeed survived Satan's wrath, I think they might be hiding in the Catskill Mountains."

"I'd have to agree." He paused in thought. "I know a place of virgin forest within Sullivan County where their kind, as well as The Woods People could live peacefully hidden from the mortal world."

"Isn't that where one of our portals is located as well?"

"Yes. It's a very magical and enchanting place." He nodded. "Have you received any news of her sister, Claudiana?"

"I've heard through telepathy that she is safe in The Northland."

"Good. I can always visit her at another time." He stated. "But for now, it's vital that we find both Nebriana and The Green Man. Once death passes, we need to let them know that they don't have to hide anymore."

Linda reacted with a perplexed expression. "Where else could they go, and what could they do?"

"They'll be free to do as they wish." He proclaimed with a smile. "The days of immortal gods are over. They should have a choice to remain here as mortal ambassadors, or go back to their native planets."

"Are you saying...?"

Philip nodded joyfully. "That offer extends to you as well, Linda."

She was speechless, and taken back by the revelation.

"I'm sure you would serve as an excellent ambassador of peace for your people." He concluded with a grin, as he strolled away to continue mingling with the others in the room.

As midday approached, the sun became obscured as though a cover were being pulled across the sky. The street lights activated, and it was soon as black as night. It was all accompanied by a mournful moan that carried on the brisk wind. If death had a voice, it would no doubt have a similar sound. Agonizing wails, and cries arose in its wake, mingling with terrified screams of the impure souls that were being carried away.

At Branchview South, Philip and Eno now sat in the Great Room with Gerard LeRoux, Alton Sinclair, and Agent Guitierez. Philip had just finished giving them the joyful news that their families were safe on the planet of Lyra when the lights suddenly flashed off and then back on. Everyone paused to acknowledge the strange pall that fell across the house.

"It's passing over us now." Philip announced.

"I think it might be a good time for all of us to say a silent prayer." Gerard suggested.

"I couldn't agree more." Alton added.

Though confident they would all be spared, Philip could still sense the nervous anxiety among the men as they sat quietly with their eyes closed. This was a supernatural event like no one on earth had ever witnessed or experienced since the days of The Bible.

As the angel of death passed over the earth, every building and house in its path that had a connection with the Elite Society, or with any of the other dark forces ignited into flame. Every other structure was spared from the wrath.

At the medical rehab center, Linda calmed all the patients with the help of Owen, Katiera, and Mahkta. They paused occasionally with controlled anxiety as the lights flickered, and the dreadful, foreboding sounds from the outside permeated through the walls of the building.

Several hours after the fire and winds had passed, huge lightning storms followed, and swept the entire earth. It brought along with it, drenching rains that quenched all the fires, and cleansed the air of the smoke and residue. The crashing lightning woke both Philip and Eno at the same time. The others stirred, but were too exhausted to totally wake up.

"It will be a whole new world when everyone wakes in the morning." Eno whispered.

"It's definitely a new era that has been long overdue." Philip replied.

The storms raged outside until just before sunrise. They then trailed off, leaving in its wake a peaceful silence. The task was finished.

13

A NEW WORLD

The Sunrise brought a new day to the Gulf Coast, and its light eventually permeated through the shuttered eastern windows of Branchview South. The small group who had slept through the long night, right in their chairs within the Great Room began to stir as they awakened. As they opened their eyes, all sensed a strange positive shift within the energy of the room.

Philip and Eno were already out in the enclosed sunroom that overlooked the Gulf. As the light smothered out the darkness of night, it revealed a splendid, cloudless sky over the vast waters. They stood, gazing silently as the first light bathed their faces.

"I savor my new position in the kingdom of Paradeisos. But I do miss the ocean very much." Philip commented as he continued to longingly stare out to sea.

"Perhaps you can plead that passion to our creator." Eno suggested.

Philip only answered with a thought filled grin before the duo was joined by Gerard and Alton.

They wiped the sleep from their eyes, and stretched as they too became mesmerized by the serene sight before them.

"It looks like it's going to be a beautiful day." Gerard stated.

"In more ways than one." Eno smiled. "Gentlemen! It's a new world."

"Where's Agent Guitierez?" Philip asked.

"He went to check on his team in the south wing of the house." Alton answered.

"He's a good leader." Eno sincerely proclaimed. "He'll be a valuable asset to the reconstruction of this country."

"Who's making the coffee?" Philip exuberantly inquired.

"I'll gladly volunteer." Gerard replied.

Before he departed, he paused to look out toward the Gulf with great emotion. "I wish that Steven was here with us."

"I was thinking the same thing." Alton added.

Philip looked upward in conclusion. "I guarantee he's here with us in spirit."

In another building a short distance away, Owen awoke from his makeshift bunk, and looked around the room. He was all by himself. In a panic, he threw the blanket aside, and stood.

"Katie!" He yelled out in desperation.

Just then a mellow, comforting voice rang out. "It's alright, Owen." Mahkta replied as his large, imposing frame entered the room. "Her and Linda went out to take in the morning air."

His answer calmed Owen. "Is it finished?"

Mahkta gave an assuring nod. "I stepped outside to check on things. The birds were joyfully singing, and the air never smelled as fresh. It was beautiful." He smiled. "Perhaps you should step outside and experience it yourself."

Owen answered his friend with an expression of anxious agreement.

A bit later that morning, there was a pleasant breeze blowing in from the Gulf as Philip and Eno casually strolled along the beach. Many of the large estates that once lined the shoreline were now gone, and so were their inhabitants. Only the ruins remained, like structural ghosts soon to be reclaimed by nature. Yet others such as Branchview South stood regally untouched as though no event had ever taken place.

Further down the beach, two women sauntered toward them, their bare feet catching the surf as it rolled onto shore. A smile graced the men's faces when they realized who they were. They all exchanged joyful waves as they approached each other.

"I think we found a couple lovely mermaids." Philip quipped with a smile.

"I couldn't resist taking a morning swim in the Gulf." Linda stated as they came closer. "It's amazing how much cleaner the water is."

"I wished I could've joined her." Katiera sadly remarked. "I'm afraid my body still won't react well to the salt water."

"At least you got the chance to see a school of dolphins swimming in my wake." Linda added.

"Oh yes! It was wonderful!" She proclaimed.

"I do love to watch them when they leap out of the water." Eno stated. "It's quite entertaining."

"You should witness a school of Mermaids frolicking in the surf sometime." Linda said. "We'll have to arrange a show before you have to leave."

"Of course, They'll all need to wear bikini tops." Katiera quipped. "You wouldn't want to put on too much of a show."

Everyone shared a good laugh over the young Oceanid's comment.

"I know I shouldn't be asking this. But is all the evil really gone?" Linda sincerely asked.

"Most definitely!" Philip answered. "They've all been relocated to lower frequency planets where they'll be subject to the same abuse that they inflicted on others during their long reign here on earth."

Eno looked out toward the water as if listening to some unheard message. They all respectfully paused conversation, full knowing that he was receiving some sort of telepathic message.

After a few short minutes, a broad smile appeared on his face.

"I have wonderful news." He announced, as they all listened with anticipation. "We found Owen's parents."

"He'll be so happy." Katiera replied as she bounced up and down with excitement. "I can't wait to tell him."

"I'll take you there, and we can both tell him." Eno exuberantly added.

Linda then turned her full attention to Philip. "I believe you and I have some business to attend to in the Catskills."

221

"The sooner the better." Philip smiled, as he turned to Eno and Katiera. "After we're finished with that, I'll need to pay a visit to an old friend in the parallel world."

"Steven Spencer's twin identity?" Eno questioned.

Philip answered with a sympathetic nod. "It's high time his mind is cleared of his past parallel life here, so that he can move ahead happily in his present life there."

"Will you be back in time for the great arrival?" He further questioned.

"I wouldn't miss it for the world." Philip grinned as he took hold of Linda's hand. "In fact, I'll be accompanying the Branchview family on their return from the planet Lyra."

"Sounds like you have quite a busy schedule, my friend." Eno concluded.

"Indeed." Philip replied, as he and Linda turned away, and gave a departing wave.

"It's been quite a while since you and I travelled in this way." Linda remarked.

"And, there's no doubt that it will probably be the last time." Philip added with a wink.

"Shouldn't we have more appropriate clothing. I understand it's quite cold in the Catskills this time of year."

"You're absolutely right." Philip answered as he made a quick gesture with his hand, and they were suddenly clothed in winter attire.

Eno and Katiera both watched as the duo then strolled further along, and disappeared into the crisp morning air.

"That is so cool." Katiera marveled.

"Now you can have the same experience with me." Eno chuckled as he took hold of the Mermaid's hand. "Hold on tight. We'll be there before you even realize it."

As they both disappeared, only Katiera's joyful, echoing giggle still lingered along the quiet, serene beach.

14

THE LAST OF THE ANCIENT GODS

Philip and Linda stepped into a barren winter scene as though departing from an invisible portal in the air. The bright sun added little warmth to an otherwise snowy scene. They both stood for a moment, and scanned their surroundings. The trees were all stripped of their leaves, and a chilly breeze blew across the landscape. The sound of crows cawing filled the cold air, and a lone hawk flew high in the air, searching the ground below for its' breakfast.

"The Catskills certainly aren't very appealing this time of year." Linda remarked with a shiver.

"I guess beauty is in the eye of the beholder." Philip replied. "Although the winters are quite cold, I find the sights to be quite appealing to the eyes."

"I think I prefer a tropical beach instead." She sighed.

"You'll be home and warm in no time at all."

"This is definitely the place that the elders said I would find them." Linda stated with a quiver in her voice.

"I don't understand why Nebriana didn't fly to the hidden world with the other faire's, and remain there." He replied.

"I know. It's a wonder the poor soul hasn't froze to death by now." Linda added.

"Nebriana!" Philip called out loudly, as they moved ahead.

Linda joined him in calling out her name as they continued on. A short distance ahead, they noticed chimney smoke rising above a grove of bare trees. As they got closer, they noticed a weathered, dilapidated cottage that would've been completely hidden had foliage been on the trees.

They proceeded to call out her name as they trudged through the snowy terrain in the direction of the dwelling. Their voices echoed loudly through the cold air. Suddenly the front door slowly opened, and a heavily clothed woman stepped out to look toward the approaching duo. As they got closer, they initially couldn't recognize the gaunt face of the woman who shivered underneath the thick wool coat. Her hair was matted, with patches of it missing, and her face was grossly disfigured, and scarred by what appeared to have been burns. She burst into tears as she recognized the visitors.

"I never thought I'd ever see you two again." She sadly remarked. "Please come in."

When the reality of who she actually was became evident, both Philip and Linda were horrified to see what had become of their beloved friend.

"Those terrible storms that came through last night brought at least three feet of snow." She breathed hard as she leaned against a table. "I've never heard the wind howl so ferociously."

Once the duo knocked most of the snow from their boots, Nebriana ushered them further into the house. There was a roaring blaze in the fireplace, and a pot of stew hung above the flames. She shuffled over, and stirred the contents as she talked.

"I thought you were both dead." She began.

"I was killed by Satan." Philip replied. "But Linda escaped his wrath."

"How…?"

"We'll explain later." Linda interrupted, and moved to embrace a somewhat apprehensive Nebriana. "I'm so sorry I didn't come find you before now. I believe you and I might be the only ones left."

"Did Green Man perish in the fire?" Philip inquired.

She remorsefully shook her head, and motioned to an adjacent room. "He stays in that room most of the time."

"Why…? Linda attempted to ask as Nebriana cut her short.

"Like me, he was badly burned in the fire." She painfully remarked as she gestured toward two hard wooden chairs. "Please! Have a seat."

She scooted a chair up for herself, and continued with a sigh. "We almost made it safely to the other side of the Old Post Road, but the flames moved faster than we could on foot." She paused emotionally. "As you can see, the fire consumed me, and burned my wings. Despite the agonizing pain, I refused to abandon my old friend. Somehow, we made our way to safety, but much damage was already done." She paused to weep. "Without my wings, I had none of my powers. I was reduced to this hideous freak you see before you."

"Please don't say that, Nebriana." Linda pleaded, but was silenced from speaking further as Nebriana raised her withered hand to stop.

"It's the truth." She winced at the terrible memory. "We may have survived, but Satan destroyed who we once were."

"How is it that you found your way here?" Philip asked with great concern.

"Though we were both in great pain, we traveled under the cover of night. The Faire's and The Woods People helped us along, soothing our burns with their natural ointments." She paused to cough. "We found our way to this abandoned cottage." She motioned to her surroundings. "This is a secluded part of the Deep Forest where humans never visit purposely. She paused before continuing. "Legend has it that this portion of The Catskills are haunted, and people tend to stay away. The seclusion is what has kept us safe for all this time."

"Do you have any idea what year this is?" Linda questioned.

She looked downward in sorrow, shaking her head. "We lost track of time long ago. We were afraid to venture far from the cottage in fear that Satan or his demons would find us."

"It's been nearly five years." Linda stated, leaving Nebriana to stare off in disbelief.

"Satan, The Elites, and all that was evil in this world have been removed from the Earth." Philip added.

"He's actually gone?" Nebriana anxiously inquired.

Both Philip and Linda gave an assuring nod.

"Please ask Green Man to come out." Philip pleaded. "I am now a Warrior Angel in the army of Paradeisos. I want to help you both."

She stood slowly, and reluctantly walked over to the closed door. "Green Man! It's alright! Please come out!" She called.

After a few moments, a sad, disfigured being emerged from the room. He was no longer the robust man beast that they remembered. His bark was deeply charred, and his leafy face was now a barren, browned surface with sorrowful eyes, disfigured nose, and a drooping mouth. Both Philip and Linda were horrified by the sight.

Nebriana gently took hold of his charred hand, and slowly led him further into the room.

"I'm so sorry this happened to both of you." Philip sincerely stated as he stood, tears welling in his eyes.

He moved closer to both of them as the two burnt figures glanced at each other with much emotion. Philip then carefully placed his hand to the side of Green Man's face.

"The nightmare is over, my friends. Both of you no longer have to hide, or carry on with your former roles as natural gods. You're now free to do as you choose."

They once again exchanged puzzled expressions.

"You know full well that Green Man was genetically created by the Anunnaki, and mercifully rescued by you and Zeus himself." Nebriana reasoned. "I, myself was very young when I left my planet. Earth is the only true home I've ever known."

"We're useless beings as we are." Green Man lamented. "Even in this so called new world, our only destiny is to hide away in these mountains for the rest of our lives."

"Then what is it that you both wish to do?" He asked with much empathy. "Have you forgotten that if you simply believe, anything you want can be possible?"

After a few fleeting thoughts passed between them, Green Man spoke up first with a faint sparkle in his eyes.

"I would wish to live my life as a handsome man instead of being in this beastly body that I've had to hide from the outside world for all my existence." He answered with much frustration.

"What about you?" Linda inquired of Nebriana, who answered with a deep sigh.

"I simply want to be restored to the woman I once was." She vented. "Since I'm now free to do so, I also wish to know what it's like to love a man, and be loved in return."

Linda answered with a sympathetic, and understanding nod, while Philip turned his full attention to The Green Man.

"I can grant your wish, Green Man" He began. "I know you've always harbored feelings for Claudiana. If you want to be with her, I'll be glad to escort you to The Northland.

"No!" He intently replied, much to Philip's surprise. "After all this time, I now realize that I loved the wrong sister." He glanced longingly toward Nebriana. "If she'll have me, I want to be the man she needs in her life."

"Do you feel the same way toward Green Man?" Philip gestured to Nebriana.

"After this ordeal, I can't imagine being with anyone else." She expressed in a shaky voice.

Philip and Linda exchanged an enlightened glance.

"So be it." Philip simply stated as he took hold of both their hands. "Close your eyes, and imagine what you wish."

Philip closed his eyes as well, and muttered an inaudible prayer. He opened them once again when he felt the change pass between them. Even Linda gasped with surprise at the transformation taking place. They both slowly opened their eyes, and first noticed their hands, and fully restored bodies. Then as Philip moved to the side, the couple embraced each other with emotional exuberance.

"You're such a handsome man!" Nebriana marveled.

"And you're even more beautiful than I remember." Green Man replied.

Philip approached them both once again.

"Since you'll both be living in this world as humans, you'll need to adopt more appropriate names." He thought for a moment before turning to Green Man. "From now on, you'll be known as Gregory." He then looked fondly to Nebriana. "And you my dear shall be known as Brianna."

"I like it!" Gregory exclaimed.

"I do too." Brianna added.

The two surveyed each other for another stunned, awkward moment before embracing once again.

Linda exchanged a sly grin, and a thumbs up with Philip as they savored the happy scene.

"We'd like you two lovebirds to come with us." Linda expressed.

"Where would we go, and what could we do?" Brianna anxiously asked. "We've never known life outside of the Deep Woods."

"For starters, you can come to live with me in Florida." Linda confidently replied. "I can help you both adapt to your new life."

"You can always come back to The Catskills in the summer to be among your people." Philip suggested. "You'll never have to worry about evil ever intruding into your world for the remainder of your existence, and you'll never have to endure another long, cold winter."

"And we'll always be there when you need us." Linda assured.

The couple's thoughts raced quickly as they listened. There were so many questions.

"Is there someone in Florida who can unite us in marriage?" Gregory eagerly inquired.

"I know a few Greek Orthodox Priests." Philip answered with a surprised grin that graduated into a chuckle. "But first, you need to ask her to be your wife, big guy."

Gregory looked to Brianna with anxious anticipation, then went down to one knee.

"Brianna, will you marry me?"

"Yes! Yes, I will!" She exclaimed with great emotion.

Philip and Linda glanced at each other with overflowing happiness as the smitten couple kissed with amorous vigor.

"Another miraculous ending." Linda proclaimed to a beaming Philip.

"Now, you're the only immortal goddess that remains on this earth. Have you thought about your future?"

"I really haven't had the time to give it serious thought." She stressed. "Hopefully, I'll find a happy ending as well."

"Your powers will be intact until you decide, or the council of elders decides for you."

"I know I'll probably remain as the caretaker at Branchview South for the time being. But I'm not quite sure what my role will be as an immortal Mermaid." She stated with a sad smile.

"I can send you all back to Florida through the portal, but I won't be able to accompany you there."

"Are you going right now to see Steven in the parallel world?"

Philip answered with a serious, and definitive nod. "I can't let this go on much longer. This task needs to be promptly handled to seal the time lines, and avoid any future complications between the two worlds."

Linda concluded with a simple, understanding nod, as she motioned for Briana and Gregory to join hands with her.

"Are we leaving so soon?" Gregory asked.

"We have to." Linda stated with urgency.

"But what about my stew?" Briana gestured toward the fireplace. "I've been cooking it all morning."

"Don't worry." She laughed. "I'll feed you both very well when you get to Florida."

At that, they stood hand in hand as a portal opened near the ceiling of the cottage. It appeared as what looked like a circular vortex of water that descended around them. In a split second, they were all gone, and only Philip remained.

"On to another assignment." He spoke out loud to himself as he closed his eyes, and disappeared as well.

Back in Florida, Katiera and Eno Calta had just shared the happy news with Owen about his parents.

Eno turned his attention to Mahkta, who was attending to a few patients nearby.

"They look like they're ready to be released back into the Gulf, Dr. Mahkta."

"They've all made a miraculous recovery." He replied.

"Our work is just about done here." Eno proclaimed. "We'll be ready to go join our ship shortly. The crew is waiting on us at the bottom of the Gulf."

The large lion shuffled forward with his paws humbly cuffed in front of him.

"Commander Calta, I'd like to receive your permission to remain here on earth. I feel I have much to offer to this new world."

Eno began with a regretful sigh. "I'd be losing one of my best doctors."

"He could be under the supervision of my father." Katiera suggested. "There's much knowledge that they could share with each other."

"We could sponsor him as an ambassador from the planet Achta." Owen added.

Mahkta smiled at the comments of his friends, while Eno carefully considered the request.

"Very well." He shook the large paw of the lion. "You'll be greatly missed by myself and the crew."

"Will I be able to visit from time to time?" Mahkta inquired.

"Absolutely, my dear friend." Eno smiled. "I'll communicate with Xander before I leave, and you'll report to him when you arrive at Station 37 with Katiera and Owen.

The lion's green eyes sparkled, and he patted his large paws together with overwhelming excitement.

On the beach at Branchview South, the portal opened, and the trio of Linda, Briana, and Gregory stepped through. The two newcomers looked around with wonder at their new surroundings.

"It's beautiful here." Briana proclaimed. "It makes me think of the beach at Lighthouse Point."

Linda paused to remove her heavy parka, and took notice of the raggedy, worn clothes that the couple wore.

"There will be ample time to get acquainted with your surroundings. But right now, we need to get you both showered, and find some fresh clothes for you to wear. I'll also have our cook prepare a good meal. She intently stated. "Follow me."

The couple exchanged anxious glances as they trudged through the sand, following her toward the beautiful house that was just ahead.

A few minutes later, they arrived at the front of the grand estate, and Brianna smiled when she saw the engraved sign near the front door that read Branchview South.

There was also a moving van parked in the driveway, and Agent Guitierez and his crew were carrying boxes from the house, and loading them into the truck.

"Leaving so soon, Agent G?" Linda asked.

"Our work is done here." He replied as he balanced a large box in front of him. "We'll be moving our operations to a new building on the grounds of Branch Consolidated Industries." He motioned back toward the house. "Gerard and Alton will be staying on for a few days until the great arrival."

"Will you be there?" She asked.

"I wouldn't miss it for the world." He smiled as he curiously shifted his attention to the couple standing behind Linda.

"This is Gregory and Briana. They're dear friends of mine that desperately need a helping hand." She stressed. "This is my good friend Agent Guitierez.

They all exchanged cordial nods.

"They've definitely found the right people to help." He answered with an assured wink.

"Be safe, and have a wonderful new life, Agent G." Linda concluded as her and the couple continued on into the house.

"You as well." He emotionally replied.

15

A VISIT WITH AN OLD FRIEND

Philip arrived that Saturday afternoon on the quaint residential street in the Parallel World that the portal had brought him to. He paused along the sidewalk to reset his bearings, and to take in all the scenery that surrounded him. Although it was winter in Connecticut, there was a warm vibe among the older, but immaculately kept houses of the neighborhood. He looked at each one as he proceeded to slowly stroll along, trying to guess which of them belonged to his old friend. He came across a modified Craftsman style home that had a small captain's watch added to the roofline. On either side of the steps leading to the open porch there were two medium sized statues resting on concrete pedestals. One was a lion, and the other was a mermaid. He smiled to himself, knowing that it had to be the right house.

He casually walked up the brick walkway, and gave a hesitant knock on the varnished oak wood door. He was shocked, speechless at first when the stunning red head with ocean blue eyes answered the door a few moments later. It had been a very long time since he had last seen her.

His heart raced, wondering if she might recognize him from their past life, but it appeared that she didn't.

"Can I help you?" She asked in almost an annoyed fashion, while they curiously eyed each other.

"I'm sorry to intrude." He stammered. "Would Steven happen to be home?"

"He's working in his office. Could I ask your name?" She further inquired.

"Oh uh, Philip." He nervously replied. "I'm an old friend of his."

"Please come in." She stated as she stepped away from blocking the door. "I'm Steven's wife, Amy."

"It's a pleasure to meet you." He politely replied as he stepped into the house, and scanned the room with his eyes.

He smiled when he noticed the collection of ceramic mermaids that lined the shelves and table tops.

"Mermaids." He commented with fondness.

Amy smiled, replying. "I've always loved Mermaids for some strange reason."

"Perhaps a memory from a past life."

Amy thought about his response for a moment before answering. "Perhaps."

There was an awkward moment that fell between them until she broke the silence.

"I'll tell Steven you're here."

Philip examined his surroundings further after she departed the room. It was a comfortable classic style home that was absolutely pristine in appearance. He couldn't help but notice a few items such as the music box that had always been present in the Branchview sitting room. The ticking grandfather clock on the other side of the room chimed at the top of the hour. It was a familiar sound he remembered hearing quite often as he stood in the foyer of the old house. In fact, everywhere he looked, he saw a reminder of The Branchview Estate.

Eventually, Amy returned to the room once again diverting his attention back to the present. "Please come this way."

He followed Amy up the short staircase that led to the captain's watch. There were windows on all four corners of the room. One direction offering a distant view of the Long Island Sound. It was the perfect workspace for a writer.

At the large, walnut writing desk in the center of the room sat Steven, immersed heavily in his work.

When he looked up, and saw the familiar figure standing in the doorway of his office, he was almost speechless with surprise.

"Hello Steven." Philip smiled.

"Philip?" Steven stood up, and his shock graduated to a warm smile. "I don't believe it."

Amy ushered him further into the room, and she took alert notice of her husband's awkward reaction.

"Could I get you two some coffee?"

"Chock Full O' Nuts?" Philip quipped.

Amy laughed at his question. "You really are an old friend, aren't you?" She replied with a clever smirk as she departed the room.

"She's just as lovely as I remembered." Philip fondly stated, prompting a warm grin from Steven.

"Please sit down." He motioned to a nearby chair, before sitting back down himself. "You're the last person I ever expected to see again."

"It's a visit that's long overdue." He paused. "I'm sorry I wasn't there for you that last day of your other life." He paused again, while Steven intently listened. "Satan killed my brother and I the night before."

"I didn't know." Steven reacted with further surprise. "If you're truly dead, how is it that you're here now?" He questioned.

"I'll begin by saying this. I'm now a Warrior Angel of the Planet Paradeisos." He explained. "Your twin spirit is there as well." He smiled. "We're still friends as we were in that other life."

"This Paradeisos that you speak of. I assume it's Heaven."

"Yes! That's the earthly name for it."

Steven looked to the corners of the room with wonderment.

"Do you and I still meet for coffee in Paradeisos?" Steven grinned.

"Oh yes!" He chuckled. "At least when I'm on the planet." His expression turned more serious.
 "I'm presently helping The Galactic Federation to bring in the 5th dimensional energy to the parallel earth."

Steven looked toward Philip with a perplexed expression as he listened to him further explain.

"Satan, The Secret Society, and all that was evil have been banished and removed from the planet. It's the beginning of a new reality that before could only be imagined by the most creative minds."

"Did Loraine survive?"

"Her and Stargazer escaped into the mirror of the Grand Ballroom the day that you died. We have no idea where they are in the spectrum of time." He sighed with disappointment.

"What about the others?"

"They were taken to a safe place, and now are ready to return to the new world."

"Does that include my children?"

Philip nodded in reply. "If they wish to come. They've been well taken care of by my son Tri…uh..Tony and his wife Andrea."

Steven showed fond amusement of Philip's near stumble, but allowed him to continue.

"They've been on the Planet Lyra for almost five years now."

They both abruptly stopped conversing when they heard the approaching footsteps.

There was a casual, yet tense feeling in the room that Amy quickly detected as she entered, holding a tray with a carafe of coffee, two cups, sweetener, and cream.

The two men continued to cease conversation while she carefully set the tray on the desk, then backed awkwardly toward the door.

"If you need me for anything, I'll be in my office." She looked toward Steven as though trying to read his thoughts. "I have some research work I need to do." She paused again before leaving, waiting for one of the two men to break the silence.

"Thank you, sweetheart." Steven smiled.

They waited for her footsteps to fade into the farther reaches of the house before they commenced their conversation.

"Does she know everything?" Philip asked.

"A good bit of it. But not all." Steven answered. "She's been very understanding of the situation, and has helped me greatly."

"Are you happy in this life?" He further inquired.

"Happier than I could ever imagine." Steven answered with enthusiasm.

He pointed to a picture on a side table.

"We have a daughter. Her name is Danielle."

Philip raised from his seat to take a closer look. "She's beautiful."

"It's hard to believe she's thirteen already."

"Sometimes the years go by too fast." Philip replied as he settled into his seat once again.

"Even though I have a great life here, I was happy in that other life too." Steven revealed.

"That often haunts me."

"I can fix that, Steven." Philip said before taking a sip of his coffee.

Steven looked upward in thought, and sighed. "Can you at least explain how I got there from here?"

"There was a portal out in the Long Island Sound that connected to the parallel world. It would open from time to time, usually during a storm or perhaps a full moon." He took a deep breath. "When it did, it would take in anything that was in its path."

"There was a storm that day." Steven recalled with intense thought. "It came up so quick, I wasn't able to get back to shore." He paused in further thought. "I can't remember anything after that."

"You and your boat were suspended between two worlds when the portal closed once again." He explained. "Your spirit flame could not get back here, so it moved on through the portal to the other world." He paused. "There could not be two of you physically in that world, so your spirit entered into your other identity.

Steven stood, and paced behind his desk, distressfully holding his hands to his head.

"This is a lot to digest." He paused to look straight at Philip. "How did I get back here?"

"When your other identity died, your twin spirit had nowhere to go once again." He paused, making sure that Steven understood. "The Nereids had the key to the portal, and they brought you back to this world."

Steven was flabbergasted, and overcome by anxious thoughts.

But he allowed Philip to continue.

"From that time on, the portal was permanently sealed so that no one else could enter or leave this world."

"There were others you know." Steven revealed. "Some of them were my patients." He sat back down. "My colleagues and I, including my wife have investigated the theory of a parallel world for years now. We've even written fiction novels about it."

"It needs to remain as fiction. The people of this world should never know that the portals actually exist." He sternly warned. "Whatever research you've compiled needs to be destroyed, and you must cease to ever revisit that theory again." He stressed with further emphasis. "It's for the protection of both worlds."

Steven gave an understanding nod, and Amy then casually sauntered into the room from where she was listening just outside the door.

"How much did you hear?" Steven asked with a weary sigh.

"Enough." She replied as she sat down on another chair in the room. "I sensed something was wrong, so I took off my shoes, and tiptoed just outside the door to listen."

"You always were curious, and very clever, Amphitrite." Philip smirked.

"What?" She sarcastically asked.

"It's not of importance now. But you and I did know each other in another lifetime."

Amy looked toward Steven with a perplexed expression.

"It's a long story." He rolled his eyes, and then focused his full attention back on Philip. "You have my word that there will be nothing else said or researched on this subject."

"In return, I promise you that I'll erase all memory of your life in that other world."

"Thank you." Steven spoke as he clenched his eyes shut. "I'm ready to forget, and move on with this wonderful life I have here." He and Amy exchanged an amicable glance.

"Unfortunately, I'll have to erase both of your memories of me, and this visit." He sighed. "However, you will retain the details of your mission. As I mentioned, all chronicled details of the parallel world need to be removed."

Both Amy and Steven gave an agreeing nod.

"I've really missed you, old friend." Steven stated. "I wish you could stay a bit longer."

Philip emotionally replied with a nod.
"I wish I had more time as well. But I really need to go now."

He then rose from his seat.

"Wait! Amy exclaimed. "What about all the others here that have knowledge of this parallel world? We have no control of what they might do with that information."

"As soon as I leave this dimension, all of their memories about this subject will be wiped clean as well."

"Will we ever see you again?" Steven inquired.

"Not in this world." He bluntly answered.

Philip turned to Amy first. "Thank you for your hospitality. Be sure to take good care of this guy." He then turned his full attention to Steven next, not able to hold back a fond smile. "Goodbye for now, Steven!" He quickly glanced at both of them. "I hope both of you have a wonderful life."

As he went to depart, Steven replied with a grin. "Goodbye Poseidon!"

Amy reacted with shock and surprise, now knowing exactly what Philip had meant by his earlier remark.

Philip simply addressed her with a humorous shrug as he left the room.

Amy then stood, and approached Steven with enlightenment, pointing toward the door where Philip had just exited. "I think he and I were married in a past lifetime."

Steven stood as well, and sighed. "And yes, you were indeed the storied goddess of the sea."

"I was Amphitrite." She declared with amazement.

Steven gave a definitive nod. "It doesn't matter now. You and I are married in this lifetime, and that's all that's important." He embraced her. "I love you, Amy."

"I love you too, Steven."

The couple nuzzled, and kissed. In that short moment of bliss, their memories were magically erased of the whole prior incident, as well as everything they ever knew about Branchview and the parallel world. They awkwardly pushed apart for a moment as though just waking from a dream.

"It's funny." Amy remarked as she cluelessly glanced around the room. "I can't seem to remember coming in here. The last thing I recall was going to answer a knock at the front door."

"I can't seem to remember anything either." Steven laughed as he glanced at the clock on his desk. "The last thing I recall is working right here, and there seems to have been a lapse of time since then."

The couple spent a few silent moments trying to sort the situation out before Steven moved to change the subject. He took notice of the picture of their daughter on the side table, and noticed it was placed different from what it was before.

"Where's Danielle today?"

"She's over at Jeannie's house. The girls are having a sleepover tonight."

Steven mulled over her answer for a moment, still feeling rather discombobulated.

"Since it's Saturday, why don't you and I go out and do something fun for a change?" He suggested. "Whatever work we have to do can wait."

"Or, perhaps we can just stay here, and have some snuggle time." She countered with a mischievous raised brow.

"That sounds like an even better idea, Mrs. Spencer."

He took hold of her hand, and she giggled like a school girl as they hurried from the room.

16

LEARNING TO SWIM

Back in the other parallel world, Xander and his wife Tabitha arrived to take Katiera and Owen back to Station 37 prior to The Great Arrival. They all gathered on the beach along with Mahkta, Gerard, Alton, and Linda.

After greeting her parents, Katiera began introducing them to her new friends.

"Mother and father, this is Gerard LeRoux and Alton Sinclair. They are both chief executives at Branch Consolidated Industries, and will be key figures in helping to rebuild the new world economy."

They all cordially shook hands.

"Katiera has shared much about your world." Gerard stated, "We both look forward to seeing it for ourselves."

"Why wait?" Xander replied. "You can go along with us while we return to prepare for The Great Arrival. Perhaps someday you'll be able to visit with your reunited families as well."

"By all means." Tabitha added. I'm sure you two gentlemen would enjoy a few days off before it's time to get back to business as usual."

After exchanging glances, Alton spoke first. "We accept your invitation."

Katiera moved on to Mahkta next.

"This is our new friend, Dr. Mahkta from the planet Achta."

Tabitha gave a cordial nod, and Xander gave his huge hand a vigorous shake.

"My daughter, and Eno Calta have told me many good things about you." Xander smiled. "I look forward to learning and sharing the newest innovations of the medical field during your stay in our world."

"As do I, Dr. Torrance." Mahkta replied.

"Well! I'm more than ready for a good afternoon swim." Linda stated. "Before you leave, would you like me to teach you how to swim, Owen?

Owen shook his head with frustration. "You know I can't swim like you, and the others."

"Yes, you can." She said, as she reached for his hand.

Mahkta rested his paw sized hand on Owen's shoulder. "You can do anything if you just put your mind to it, my friend."

"Now's as good a time as any." Xander urged him further. "After all, you are one of us now."

"You will not fail, Owen." Tabitha assured.

Owen looked to his wife for further encouragement.

"Could you, and your parents do this with me?" He asked with pleading eyes.

"Owen, we can't. Our bodies are used to fresh water. The salt water, and warmer temperatures would be too much of a shock." She gestured toward the water with a loving smile. "Let Linda do this."

He answered with only a hesitant nod as he took hold of Linda's outstretched hand. Together they rushed into the Gulf waters while the others cheered him on.

"Hold your breath, and follow my lead." Linda instructed. "I promise I won't let you go."

They hit the water, and quickly went under. Linda transformed, but Owen did not. Instead, he thrashed to the surface in a panic, while she rose from the depths to support his body.

On shore, the others continued yelling out encouraging words.

"Did it happen? Did he shapeshift?" Alton anxiously asked.

"I can't tell." Gerard answered as he squinted his eyes against the bright sun.

"He'll do it." Mahkta confidently replied. "I know he will."

They all breathed a sigh of disappointment as he paddled back to shore gasping desperately for air, and stumbled onto the beach.

Linda emerged as well, and followed him onto the beach.

"It's no use. I can't do it." Owen sputtered in frustration.

"After everything you've seen and experienced, do you not believe that anything is possible?" Xander calmly asked.

Katiera placed her hands on either side of Owens face. "You can do this, sweetheart. Do you remember how we merged our souls on our wedding night?"

"How can I forget it?"

"Put all the doubt from your mind, telepathically listen to me, and just believe." She spoke with encouragement before kissing him.

All the others placed a hand of confidence on him before the duo once again headed toward the water.

"Let's try this again." Linda said as they waded waist deep.

Owen closed his eyes as Linda pulled him under once more.

Under the water, Owen vigorously paddled his feet. He clenched his eyes, and concentrated. On shore, Katiera spoke to him with her mind. Her eyes clenched shut as well. This time something miraculous happened. His legs slowly transformed to fins as Linda slowly let go of his hand.

Owen opened his eyes, and swam with confidence on his own. Linda then motioned for him to follow her lead to the surface. With precision synchronicity, they leaped side by side out of the water in an arc, before diving once again below the surface.

"Look! He did it!" Alton cried in amazement as they all continued to cheer wildly from the beach.

"That's my son in law." Xander proudly proclaimed.

"I have a feeling we'll have a hard time keeping him out of the water from now on." Tabitha mused.

Owen and Linda surfaced briefly, and waved to the others on shore.

"I did it! I really did it!" Owen emotionally yelled back to shore.

"I knew you could, sweetheart." Katiera yelled back with enthusiasm.

"Come on! I'll teach you a few more underwater maneuvers." Linda urged him on with joyful eagerness.

"Thank you so much for this gift, Linda."

"It was all you, Owen." She stated with a smile before they submerged below the waters once again.

Later, when Linda returned to Branchview South, and slowly sauntered through the front door, the house was quieter than it had been in quite time. She relished that peaceful feeling. As she strolled into the kitchen, she surprised Briana and Gregory who had been embraced in a kiss.

"Well! Where have you two been all day?"

"We were out exploring along the beach, and enjoying the sights." Briana answered. "We were just getting ready to go out again."

"This priest that Philip spoke about. Is he anywhere near here?" Gregory asked.

"I'm afraid not." Linda replied. "Father Narcopolous is in Tarpon Springs, which is a good distance north of here."

"Can you take us there as soon as possible? We want so much to be married." Briana inquired.

"I promise I'll take you there. But it will have to wait until after The Great Arrival." Linda firmly answered.

They both replied with a disappointed, but understanding nod.

"I'll leave you two lovebirds to carry on for now." She stated before departing the room, while also continuing to speak under her breath. "I could use a bit of alone time for myself."

Moments later, as Linda exited the house once again, she strolled down the long driveway of the estate, lost in her thoughts. She took in the sweet smell of the flowering bushes that lined the drive, and proceeded to quietly converse with herself.

"Oh, how I wish I could have a happy ending as well." She sighed, while looking upward. "If you can hear me, please send me a strong man with the character of a Philip Seagraves or a Steven Spencer."

Only a moment had gone by before an SUV pulled to the head of the driveway, and a tall, athletic built black man got out, and waved to her.

"Good heavens!" She exclaimed, glancing upward once more. "Ask, and you shall receive."

As they met halfway up the drive, he offered her a flyer.

"I'm Nathan Cook. My church is inviting all the survivors from Long Boat Key to a celebration of life this evening."

He paused to respectfully, and discreetly eye the lovely woman in front of him. But his amicable attention failed to escape Linda's notice. Neither did the fact that he had no wedding ring on his finger. She grinned as he nervously stumbled to continue.

"I won't take up any more of your time, ma'am. I hope that you'll join us."

Linda quickly glanced at the flyer before speaking up.

"Obviously, you must be a true man of God to have survived, and to be out here handing out these flyers."

Her words brought him to a pause

"I certainly hope so, ma'am. I'm the Pastor of the church."

They both chuckled as the tension of the encounter eased.

"Excuse me for being so bold. But how is it that a handsome man of God like yourself doesn't have a woman in his life?"

"How would you know that to be true?" He tactfully countered with a grin.

"Well. It's quite obvious that you're not wearing a ring. Women do tend to notice those things."

Nathan reacted with shy embarrassment as he conceded. "Fair enough. I suppose you could say that the right woman just never came along."

Linda gave a quick glance back toward the house, then looked back toward Nathan.

"Would you be willing to join two people who wished to be married?"

"Of course! Do you know these people?"

"Yes, I do. Quite well as a matter of fact."

"Well. Whenever they're ready, I have a clear calendar." He smiled.

"I have to also ask." She paused with a mischievous smile. "Do you believe that Mermaids exist, Reverend?"

Initially, he couldn't hold back a laugh. But when he realized she was serious, he quickly regained his composure.

"My gramma used to tell me stories about the mysterious Caribbean water people when I was a kid." He paused in thought. "After all I've seen in the past few days, I might have reason to believe those stories might be true." He answered with a puzzled tinge of humor.

She displayed a thought filled smile at his answer before speaking again.

"It's quite warm out here today." She began. "I have a nice lanai that overlooks The Gulf. Would you care to join me for a cold drink, Reverend Cook?

"I am quite thirsty, ma'am. "I do believe I will take you up on that invitation."

"Please! Call me Linda." She requested as she motioned him to follow along.

"Very well, Linda. You can call me Nate." He cordially stated, as they continued up the walkway side by side, conversing as though they were long lost friends.

255

17

THE GREAT ARRIVAL

A large contingent of surviving dignitaries, and those hoping to be reunited with loved ones who were taken five years before, gathered in the New Mexico desert on a beautiful moonlit night. Members of the nearby Navajo tribe, as well as anyone else willing to travel the many miles to witness the historic event were in attendance as well. Hardly a conversation stirred as they all looked anxiously into the night skies. One could hardly resist to be dazzled by the clarity of the canopy of stars above.

Suddenly, a blinding bright light shattered the darkness, and a sound similar to a sonic boom shook the still desert, as the enormous starship broke through the spectrum of time that separated the Earth from the unknown frontiers. The lights around the perimeter blinked in various color hues from red, blue, green, purple, and yellow. The lights were accompanied by various loud bass tones that echoed throughout the barren area. As they began their slow descent toward the earth, it became evident just how large the craft actually was. It measured the equivalent of one mile long, and at least a half mile in width and height. It was like a flying city. It was understandable as to why they chose to land in the desert. No populated area could ever accommodate the enormity of the craft.

The descent took some time, until it finally came to a hovering halt several feet above the ground. The lights around the width of the craft continued to blink in synchronicity. Everyone watched in wonder, and anticipation as the quiet engines fired down to almost complete silence. A loud whirring noise filled the silent desert air as the large ramps opened at the front of the craft, and slowly lowered to the sandy ground below.

There was anticipation in the air as a succession of higher octave musical tones ushered in the first group that came down the ramp. These were the children who had been spared. Many were now teenagers, and hardly recognizable to their parents. Still many more were now orphaned since their parents had been purged from the earth. The youngest were accompanied by their sponsors. They all fanned out in the crowd, desperately trying to find their loved ones in the darkened landscape. Slowly but surely, the joyful, and tearful reunions began to unfold.

Next came the adults. Among the first of that group to depart down the ramp were Sharie Le Roux with her daughter Deanna, and her now husband Tre' Russell who was carrying a young male toddler.

Gerard stood stoically stunned by the sight of his family. He walked to the front of the crowd to greet them, then rushed the rest of the way when they caught sight of him.

"I missed you all so much." He expressed as he emotionally embraced his wife.

He then turned to his daughter who stood shyly nearby, and greeted her with the same enthusiasm. As they broke their embrace, Deanna gestured to the young, bright eyed child that Tre was carrying.

"Daddy! Meet your grandson, Elijah." She beamed. "We named him after great grandpa Wallace. Gerard was rather stunned and perplexed. "Tre and I were married on the planet Lyra."

He gently, and proudly took hold of the child as Tre passed him over. "He's one handsome young man."

257

He carefully cradled the baby, and the child giggled with joy. Gerard then scanned the others who had come down the ramp behind them, looking for familiar faces.

Just then, Alton raced by them, catching sight of his family. He scooped up Audrey in an emotional embrace. Daniel and Heather, who were now young adults, waited patiently behind to greet their stepfather. Surprisingly, Tony Freeman, his wife Andrea, and all the children of Branchview followed along next.

"Where are the others?" Gerard questioned.

"The others decided to stay behind in Lyra." Sharie sighed. "Philip convinced Tony, Andrea, and the children to come along at the very last minute."

Gerard gave a sad, regretful nod. "Nevertheless, those of us who are here will all continue on as a family." He declared as the group came together for a happy reunion.

Nearby, the Nereid contingency of Queen Hermia, her husband Heroditis, and the sentry Damarus took in all the happy reunions taking place around them. Damarus looked with anxious anticipation among the sea of faces that still poured down the ramp, and onto the sandy desert floor.

"There he is!" She suddenly squealed with excitement as she spotted the perplexed young man that was accompanied by Nera Calta. She broke through the crowd, and met them at the bottom of the ramp.

The two young lovers embraced, while Nera stood close by.

"I had a hard time finding this guy." Nera stated. "He was among a small group that was being harbored on a planet just outside of this solar system."

"I never thought I'd see your beautiful face again." Stuart lamented as he cradled Damarus head in his hands, before once again kissing her.

Damarus turned to Nera with tears in her eyes. "How can I ever thank you?"

"Simply by loving each other, and doing what you can to make this new world a better place." Nera smiled.

Hermia drew a sigh as her and Heroditis watched the reunion from a distance.

"Looks like we've lost the chief sentry of the Nereids." She sadly stated.

"We have other worthy candidates to take her place." Heroditis smiled. "Damarus will now hopefully become our chief liaison to the United States."

"I never really gave that much thought." Hermia answered with a keen expression. "I'm sure she'll be a wonderful representative for the people of our world."

A bewildered Owen stood with Katiera, her parents, Linda, and Mahkta. "Where are they?" He asked with frustration. "Eno and Philip promised they'd find my parents."

"There's still people coming down the ramp." Katiera replied as she pulled her husband closer.

Just then, they appeared at the top of the ramp flanked by both Eno and Philip.

"There they are!" Owen cried out with joy.

They all stood at the top for a moment, and looked over the crowd in amazement.

As they ascended the ramp, and into the ocean of receptive people, Owen waved his arms, and yelled their names vigorously to get their attention. Philip noticed them first, and pointed the way.

Owen ran to embrace his parents, and led them the rest of the way to where his new family waited.

"Mom, Dad, I want you meet my wife, Katiera."

They both reacted with joyous surprise as they embraced her as well.

"It appears you've been rather busy while we've been gone." His father stated with amusement.

"In more ways than one." Xander chimed in, taking Kevin totally by surprise.

He had been so wrapped up in the reunion with his son that he hadn't noticed him standing there. He vigorously shook his hand.

"Xander Torrance! How are you, old friend?"

"Very happy now that I'm among my new found family." He answered with a sly grin, which prompted a puzzled look from both Kevin and his wife Joyce.

"Xander and Tabitha Torrance are Katiera's parents." Owen announced.

"We're now in-laws, Kevin." Xander chuckled.

Kevin curiously looked toward his beaming new daughter in law. "You look so familiar to me, Katiera? Perhaps you accompanied your father on one of our secret meetings."

"You'll have a hard time believing this." She began. "But you and I first saw each other many years ago when you were a little boy, and I was just a teenage Mermaid." She replied.

A look of enlightenment came across Kevin's face as he realized who she was. "You were the Mermaid I saw that night on the beach."

"You might also be surprised to know that your grandmother Thea was an Oceanid. I knew her before she went to live on land with your grandfather. Tabitha added as she strolled forward.

"How...?" Joyce Gustafsson began with a very perplexed expression, before Xander cut her short.

"It's a long story that we'll have to explain later." He chuckled.

"But that would mean Tabitha would be close to one hundred years old." Kevin reasoned.

"97 actually." She answered.

Kevin's eyes then wandered curiously to Katiera once again, and she responded with a sigh.

"I'm actually 72 in earth years."

"You mean to tell me that my daughter in law is older than I am?" Joyce further questioned, looking as though she were ready to faint.

"Oceanids do have a much longer life span than humans, mom." Owen explained. "We'll have more than enough time to bring you both up to speed on everything."

"And our friend, Dr. Mahkta can bring us up to date on all the newest advanced technologies in the medical field." Xander added as he gestured toward the large lion that stood patiently nearby.

"I can't wait!" Kevin proclaimed with exuberance, as both he and his wife marveled at the stature of the lion being.

Eno, now joined by his wife Nera, stood with Philip who had reunited with Linda Sanchez.

Linda clutched a large, old and weathered journal with both arms.

"This is a day I'd hoped would happen for a very long time." Eno proudly stated.

"Indeed! All is definitely well on earth tonight." Philip added, before glancing curiously at Linda, who stood silent with a large smile on her face. "You're unusually quiet."

"I'm just busy taking in all of the happy reunions." She replied nonchalantly.

"No, there's definitely something else that's different about you tonight. A certain glow."

"Oh! Really!" She grinned, as he continued studying her expressions.

"Are you in love, Linda Sanchez?"

"I don't know. Am I?" She quipped, prompting him to simply roll his eyes in frustration. "Come along, I do believe we need to give this journal to Gerard LeRoux and Alton Sinclair." She commanded, while tugging on his sleeve, and leading the way.

"Of course." He replied.

"After exchanging greetings with the returning family's, Linda presented the tattered and fragile journal to Gerard.

"What's this?" he questioned as he opened it to scan the yellowed pages.

"That is a journal that chronicles all the locations in the world where my brother and I kept our gold and silver throughout the centuries. No one else has knowledge of this." Philip grinned. "There's enough riches in that very book to make the new earth a very prosperous place seven times over."

"That's amazing! But why are you giving this to us?" Alton further questioned.

"Because we are entrusting you and Gerard to be the caretakers of that gold and silver." He paused to gauge their shocked reaction. "A new economy must be built worldwide with the guidance of some of the brightest minds in the Galactic Federation." He gestured toward the space transport as he spoke. "That gold and silver will be the basis of that new economy."

Eno and Nera gave an assuring nod, while Gerard and Alton exchanged looks of disbelief.

"We don't know what to say." Gerard replied with great astonishment.

Linda smiled as she stepped in closer to add further comment. "The Nereids, the Oceanids, and the other Water People possess all the wealth of the underwater regions that are not listed in that journal. We hope to join forces with you to combine those riches, and make this world a better place for all."

"We'd be honored." Alton sincerely replied.

Another sequence of musical notes emerged from the large craft, as the new ambassadors began their descent down the ramp. There were hundreds of individuals from other worlds within, and outside of the earth's galaxy. Areas previously unknown to those on earth. Some looked similar to humans, while others were beings that were totally foreign to the human eye, and beyond imagination.

Two by two, they descended the ramp to a world that was just as foreign in their eyes. Among them were a pair that resembled domestic housecats that walked upright. Others also looked like a mix between other certain animals and humans, while still more had features that could not easily be explained. The crowd on the ground watched with awe striken silence, as the newcomers took in their new surroundings with apprehensive wonder.

There was no fear or prejudice among either side. Only an eagerness to embrace their differences, and learn from each other. As the first group, made their way to the bottom of the ramp, they were warmly greeted by the people of the new earth. As they mingled in the crowd, new friendships were forged, and the initial differences faded away.

"I wish I could stay longer to experience what this group will accomplish." Philip expressed to Eno. "Somehow the universe just became a bit smaller."

"I'm sure you can always find time in your busy schedule to come back and visit." Eno replied.

"You can count on that." He smiled as he set his eyes on his sons Tony Freeman, and the much younger Dimitri. "Please excuse me for a moment."

He greeted both with a warm, fatherly hug.

"I'm glad you talked us into coming back, father." Tony expressed. "I look forward to rebuilding this great new earth."

Philip then gestured to Dimitri, and the other children. "These children are the important keys to the future. It's up to them to make sure evil doesn't seep its way back into society."

"Evil eventually does makes its way back into humanity. You and I know that all too well."

"Hopefully that won't happen for many years to come."

Dimitri looked up at Philip with sober, wide eyes. "Will mother ever return to earth?"

Philip shook his head no as he went down to one knee to be closer to the child. "We'll all be together someday in another place and time. Until then, be sure to always keep her alive in your heart and mind. With that, she'll always be with you." He gave an assured pat to the boys' shoulder as he stood once again and turned his attention back to Tony.

"Were there any new developments concerning Loraine Spencer?"

"Sonja scoured the Akashic records, and found a few abnormalities." Tony seriously replied. "In different decades over the past one hundred years, a woman with seemingly no prior history had sought out help from both you and my mother, Amphitrite. Whether she assumed aliases or not, it's evident that she didn't identify herself as Loraine."

"Which was a very wise thing to do." Philip answered with great thought. "What about Stargazer?"

"He's made such a habit of jumping timelines that he's like a ghost." He laughed. "There's no way to pinpoint his presence in the library of time."

"This woman you speak of has to be Loraine." Philip proclaimed.

"If so, what can we do to bring her back?" Tony asked. "It's vital that she's reunited with her children."

"At present, we can't do anything. In the past, perhaps there's something Amphitrite and I can do." He concluded with much concentration. "I'll be sure to keep in touch with Sonja for any further developments in the timelines."

"Should I tell Olivia and London?"

"Not yet, until we know for sure that it's her."

Suddenly a very bright light shone down on them from the top of the ramp. Within that light was the figure of a celestial being. Those who were aware of who the illuminated figure was, immediately went down to one knee, and respectfully bowed, while others were clueless.

Gerard who was still holding his new grandson, quietly approached Philip and Eno.

"Is that who I think it is?" He humbly asked.

"That is our Supreme Commander, Yesua." Eno answered.

"Jesus." Gerard spoke with amazed enlightenment. "He finally returned as he had always promised."

"And that's the grand finale of the great arrival." Philip smiled.

A loud, pronounced musical note then echoed out from the giant transport, and all eyes turned toward it. Eno and Nera looked to Philip.

"That's our cue. It's time to go." Eno announced.

Philip turned to Xander. "You and your people are now free to come and go from your world any time you'd like."

"I'll spread the word to the other colonies in the Great Lakes and beyond. We plan to introduce ourselves to the new earth as soon as the lakes thaw in the Spring."

"Why wait?" Philip inquired.

"Would you want to come to the surface during a Great Lakes winter?" He countered with a chuckle. "My colony will swim ashore at Presque Isle. Will you be there to greet us?"

"We'll all be there." Eno spoke up in reply, while Xander exchanged a firm handshake with both men, before giving a quick hug to Nera.

Philip then turned to Linda before departing. "Would you like to come with us?"

"There's too much for me right here. I could never leave now." She firmly answered.

"You really are in love. Aren't you?" He quipped with a sly wink.

"I guess you'll find out in the Spring." She smirked.

Philip shook his head and laughed as he turned away to follow Eno and Nera up the ramp of the enormous craft. At the top, Yesua greeted them. Then they all turned to give a departing wave to the crowd before entering into the belly of the vessel. Another series of musical notes accompanied the ascending ramp. Yet, another series of deeper bass notes with a blinking sequence of colored lights preceded its' departure as it rose from the desert floor. Then with lightning speed, it shot upward. A sonic boom, and bright flash signaled its' exit through the portal of the stars, and into another dimension.

All eyes continued to look upward with wonderment, even after the transport had disappeared. The newcomers were struck with the reality that they were now a part of this world. The survivors of the old earth realized that it was a new beginning. A chance to start all over in a pure, positive world. The blanket of stars seemed to shine brighter than ever in that clear, dark desert sky. All in attendance were now fully convinced that they in fact were not alone in this massive universe. They were never alone.

"What a magical night!" Owen proclaimed as he affectionately squeezed Katiera's hand.

"There will be many more like this to come." She countered with a smile as they snuggled close.

18

ALL ASHORE TO THE NEW WORLD

March 31, 2028.

After a very harsh and cold winter, the Spring had finally arrived with a refreshingly warm thaw in the northern hemisphere. Though a noticeable chill still remained in the air, the skies were clear and blue, and the sun shone brightly. It was as though the Oceanids had foreseen this as being the perfect time to rise from their hidden colonies to swim ashore to the new world.

All along the shores of the Great Lakes region, the survivors of the new world, and their new friends from the previously hidden worlds gathered in anticipation of the arriving newcomers, who had actually been secretly among them all along.

At Presque Isle near the Port of Erie Pennsylvania, a welcoming committee that included Philip, Eno and Nera, along with Linda, and her new love Nathan Cook waited patiently on shore. They occasionally peered through binoculars hoping to catch sight of the first wave of Oceanids on the horizon. Kevin and Joyce Gustafsson along with Mahkta had been transported ahead of time from Station 37 to land, so that they could partake in the welcoming festivities.

"I honestly don't know how anyone can live in this part of the world." Linda said as she shivered against the chilly north wind, and pulled the top of her heavy winter coat tighter against her chest. "I'm about to freeze to death."

"It's definitely not the tropical weather we're accustomed to." Nathan soberly replied.

Nearby, Joyce complained to her husband, Kevin. "I don't understand why Owen and Katiera couldn't come here on the transport with us."

"Maybe they just decided to get a later ride." He reasoned. "I'm sure they'll arrive shortly."

"I think I see something." Eno proclaimed, as everyone looked out over the lake with excitement.

Instead of a sea of Oceanids, they saw what looked like a dragon like creature swimming swiftly toward the land. Alongside it, a holographic type figure that looked almost like the face of a woman appeared as an onrushing wave.

"What in the world is that?" Joyce inquired with much alarm.

"That is the fabled Lake Erie Monster, and the Lake Erie Storm Hag. They've lived in these waters for centuries." Philip calmly answered.

The Storm Hag announced her arrival singing in her beautiful operatic voice that had hypnotized mariners for centuries.

Both creatures came to a halt about two hundred yards out from shore. The Monstrous Dragon let out a roar, while the Hag continued her serenade. Philip and Eno stepped forward to the water's edge to telepathically communicate with them, and they both immediately calmed to silence as though understanding.

"What should we do?" Kevin whispered. "They look quite ferocious."

"Absolutely nothing." Nera replied. "They come in peace. They simply want to introduce themselves."

"How do you know?" Joyce further inquired.

"They speak the universal language that we understand." Mahkta assuredly replied. "We tune into each other's frequencies."

After a few long moments, the creatures appeared to slightly bow to those on shore, then they swiftly retreated in the opposite direction, swiftly disappearing below the depths.

"That's beyond anything I could ever fathom!" Nathan enthusiastically proclaimed.

A few moments of silence prevailed on the shoreline as the group reeled with awe at what they had just witnessed.

Suddenly, the faint joyful chatter of Oceanid clicks could be heard echoing over the water, and a long line of swimming figures appeared across the horizon. It looked like an enormous school of dolphins swiftly approaching across the surface of the lake as far as the human eye could see. Their tail fins looked like a moving wave of green as they approached, and their chatter grew to a deafening pitch.

"Here they come!" Philip enthusiastically announced.

Xander, Tabitha, Katiera, and Owen led the way, and were the first to appear just off shore. They were followed closely by Ana Pare', and the other advisors of Station 37. They shook their tails one final time above the surface, before submerging, then re-emerging to walk the rest of the way toward shore.

"I know I've seen you do it several times. But I still don't understand it." Nathan lamented to Linda.

Linda took hold of his hand. "You'll get used to it."

Owen walked proudly to shore with Katiera by his side.

"That was a cold swim. I'm ready for a good cup of hot chocolate." He remarked as he paused to catch his breath.

"That was your longest swim yet, sweetheart." Katiera beamed.

The group was soon followed onto shore by a multitude of mermaids and mermen from their world. They also took legs as they waded to the beach, and immediately began mingling with the humans who lined the shore to greet them.

Kevin sprang forward to greet his son with much surprise.

"How did you ever learn how to do that, and why did you keep it a secret from us?"

"It's in our genetics dad. I wanted to surprise you." Owen looked around. "Where's mom?"

"She's over here." Mahkta replied as he leaned over to offer her aid. "I believe she simply fainted."

"I guess she's got a lot to get used to." Owen laughed.

"She's not the only one." A perplexed Nathan commented as he and Linda casually strolled by.

Owen and Katiera happily watched as the last group of their Oceanid contingent walked ashore.

"I'm so glad I found you, Katie."

"I'm glad you found me too." She smiled.

"Do you think we should tell everyone now?" Owen asked.

"I think it's a great time to do it." She replied.

Owen stepped forward to get the attention of his family, friends, and anyone else within earshot.

"Hey everybody! Katie and I have an announcement." He then yielded to his wife.

"We're expecting a baby." She announced joyfully. "And we just found out this morning that it's going to be a boy."

Everyone gathered around the couple to offer their cheerful congratulations, and applause.

Eno commented as he and Nera took their congratulatory turn. "A male Oceanid. That's quite special and rare."

"Yes, it is." Katiera proclaimed.

As Owen and Katiera's parents moved in to share the joy, Kevin winked at his son. "I'm so proud of the man you've become."

"I'm proud of you too, dad."

"Well Kevin!" Xander intervened. "Looks like we'll have a grandson to spoil."

"Don't forget about us." Tabitha said with amusement as she placed her arm around Joyce.

Mahkta approached them next with a benevolent smile. "I thought you weren't going to tell them until a later time."

"We just couldn't keep the secret to ourselves." Katiera answered.

"I totally understand, my friends." He concluded with a chuckle.

As the couple took in all the happiness around them, Owen gave his wife's hand a gentle squeeze.

"You know, summer is just around the corner." He remarked. "We'll have to visit here as much as we can before you get too far along in your pregnancy."

"And, we can ride the merry-go -round at Waldameer." She enthusiastically added.

"Yes, we can!" He laughed with amusement as he embraced his wife lovingly, and they kissed.

Philip and Eno stood apart from the crowd, also observing all the happiness around them.

"It certainly is a great day to be alive." Eno proclaimed.

Philip gave a single solemn nod in response, and seemed to have a moment of deep reflection.

"Did I say something I shouldn't have said, Philip?"

"No. It's just that I remember someone special that used to sing a tune with those words in it. Unfortunately, she's no longer with us."

"I'm sorry! I didn't know."

"No issue, my friend." He replied with a cordial smile.

"Shall we mingle with the newcomers?" Eno suggested.

274

"Yes, we most certainly should." Philip answered with a quick shiver. "I could go for a piping hot cup of coffee as well."

"Ah, yes!" Eno chuckled. "I've also grown rather fond of that beverage in my many recent visits to earth."

Philip replied with an agreeing nod. "I believe they're serving hot drinks over at the reception area."

"Then lead the way, Warrior Angel." He motioned with a grin as the two men continued on.

After just a few steps, Philip turned once more to look back over the choppy lake waters where the sun reflected like diamonds on the surface. It was as though he was searching for someone else who might appear on the distant horizon. Eno also curiously turned to see what he was looking at.

"Do you see something else out there?"

Philip shook his head no. "I just need a few moments to myself. I'll be along shortly."

Eno gave him an understanding pat on his muscular shoulder before moving on.

Philip then continued to look out over the water, and spoke softly.

"I promise I'll do everything in my powers to find you, and bring you back, Loraine Spencer."

Concluding with a determined nod, he turned once again, and continued up the beach to join the others.

Author Bio

Author Bio: Brian was born and raised in Erie Pa., and has also lived in New York State, North Carolina, and Florida. He wrote scripts part time for the movie industry for several years, while also working full time at FedEx. Upon his retirement in 2017, he began turning much of his archived work into novels. A few years later, he formed Large Lion Entertainment as a platform for his work.

In his spare time, he enjoys exercise and fitness, and is also quite active in charity work for animal rescues, and veterans causes. Brian and his family presently live on the Gulf Coast of Florida.

Books by Brian Jay Nelson

Branchview Series

- The Unexpected Journey
- The Epic Showdown
- The Portal of Time
- The Fall of the Secret Society
- Coming late 2026….. A Passenger In Time

Stories from the Hidden World